D1149131

TRANSPARENT

TRANSPARENT

NATALIE WHIPPLE

HOT
KEY
BOOKS

First published in Great Britain in 2013 by Hot Key Books
Northburgh House, 10 Northburgh Street, London EC1V 0AT

First published in the US in 2013 by HarperTeen, a division of
HarperCollins

A CIP catalogue record for this book is available from the British Library.

ISBN: 978-1-4714-0076-6

1

Typeset by Palimpsest Book Production Limited, Falkirk, Stirlingshire
This book is typeset in Berling LT Std 10.5pt/15.5pt

Printed and bound by Clays Ltd, St Ives Plc

Hot Key Books supports the Forest Stewardship Council (FSC), the leading
international forest certification organisation, and is committed to printing
only on Greenpeace-approved FSC-certified paper.

www.hotkeybooks.com

To my mom, who taught me how to dream.
To my dad, who taught me how to catch them.
And to Nick, who made them all come true.

Prologue

I nearly died the second I was born. The doctor dropped me, but it wasn't his fault. When I smacked the floor and let out a screeching cry, all anyone could see was the semi-transparent umbilical cord. The poor guy scooped me up, gasping in shock at my invisible body.

I spent a year in the hospital—not because of injuries. They had to study me, cure me. Mom wanted a normal baby, one with a non-dangerous ability like glow-in-the-dark hair or breath that smells like chocolate. Then I wouldn't have been so important to my father. Instead, she got the first ever invisible child.

Not only was I famous, but I was infinitely, dangerously useful.

When they gave up on a cure, Mom took me home. The paparazzi tried to get pictures, which was stupid because they couldn't actually see me. They wanted a glimpse of the girl with no face, but my dad's people made sure that didn't happen. He made sure the world saw as little of me as possible, and more importantly, that they never realized what I could really do.

Hiding an invisible girl. Go figure.

Chapter 1

It's a good thing summers in Vegas are so hot, considering how often I walk the streets naked. Even at night the dry heat lingers, especially on the strip where lights and people and cars move nonstop. Mom walks beside me, her gold dress one sequin short of overkill. With her auburn hair doing that blowy model thing, people can't help but look at her. No one looks at me.

Of course, they can't see me, but still.

The old Sahara Hotel is in sight, with its Moroccan dome and vintage sign. I can't believe the thing hasn't been torn down yet, but people tend to hang on to places like this now. They are relics of the time when normal existed.

"You remember the room number, right?" Mom whispers in the wake of a taxi's honk.

I tap her shoulder to say yes. Talking while I'm on a mission is too risky. There must never be proof that I was anywhere near here tonight, because as far as the world is concerned I'm just a spoiled syndicate baby, born into crime but not actually participating. Someone to be loathed, sure, but not a real criminal.

The doormen acknowledge my mom tentatively, as does everyone who lives in Vegas, and we stride into the foyer.

Clinking coins and Middle Eastern music assault my ears, and the smell of smoke forces me to hold in a cough.

Mom heads for the bar, since she has to make it look like she's just treating herself to a night out. She takes a seat, and the bartender drops everything to wait on her. "What can I get you, Lauren?"

She smiles. "The usual."

As he mixes her drink, I scan the room for our targets. They shouldn't be too hard to spot—Juan Torres's people never are. Dad says they're fools, marking themselves the way they do, but not all syndicates work like us. Juan may not have Dad's stealth, but he has a gift for instilling terror in people. His henchmen flaunt their depravity and smear it across the news so even the cops run the other way, while Dad makes sure the "authorities" can never pin a crime on him.

"Thank you." Mom sips at a neon-pink concoction, carefully watching the lobby like me. Men eye her hungrily, but they know better than to mess with my dad's women.

Then I spot them. Even with their long sleeves I can make out the tattooed claws on their hands, which are surely connected to jaguars, Juan's signature mark. I slink through the crowd as Mom finishes off her drink. We've done this enough that she knows I'll be where I need to be, even if she can't see me.

They wait for an elevator, just like our intelligence said they would, and speak in hushed Spanish. I run my tongue over the recorder in my mouth, which is smaller than a stick of gum. Once their elevator comes and goes, Mom walks up. She presses a button and waves her hand slightly in the process. Our ride is there in seconds.

Telekinesis. The reason Mom is my perfect criminal partner.

She presses the button for a different floor than the one we want, but she uses her power to take us to the right one. Up, up, up we go, until we reach the restricted VIP floor. She opens the door, and then it's me and a long, quiet hallway.

The carpet is lush, making it easy to creep along in silence. I find the door I'm looking for and hear muffled voices. Now I just have to get in and figure out what they're doing here. I knock.

The door opens wide, and the idiot who answered holds a small pistol as his eyes search the empty hall. Crouching, I slip inside before the moment's lost. I find a concealed corner and pull out the recorder, while the door guy goes back to the table and takes a swig from a tequila bottle. With one flick of the recorder's switch, I'm in business.

The whole job is child's play, really—nothing I haven't done before. My shoulders slump as the thought sinks in. Sixteen, spying on criminals for a criminal, and here I am thinking it's no big deal. Sad.

" . . . Radiasure . . ." one of them says.

The word makes my ears perk up. If this has anything to do with Dad's drug stash, he'll be pissed. Then the bald one pulls a tiny bag from his pocket, and I can't breathe.

Glowing blue pills.

Radiasure may not look like much, but each one of those goes for over a thousand bucks on the black market. They are what make this twisted world go round.

They are mine.

I take a small plastic cylinder from under my tongue. Carefully, I pull out three minipins, their points colored purple to indicate their use: knockout needles. Dad has these made especially for me, for emergencies, but I'm sure he wouldn't mind if I use them now to bring the pills back for him. He'll be happy. I want to make him happy.

By the time one of them catches sight of the pin, it's too late. I stick the closest person in the neck, and he writhes before going limp. Guy number two gets pricked before the first hits the floor, and the third fumbles for his gun. I pull the final pin from my teeth. Ever so smoothly, it sinks into his skin.

"You . . ." he says before falling on the bed.

Thanks to the nearly empty tequila bottles, I'm not worried about him remembering the exact details.

I grab the pills from the table. They are beautiful, like gleaming jewels. Consuming Radiasure boosts your ability, but it's not like I can get any *more* invisible, so taking one would be a waste. The bag fits in my mouth without a problem. Slipping through the door, I knock on the hijacked elevator to signal to Mom that I'm done. It opens, and Mom guides it down without a word. She has a few more drinks, and we're back at The Clover just after midnight.

Dad is already at our penthouse, sitting on the couch with Petra, the resident speaker of tongues. His dark brows are pulled over his eyes, and he frowns. I can't wait to change that.

"So?" Dad stands, and though he's not a large man, he's still intimidating.

4

"Fiona?" Mom looks for me, her voice high, as if she fears I might have gone missing on the way back.

"Here." The things in my mouth garble the word. "And I have a present."

I spit out the Radiasure, and Dad's eyes light up. Then he's smiling, and I can't help but do the same. I made him happy. I am useful to him. That makes me the luckiest girl in the room. "You darling girl. Juan's men had this?"

"Yeah." I grab the sundress I left on the couch, since the AC in the penthouse is freezing me out. "And they talked about Radiasure a lot. They were obviously planning to use this bag for a power boost, but after that I don't know. It was all in Spanish."

He grabs the recorder and thrusts it at Petra. "Translate."

She takes it, touching my dad in a way that makes Mom look away. It's one of those things you never get used to, but this is what Mom got herself into when she fell for a Charmer. Petra listens to the Spanish and then she nods. "Your daughter is right—they were going to use the extra power to break into your vault at The Bellagio."

His nostrils flare. And with good reason. The Bellagio vault has at least a ten-billion-dollar stash of Radiasure. "They *knew* where it was?"

"It seems Juan paid Spud millions for a hack."

"Damn her!" He grabs the recorder and almost throws it, but then thinks better of it. "If I ever find that hacker, I'll make sure she dies slowly."

Except no one ever finds Spud, the computer savant that some say could control the entire world if she felt like it.

5

"It's a good thing I grabbed the pills," I say. "They don't stand a chance without them."

Dad shakes his head, anger reddening his face. "It's not enough. Juan sending his men into *my* city? Plotting to steal *my* Radiasure? He needs to be taught a lesson. No one touches the O'Connell syndicate."

"Should I call Graham?" Mom says. Graham is my oldest brother and head of Dad's beat squad. There is no one I hate more.

"No. Juan needs to understand that he's never safe. We'll take the fight to Phoenix. See how powerful he thinks he is when we kill his daughters." He points at me. "It's time to show him death he'll literally never see coming."

My heart stops. "Me? You want me to do it?"

He nods.

I've spied on people. I've stolen millions. I've knocked people out, destroyed their cars. But I have never killed someone, and the thought makes it hard to breathe. "I . . . I can't."

He raises an eyebrow. "Excuse me?"

"Please don't make me." I regret saying it, because now he's really angry.

He grabs me by the shoulder, and his fingers dig in. "You'll do what I say, and you'll do it on tape for every wannabe criminal to see. Do you want people questioning our power?"

I don't answer fast enough, and it earns me a slap to the face. Mom flinches, but stays where she is. Dad takes out the Radiasure and swallows two. He sucks in a breath, and in the silence I can feel his pull. His happiness is the only

6

reason to live. There's nothing better than making him smile.

"You're going to kill them." His voice is firm, and it fills me with resolve.

"I will, in front of Juan if I have to," I say.

He smiles. "That's my girl."

Later that night, when the penthouse is dark and Dad's charm has worn off, I shake and cry and curse myself for what I promised. It's always like this. Why didn't I say no? Why didn't I disappear into the Vegas crowds when I had the chance?

My door clicks, and I go silent.

"Fiona?" Mom says. "Are you awake?"

"Of course I am." I never sleep the night after a job. Too much guilt. Too much self-loathing for giving in to Dad's power once again.

"Good. Pack your things."

I sit up. "What?"

"We're leaving."

Normally, I would groan at yet another one of her pathetic attempts to escape, but not tonight. Tonight I am running; it's the only way I won't become a murderer. I grab the nearest bag and shove things into it. She doesn't say anything else, only watches me in the scant moonlight. We work better without words, anyway.

Once I have what I need, she leads me to the garage, disabling cameras and locks all along the way. She revs the engine without a key, and we're gone.

Chapter 2

I run a brush through my hair, checking out my clothes in the mirror. At least the bright yellow shirt and eggplant-purple jeans show off my figure. I grab a few strings of black beads and wrap them around my neck. Then I pick some cat-eye glasses. They don't have lenses, since my vision is perfect, but I wear them so people know where to look. The more I stare, the stupider I feel. Sure, the clothes look great—I still look like nothing.

All I know about myself is that I'm five foot eight, a hundred and forty pounds, and the owner of one rocking wardrobe. When all anyone sees is your clothing, it's important.

Eye color? No clue. Skin? I try to keep it soft. Hair? A wavy mess. It might be curly if I had any clue how to style it.

It's not so bad. That's what people say if I complain, but there's no way they can possibly understand how it feels. Sure, no one can ever tell me I'm ugly, but no one will ever call me pretty, either. It's easy to be comfortable naked, but I don't even know what my own body looks like. I can literally disappear when I don't feel like dealing with stuff, but sometimes it seems like I wouldn't have problems in the first place if people could see me.

Letting out a long sigh, I debate changing outfits. I can't believe Mom's making me go to a real school after just three weeks away from Dad. I wish I could at least take a stand by putting on sweats and refusing to leave, but I can't. The truth is, a little part of me wants to know how people live outside of Dad's syndicate. The normal world seems so foreign, without constant threats and fear. It's strange to think the people in this minuscule town have real jobs that don't directly involve crime.

There's a knock at my door, and then a soft click as Mom opens it. She's in her yoga gear, her morning coffee in hand. Her hair looks wild, and she seems free and untamed, even though she's the complete opposite. She holds up an untoasted blueberry Pop-Tart, the best possible breakfast. "I'm guessing you're hungry."

"Sure." I grab it, eyeing her. I hate when she tries to take care of me, like it makes up for everything she does wrong. Minus the fight over school, we've spent most of the last few weeks in silence, me vegged out on the sofa with a DVR full of romantic comedies and her in the garage sculpting. I prefer it that way.

"Ready to go?"

I stiffen. "No."

"You look ready." She takes a long drink from her mug.

"Why are you making me do this again?" I don't know why I'm asking, since she won't tell the truth.

It's always the same. Dad is a drug—a mutation in his pheromones makes him practically irresistible to women. The longer they're around him, the more addicted they get, until they'd do anything just to make him happy. Mom's known him since she was my age, so it's a joke that she tries to detox at all. Even I'm not immune, though it's not as bad. I think it's because I'm his blood. I can at least get through the withdrawals without begging him to come back.

The worst part? I *miss* him. I hate him and miss him at the same time.

"I thought you'd want to go to school, make friends," she says.

I let out a wry laugh. Why would anyone want to be around someone like me: a thief, a threat, and a freak? "Dad will find us because of this."

She shakes her head. "Not necessarily. This is a really small town, and he doesn't have much sway in Arizona. This is Juan's territory. Considering the last order he gave you, he'll assume we ran somewhere else. There's no safer place."

I stuff half the Pop-Tart in my mouth, hating that she has a point. It's true that Dad's gold-and-jewelry "business" doesn't reach this far south of Las Vegas. He covers more of the northern West, anything from Sacramento up to Seattle and over to Boise. Juan Torres controls the Southwest, and Valerie Sutton owns small-but-important Southern Cali. Technically, Dad would have a hard time getting to us here, since the news reported that Juan has tightened his borders "for unknown reasons." We only got through because we left that night. Mom and I can guess Dad killed the henchmen I knocked out, which would put Juan on the defensive.

"Don't you want a future, Fiona?" Mom says.

"I didn't realize I had a choice."

Her lips bunch up, as if she's about to cry. "Why do you think we're here?"

"Whatever. Let's get this over with." I stuff the rest of the Pop-Tart in my mouth.

"Try to have fun." Her fingers move gracefully, and a black-and-white checkered bag floats to me from the closet. "I think this goes well with your outfit, and your books should fit perfectly."

I grab the bag, hating that it's exactly what I would have picked.

Chapter 3

When I used to indulge in fantasies of normal teen life, Madison High School was not what I envisioned. It's smaller than Dad's suite at The Clover—and a lot less glamorous. The front office looks like it was plucked out of a brown-and-orange nightmare, complete with oak paneling on the walls. The yellow lights don't help.

Mom sits next to me in an orange chair, filling out papers. I blink a few times, wondering if this is some kind of dream. It definitely can't be real. She's acting too motherly, looks too normal outside our usual routine of slinking through dark alleys and stealing. Any minute she'll look up and tell me she can't believe I fell for it.

She turns to me, smiling. Here it comes. "What electives do you want?"

"Huh?" I try to find the joke in her expression—she always has this glint in her eyes when she messes with someone. Nothing. She's serious. I can't figure out if the knot in my stomach is excitement or terror. Dad never let me go to school. He didn't want anyone swaying me but him. Personal tutors sounded like a good idea when he said it. I didn't need friends or a real education or a boyfriend.

All I needed was a lockpick to open doors and a Swiss Army Knife to disable security cameras.

"Electives. I have you signed up for the stuff you need: English, math, biology, history, and PE. I just don't know what you'd like to take for fun."

"Fun?" Starting school for the first time doesn't sound as fun as it did in my imagination. Because in my dreams I wasn't the invisible syndicate baby walking into a tiny school where everyone probably knows one another. Four weeks late, no less, so I stick out even more.

"Look at the list and pick." She shoves a mustard-yellow paper at me.

The classes are just words. I don't know what I like, what I'd be good at, or whatever reason someone picks an elective. Surprisingly, there's no class called Stealing 101. I'd ace that. "How many of these do I need?"

"Two. Don't you like any of them?"

"I don't know." I hand the list back, wishing I could leave. "This is stupid."

Her brow furrows. "Can't you at least try?"

I look away, only to find the secretary staring at me. Or rather through me, as if I don't have eyes to notice how jarring she finds my presence. "What do you think I should take?"

"What about art?"

I groan. Talk about going right to her passion. No thanks.

She frowns. "Fine. Home ec? They'll probably have sewing. You could design your own clothes."

"Sure, I guess."

"Spanish?"

There's not much else on the list, unless I want to be in performing arts like dance or music or drama. An invisible girl acting? Yeah, right. "That might be handy."

Mom hands the forms to the secretary, who takes forever to print up my schedule. She holds it out for me with a wary smile. "Here you are, Miss McClean. Third period is starting shortly. You should have just enough time to find your locker."

"Great." I grab the papers, already wishing I didn't have to carry around the map like a dork.

"Do you want me to come with you?" Mom asks.

I stare at her. What am I? Five? I might die if she pulls out a camera to take a picture of my first day of school. "I think I can handle it."

She straightens, her eyes watering. "All right. Have a good day, hon."

Once she leaves, I search the halls for my locker. A few neon posters hang on oatmeal-colored walls, advertising upcoming dances or club meetings or other events I never imagined myself going to. The bell rings, and the halls fill with students. It's not a flood like in the movies. I bet there aren't even sixty students in my junior class.

Still, there are enough people staring at me. Eyes roam over my missing arms and head. Mouths gape open. Whispers fill my ears. I wouldn't be surprised if even here they vaguely know who I am, who I belong to. Which means there's no chance anyone will ever talk to me.

Normal life. Right.

I barely make it to third period on time: algebra. Seeing

as I hate math more than anything else, it's only fitting to start here. The teacher, Ms. Sorenson, is a mousy thing with bright pink eyes. She jumps when I come up to her, like I might mug her on the spot. "D-do you have your schedule?"

"Yeah." I hand her my paper, and she looks it over as I try to ignore my silent, curious classmates.

"Everyone, this is F-Fiona McClean." She turns to me. "Is there anything you want to tell us about yourself?"

"Isn't it pretty obvious?"

The class snickers, and I'm glad they can't see me blushing.

The teacher holds out an old book. "Here's the text. Take a seat next to Miss Navarro, please."

I search the classroom, not wanting to ask who that is. Instead of finding the girl, my eyes lock on the hottest guy I've ever seen. He's all muscle, with a spattering of freckles and a mop of carrot-orange hair. He oozes confidence, smiling right at me with a one-dimpled grin. At least there's one great thing about being invisible—I can enjoy the view without him knowing.

The girl next to him nods at me, which is when I realize she's probably this "Miss Navarro" I'm supposed to sit by. I rush over and plop down in the creaky desk.

"I'm Bea," she says, searching the space between my glasses.

"Or Trixy," Hot Guy says.

Bea smiles. "But never, *ever* Beatrix."

"Okay . . ." I feel bad for kind of hating her, since she's at least playing nice. But she has perfect tan legs, and her mess of dark hair makes it seem like she doesn't try. Her

15

eyes are gorgeous and playful. It's not fair for a girl to be that beautiful.

She motions to Hot Guy, who must be her boyfriend. "This is Brady."

The teacher starts class before I can answer, which is fine because I wasn't sure what to say anyway. "You have until the end of the period to finish the exam."

My mouth goes dry. A test? The blue paper lands on my desk. "But I . . ."

"I'd like you to take the test, if you don't mind," Ms. Sorenson says. "It will help me gauge your understanding."

Nodding, I turn the cover page. I was technically in a certified homeschooling program, so maybe I do know this stuff. I pick up the pencil and stare at the first problem for what seems like an eternity. Nope. Don't know this. I scribble something down. It's wrong, but I don't know how to make it right.

The bell rings, and I pass my test forward, positive I failed. Bea turns toward me, but I'm not interested in another awkward conversation. I grab my bag, rushing for history before she can begin her sentence. I make a wrong turn on the way, since I can't bring myself to look at the map. When I open the door, I'm greeted with almost the exact same faces as math, right down to Bea and Brady sitting in the back next to each other.

I get introduced. Again. The only free seat is by Bea, of course. She doesn't look at me, but she seems upset.

"Group discussion today," Mr. Abbey says. His skin is a pleasant sky blue, just warm enough that he doesn't look dead. "Topic: Radiasure."

My blood goes cold. I'd rather talk about algebra than that stupid drug, and that's saying something.

Radiasure was invented as an anti-radiation pill during the Cold War, and people popped it by the dozens in hopes of surviving a possible nuclear holocaust. About five years later, the mutations came. They weren't much at first. Most people didn't have anything close to invisibility or flying or telekinesis. A green person here. A woman with a man's voice there. People figured it was an equal trade for immunity to radiation.

At least until they discovered the mutations would affect their children. Babies who'd never had a drop of the drug were born smelling like roses or covered in a thick layer of hair. It didn't even matter if their parents had stopped using. The distorted genes were already at work, and the mutations just got stronger and stranger. By the seventies some people were flying, reading minds, and emitting fatal sound waves.

The FDA pulled Radiasure, but that didn't stop everyone from trying to get it. Most people wanted the mutations—superhuman strength, iron-tough skin, diamond-sharp teeth, infinite endurance, and mind control. They wanted to be superheroes like in the old comic books. Or supervillains. Everything has pretty much gone to hell since then. Governments try to regulate things, but everyone knows it's the criminal syndicates and vigilantes that control the Radiasure, and therefore the world.

The teacher groups me with two girls and two guys. They don't discuss; they just stare at me. I'm not starting this, so I lean back in my chair and wait.

Finally, the guys glance at each other and then at me. A boy with horrible acne opens his mouth. "I bet you know all sorts of things about Radiasure, don't you, No Face? You probably take one every day."

My throat tightens. "What are you talking about?"

"Don't think we're stupid," one of the girls says. "You're Jonas O'Connell's daughter, so you must have unlimited access to it."

I knew it. If Mom doesn't cave, someone in town will narc. "What's it to you?"

"We have enough problems with Juan," says acne boy. "You and the rest of your kind should take your shit somewhere else."

My kind. I laugh at the thought. There's no one else like me. People are so predictable—afraid, angry, jealous, whatever. They don't stop to think that maybe, just maybe, I don't have a choice in the matter. They don't realize that I'd trade places with them any day of the week for one glimpse of myself.

"Does your daddy think he can hide you here, No Face?" says the other boy.

I pause, confused. "What?"

"The news says Juan's planning a syndicate war with your father. Does he think he can use our town as a refuge for his precious daughter until it's over?"

I try to stay calm. This can work for me. They think I'm just a syndicate baby, and that Dad's trying to protect me. It makes sense, no matter how far from the truth it is. "What'll you do if he is using your town? Should I call him and say you want to tell Juan where I am?"

Their eyes go wide, and I smile. Too easy.

"Go to hell," acne boy spits.

"Already there."

That seems to make him angrier. "Good, you deserve it."

As much as I don't want it to, it stings. I wish I had something else to say, some clever reply. But I don't. All I can think is that anyone who's done what I have does deserve hell.

"Hey, Fiona." A deep voice makes me turn. It's Brady, and he's smiling. "How about you come over to our group?"

I stare at him, wondering if it's some kind of joke. Then Bea rolls her eyes. "Not everyone at this school is a royal dick like Tom. Come on."

"Suck it, Bea," acne boy, Tom, says.

"In your dreams."

The teacher clears his throat. "Do I have to send you to the office again, Miss Navarro?"

She puts on the most angelic face I've ever seen, complete with twinkling eyes. "Sorry, Mr. Abbey."

I bolt for Brady's group—anything is better than listening to Tom tell me I deserve my crap life. Brady's blue eyes gleam. I've always wished mine were blue, even if there are much more unique colors nowadays. There's just nothing more gorgeous than blue eyes.

"Don't listen to him, Fiona," Brady says when I sit. "He's just jealous, since all he can do is smell like shit when he gets scared."

Bea laughs. "And that's not a joke."

I smile in spite of myself. "How do we make that happen?"

They both grin. "Easy," Bea says.

"Brady, will you come up and tell the class what your group discussed?" Mr. Abbey calls.

"Sure." Brady pushes himself out of his desk. The metal frame bends, leaving it crooked. "Crap." He pushes it back into shape and continues on like that happens every day. Maybe it does. I haven't met many Strong Arms, since most are men and my dad is all about the women.

"Perfect distraction," Bea whispers. "Now watch Tom." She cups her hands around her mouth, her voice so low I can't make out what she's saying.

I watch Tom. He about falls out of his seat, and then comes the smell of a thousand Porta-Potties. It's awful, worse than my brother Miles's nastiest scent imitations.

"Bea!" Tom yells, which only makes his face redder. "You little shithead!"

"Look who's talking!" She laughs as Mr. Abbey tells us to head outside for fresh air.

"What'd you do?" I ask.

She shrugs. "I yelled a few obscenities in his ear."

Voice throwing—a pretty rare vocal ability. "Pretty tricksy."

Brady slides up beside us. "That's how she got the nick-name."

I watch them, trying to figure out if they're as nice as they seem. I want them to be, but I can't be too careful. Dad always said nice people are the most dangerous because you don't want to see the knife in their coat pocket. I finally get what he means.

Chapter 4

"Hey, Fiona!" Bea calls as I finish up at my locker.

"Hey." I try not to fidget with my necklace. I can't believe she hunted me down after school, as if having almost every class together (and neighboring desks) wasn't enough. "What's up?"

She shrugs. "Just wondered if you had a ride home."

For some reason, this triggers all my panic buttons. She can't know where I live. It's not safe. What if she's a spy? I can't help thinking all of Bea's and Brady's niceness means more than they're saying. It's possible they're working for a syndicate. They're too useful to have gone unnoticed by Juan, even in a small town like Madison, Arizona. He runs the Southwest with his breath—take in one puff and it triggers all your pain sensors. Some of my dad's women have come back from jobs half-dead and full-on crazy because of him. If Bea and Brady are with Juan . . .

"I'm good. Thanks for asking, though," I say.

She nods. "Cool. Thought I'd ask before Brady left. I have to stay late."

I silently curse myself for missing a ride with the gorgeous Brady, but it can't be helped. After waving good-bye, I head for the house on foot. I'm only a block from school before the heat starts to feel like the inside of a blow-dryer. It's dustier here than in Vegas, each gust of wind blowing something in my face, and there's hardly a tree to shade my way. I'll be drenched in sweat by the time I get home. After another few blocks, my mouth is dry. All I want is a cold drink. And air-conditioning. The heat radiates off the pavement so much I can feel it creep under my jeans. I like wearing pants to define my legs, but I'll have to relent and wear shorts if the heat doesn't let up.

Old cars pass me, obviously coming from the school. Some of the passengers flip me off as they go by. I duck onto a side road, hoping I can figure out how to get to the house despite the detour.

I spot the gray stucco house the second I round the corner onto my street. I have to admit it's the nicest place Mom's ever taken me on these escapes. Where she got the money, I don't know. I can guess—Mom has opened plenty of bank vaults with her ability—but I'd rather not think about it.

Hurrying across the road, I plan to chug the first liquid I see in the fridge. Or maybe I should go straight to ice cubes. The cold air crashes over me when I open the front door, but that's not what stops my breath.

Mom sits on the couch, a cell phone to her ear.

We didn't bring a cell phone.

She stares at me, mouth hanging open. I grit my teeth, not sure I can contain my anger. This whole day was bullshit. She just wanted me out of the house so she could get her hands on a phone without me questioning her. I hoped maybe this time she'd be serious about escaping.

I'm always disappointed.

"Who are you talking to?" I say through my teeth.

"Fiona, it's not—"

"Who?"

Her shoulders slump, and she looks at the little black phone in her hands. "Graham."

I swear, just because I know she hates it.

"I should have told you, but I didn't think you'd believe me." Her voice cracks. "He said he would help us."

"Riiight." My oldest brother is Dad's lapdog. He says fetch, and Graham goes shooting off at lightning speed without so much as a breath of hesitation. Graham's a Flyer, which means he could have escaped, but instead he chose to follow in Dad's bloody footsteps. At least Miles, my other brother and best friend, has some sense of integrity. Of course, Dad also deems him worthless, so it was a lot easier for him to get away.

I take a few steps forward. "How much did you tell him?"

"Nothing. I just told him we were safe."

Like I can believe her now. Graham's probably on his way here right now, or at least tracking the call. I snatch the phone from her. "I'm not going to school tomorrow."

When I get to my room, I pace the floor. Why can't she learn? The last time we ran, we ended up in the middle of the Utah desert. It was a nasty, small trailer park, but I still had high hopes. This place was truly isolated, wedged against the southern national parks. It took an hour just to reach a gas station, and two to reach a SuperMart.

After a month, I really thought we had made it out. I thought we could have a decent life there. Not glamorous, but at least honest.

On a trip for supplies, Mom called Graham from a pay phone to "tell him we were safe." Of course, I didn't know that until later. I was out running when he scooped me up like those evil flying monkeys do in *The Wizard of Oz*. I begged him to let us go. Begged. We were happy and safe, and if he helped we could stay that way.

For a second his hardened face cracked, and I thought maybe he would listen. Maybe he'd remember that he wasn't always Dad's gofer. Maybe he'd remember we were family. Then he shook his head. "You don't understand, Fifi. You will *never* be safe."

He took us back. He always took us back.

And then Dad came to see us. He hit Mom, beat her senseless as he called her a traitor for leaving. He apologized, and she forgave him because she couldn't help it. Then it was my turn. . . .

Sure, there are perks to Dad's life. Endless money. Power no one person should have. And it's not like he treats us poorly when we behave. He's too smart for that. He showers us—all his women and their children—with gifts and praise and luxury. If he doesn't have to use force, he won't. He's a Charmer, after all. Usually that's more than enough.

I stop at the mirror, searching for my face for the bazillionth time. There's nothing there.

Graham used to be a normal big brother—a tease, a pain, but protective and kind at the same time. He and Miles would play catch in the park while I watched, giggling at Graham's air flips. It wasn't until the day Dad came for him that things got bad. Graham was ten. Miles was seven.

I was five. We were just kids. None of us really understood what we'd been born into.

Miles and I were left alone in the penthouse for hours, wondering when our parents and Graham would come home. I ate a whole carton of ice cream, crying between bites because I thought we'd be trapped in there forever. They didn't get back until after midnight, but we were up buzzing on sugar. Graham's expression was different, like he'd just grown ten years older. Miles asked him what was wrong, and he shoved Miles into the wall.

"What do you care, Skunk Face?" Graham yelled. "You will *never* have to care!" He stomped to his room, and nothing was ever the same again. Dad would come for him constantly, and each time Graham's face got harder and his actions crueler. I didn't understand at first, not until it was my turn to join the family business.

When I was seven, Dad took me to one of the glitzy hotels, up to the third floor, where we could get a good view of the vast, busy lobby.

"Let's play a game," he said. "You like games, right?"

"Yeah!" He never gave me so much attention, and I wanted to soak up every second.

"Great." He kneeled down, almost looking me in the eye. "You are such a sneaky little girl. I love how sneaky you are."

I smiled. "I'm the best at hide-and-go-seek!"

He laughed. "I bet you are, but this is a really hard game. Do you think you can do it?"

"Yeah!"

"Okay." He pointed down at the lobby. "There are lots

25

of people wearing watches and jewelry down there. For every piece you can sneak away with, I'll get you a new toy."

My eyes widened. That could be *a ton* of toys. "Really?"

"Really. But you can't get caught. If you do, you don't get any toys. You lose."

"I won't lose." I started to pull off my shirt, but then stopped. "Is this called stealing?"

"No." He put his hand on my cheek, warm and fatherly. "This is just a game. Everyone's playing."

That was all it took to convince me. I snuck down the stairs naked, pulled a loose bracelet from a lady's wrist, and put it in my mouth so it would disappear. She thought it had fallen off and immediately dropped to the floor to look for it. Then I tiptoed back up to Dad and showed him.

"You are brilliant, Fiona." He dried it off and slipped it into his pocket. "Do it again."

And with that I was part of the syndicate, just like Graham. It took a long time to realize Dad was training me, so long that I was already trapped when the guilt and sadness flooded in. I'd always been a tool to him—all he had to do was wait until I was old enough to use. First pickpocketing, then simple jobs like grabbing a neglected bag or flash drive with top secret info. After that I gradu-ated to bigger crimes, working with Mom. Banks, law firms, jewelry stores, art galleries, government agencies—nothing was safe from us. We brought in millions for him, which he used to get his hands on Radiasure, the true valuable.

I shake my head, trying to erase the memories. When my dad told me to steal, it made perfect sense. My

26

conscience only hit after, when he abandoned me for another of his tools. Even though I did it against my will, the guilt is still there.

I try to find something real about myself, something not marred by Dad's influence.

Blank.

I don't know who I am or what I should be. Besides Miles and Mom, there's no one I care about, and no one who cares about me. I'm as hollow as I look. Tears escape my eyes, but I can't see those, either. I let them roll down my face, soak in the tickling sensation. Then my skin prickles as I realize there's one thing I do know:

It's not worth it anymore.

I won't be this.

Must get out.

I slip on a pair of shorts, some running shoes, and stuff the cell phone in my pocket. There's plenty of desert around here; maybe I'll disappear for a few hours and see how I feel then.

"Where are you going?" Mom asks when I enter the kitchen.

I grab a Gatorade from the fridge and gulp it down. Then I take the car keys, in hopes that she won't run out and get another phone. She asks again, but I don't answer. I don't even look at her as I drive away.

I stop the car at a park on the edge of town. After a few stretches, I'm off.

My feet pound the dusty ground, and though it's still blistering hot I don't feel it. I never think much when I run. My heart thumps and my lungs burn. Every nerve sparks with life, and it reminds me I have a real body, seen or not.

There isn't much out here, save some strange potholes and red mesas in the distance. A few cacti make for decent landmarks. I try to remember their shapes, so I know which way I came. I squint through the wavy heat. There's something else: a run-down set of buildings. Maybe it's a ghost town. It's too far to check out today, but it could be a good place to hide when Graham comes calling.

I stop when my legs begin to shake. A boulder casts just enough shade for me to huddle in, and the cooler ground feels heavenly against my skin. My stomach grumbles. I should have thought to eat something with the Gatorade I drank. I'm not ready to go back, so I'll just have to put up with it.

As the shadow lengthens, I lie down and watch the cloudless sky. Every bird makes me flinch. Graham often looks like one from the ground, and he's swooped down and grabbed me enough for me to be extremely afraid of heights. When I was younger, a little sparrow could make me scream. Graham thought it was hilarious. He'd make paper airplanes when I wasn't looking, shoot them right over my head, and watch me cry.

If Mom lied to me, he could be here as early as tonight. I wish I had more time to come up with a plan. It's not that I particularly want to stay here—I just don't want to go back. I have to find a way out of that life.

I gasp. *That's it!* Maybe the phone wasn't the worst idea. I pull it out of my pocket and flip it open.

Dang: one bar. I guess I should be grateful there's service at all.

I type in the number, hoping Miles hasn't changed it recently. He usually gets a hold of me when he does. We've always been close. Dad likes to periodically abandon his women, make them go through the withdrawal so they remember how bad it is, how guilty and terrible they feel without him around. When he did that to us, Graham would take Mom, since she'd be completely dysfunctional for days. Miles would make sure I was happy and distracted. He'd take me to girly movies, though he hated them. He's even missed a Giants game for me, and that's a huge deal.

If it weren't for Miles, I wouldn't have an ounce of sanity left. It's been hard since he went off to Arizona State last year to study graphic design, but I'm glad at least one person in our family can have some semblance of a normal life. I'm proud that he wants to be as far away from Dad as he can get.

The phone rings. And rings. Just when I think he won't pick up, I hear, "If you're trying to sell me crap, hang up now."

"Miles!"

"Fiona! Thank God! Are you all right?"

His voice calms me. "Yeah, so far."

He sighs. "Dad already called. I was hoping you'd find a way to contact me before I changed my number again. This your phone?"

"Not technically. I took it from Mom. She called Graham."

"Damn. I was starting to hope you guys had made it out of the worst."

"Me too." I tell him how Mom conned me.

"I'm sorry, Fi. That's really low."

"And now Graham's gonna find us and take us back."

"Calm down. You don't know that for sure. You could have interrupted."

My eyes sting as I fight back tears. "Miles, I can't do this anymore. I can't go back again. I don't want him to control me forever." There's a pause, and I worry I've lost him. "Miles?"

"Still here, just thinking." There's another pause. "Do you really mean that? What you said?"

My brow furrows. "What's that supposed to mean?"

"Don't get all defensive. Just answer."

"Yes. I'm dead serious. I'm out in the freaking hot desert trying to figure out how to escape. Would you like more proof?"

He laughs. "No. But don't go killing yourself in the middle of nowhere, okay? Do you need me to come? I will if you want."

My heart warms. He'd do anything for me, but I'd rather not get him mixed up in stuff if I don't have to. Besides, I'm afraid to give him our location. "I have to destroy this cell. Can I email you?"

"Sure, I'll leave my old one open for a few more days."

"Okay."

"Fiona?" Miles's voice breaks up.

"Yeah?"

"You don't have to—" The phone crackles with static, and I lose him.

Chapter 5

The apple-green sundress I put on the next morning doesn't define my figure like I prefer, but I need a quick escape outfit in case Graham shows up. I probably shouldn't wear glasses, but I feel invisible enough as it is. Scanning the dozen pairs I brought, I settle on the square purple frames, which are one of my favorites. It's lucky I packed them before the late-night escape; I miss my massive closet.

When I enter the kitchen, Mom almost spits out her coffee at the sight of me. "I thought you said you weren't going to school."

I shrug. If she can lie to me, then I can lie, too. School might suck, but the library has computers, and I need to email Miles. Perfect cover. "Maybe you were right. When am I going to have another chance at a normal life? May as well enjoy it before it's gone, right?"

She purses her lips, and for a second I wonder if she doesn't buy it. "What makes you think it'll go away?"

Oh, please. I grab the Pop-Tarts and sit at the table, not facing her. As long as I can keep my voice even, no one ever knows I'm lying. "Just being cautious."

She goes back to her coffee. Every few seconds she takes a deep breath, and I worry she'll ask about where I was last night or if I'm mad about Graham. But she doesn't. All she says is, "I was worried about you."

The words surprise me, but at the same time I bristle. "Where was your worry for the last nine years?"

She shrinks. "That's not fair, Fiona, and you know it."

"Whatever. I'm taking the car," I say on my way out. The door slams before I hear her reply, which is good because I already feel guilty enough.

The second I park, I feel eyes on me. I thought I was used to staring, but this is different. Around my dad's people, it feels like admiration. People fear me, but they also secretly want to be me. At Madison High School? It's more like they're trying to bore into my skin with their hatred. I'm not sure if I blame them or not. If I were some normal girl with freckles and pointed ears, maybe I would act the same way. Not that it's right, but I get that I'm a freak.

The second I get to home ec, I'm sure it was a bad idea for an elective. We're not sewing until winter. There's no way I'll be here that long, so I'm stuck cooking. The banana-bread mush in the mixing bowl makes me sick. I can't help thinking it looks like barf, which makes me want to barf.

English, the only other class I haven't been to yet, has the same familiar faces, including Bea and Brady. Bea smiles as she motions for me to come over. I wish I could sit in the front row so I don't have to witness the glares, but the only open seats are by her.

In math, Ms. Sorenson passes the tests back . . . except mine. "Please go over the problems you missed. Miss McClean, may I see you for a moment?"

Forcing myself from my desk, I make my way to the front of class. "Is there something wrong?"

"Have a look." She slides my test over.

I peek under the cover sheet, and a big green F stares back at me. "Oh."

"I'm assuming you haven't covered these concepts yet."

"Not exactly."

"I'm willing to let this slide, but you need to catch up, and fast." She grabs a slip of paper to write on. "I have a student who runs a tutoring class after school. You'll probably need to go for at least a month to make sure you can keep up."

The last thing I need in my life is more math, but I take the slip and my test so I can get back to my desk.

"Let me guess," Bea says. "Tutoring?"

I wish my hand would actually cover the piece of paper. I turn it over. "It's not really any of your business."

"It's no big deal." She smiles. "I'm in it, too. The tutor, Seth, is really helpful. You should come with me today."

"I'm not going. My tu . . ." I pause, suddenly unsure if I should tell the truth. "We weren't this far at my other school. I can catch up on my own."

She pauses, looks at Brady with a little frown. "Oh, well if you go tomorrow or any other day, I guess I'll see you there."

"Yeah." I stare at her, trying to understand why she's being so nice. Even with her tank and shorts, I can't see a jaguar tattoo. Maybe she's not with Juan, but that doesn't mean there isn't some ulterior motive. Other students seem to avoid her and Brady, so there has to be something up with them.

33

At lunch, they invite me to sit at their table, but the last thing I want to do is eat in the cafeteria with all those eyes on me.

"No thanks, I need to use the computer," I say as they follow me.

"Ugh!" Bea stomps her foot. "You know what, Fi—?"

Brady wraps his arm around her shoulder. "Chill, Bea." He looks at me, so close to catching my eyes I can't seem to breathe. "It's hard, huh, having people act like you're a monster. I bet it was different in Vegas, where more people have significant abilities. For what it's worth, I don't think you're a monster."

I choke down the rock in my throat. "Oh."

"You don't have to hang out with us if you don't want to, but you're always welcome, okay?"

I bite my lip. "Okay."

"Have fun at the library." Brady waves, and Bea follows him down the hall. I watch them and wonder again if they're actually being genuine. It'd be so much easier if they were frauds.

The library isn't in any better shape than the orange-and-brown front office of yesterday, but at least it's free of wood paneling. It's nice, cozy cinder block instead. Rows of books fill the long room, as well as tables and orange chairs. It's busy, too—more with adults than teens, since it serves as the community library as well. I have to wait twenty minutes for a turn, so I spend it trying to decode my math book.

When I sit at the computer, I don't bother accessing my old account. There's no way Dad's not watching it. Luckily,

Miles and I have ways to get around that. They might not be foolproof, but at least they make me feel safer. I pick a different email service and fill out false information. When it asks me to put in an email address, I think of the most awkward name possible. BrittneyBunnyGurl33 is the winner, only because BrittneyBunny33 is taken, which is kind of disturbing. Oh well; I know it'll make Miles smile.

Hey, Sweet Cheeks, had a great time talking with you in class. I'm home visiting family and can't stop thinking about you. Found your email in the campus directory. Hope that's not too stalkerish. ;)
Brittney

I hit send, grinning despite myself. I've sent way too many vague, slightly disturbing emails to my brother, but at least I can be sure no one will think it's me. Browsing the internet to kill time, I hope he'll reply so I don't have to wait until tomorrow to check. There's only three minutes before lunch ends when something pops up in my inbox.

It's not from his old account—he's smarter than that. I nearly burst out laughing as I read HotMulletMan1.

You're sick, Brittney. Love, HotMulletMan1

A small smile crosses my lips as I type.

Gotta go, but I'll be here same time tomorrow. Hope we can talk more. Brittney

The bell rings, but I wait for his message anyway. It arrives just as the librarian comes over to make me leave. I click it, and for the first time in a long time I feel truly hopeful.

I'll be here. Miss you, HotMulletMan1

Chapter 6

The best part about my lunch dates with Miles is that they've saved me from the cafeteria. He spent last week "poking around," otherwise known as milking old contacts for information. So far it seems like Graham and Dad don't know where we are. Dad has a lot of people out there looking, but they don't appear to be concentrating on any one area. That's a good sign; it means they don't have any decent leads.

It also seems like the other syndicates don't know we're missing.

There's no talk, Miles writes. We've moved to instant messaging, so it's almost like we're in the same room.

How do you know?

Trust me. I know.

I laugh.

What, do you know Spud or something?

I plead the fifth.

I stifle a gasp. Dad never took Miles's scent-imitation ability seriously, but he shouldn't have overlooked Miles's knack for making connections. He's so easy-going even the toughest people seem to like him.

Are you serious? You know her?

The fifth. Anyway, seems like you're okay. For now.

Okay. Gotta go to class.

But that doesn't put me entirely at ease. If people at school get wind that I'm not here because of Dad, it's over. They won't hesitate to sell me out, whether it's to Juan or my dad. I won't give anyone the chance, though. I have no problem acting like a spoiled syndicate baby if it keeps me safe. Better if they think there will be hell to pay if they out me.

Miles said he'd take me away if I wanted, but I won't give him our location. Not yet. He's already risked enough. If Dad hears we've had contact, he'll hunt Miles down and kill him if he doesn't give up information.

Like I have for the past week, I bolt for my car at the last bell. As much as I want to talk with Miles again, I have to leave school before Bea finds me. She keeps asking me to come to tutoring so she's not alone in there, and I can't exactly tell her I have more serious things to worry about than math. I would have thought she'd take the hint by now, but she won't give up.

I pull out my keys when I get to the parking lot. But as I look over the rows for Mom's white SUV, I realize it's not where I parked it. I scan the cars again. Maybe I'm remembering yesterday's spot. But the longer I look, the sicker I feel.

It's gone.

An average teenager would probably think it was a prank, but an average teenager doesn't have a telekinetic mother. It's not the first time she's stolen a car.

One time we snuck into a luxury car dealership in Reno.

I went first, knocked out the guard, and disabled all the cameras with a pocketknife small enough to fit in my mouth. Noelle, one of Dad's women, taught me how. She's what they call a Chameleon, able to change her pigment at will. Not shape or features, just color. It's about the closest thing to invisibility.

Mom came in, smiling at a ridiculous, gold European car. "Jonas would love this one."

"How long will this take?" I whispered.

She laughed as she raised her hands. All the cars beeped, their alarm systems disabled. Then she used a wide sweeping motion to unlock all the doors. To top it off, every engine roared to life. "How long did that take?"

I rolled my eyes, just wanting to get back to Dad, wanting to see his smile and hear his praise. "C'mon, then."

She drove all the cars with her mind, in a straight line, back to Vegas. Dad kept the gold one, which set Mom on full Jonas glow for days.

At least this time the car kind of belongs to her.

I should have seen this coming a couple days ago when she asked if there was a bus I could take to school. I told her there wasn't, except for those bussed in from neighboring towns, and she seemed satisfied. But she must be desperate to contact Graham if she walked all the way here just to take the car. She's officially cracked. Graham's probably already on his way to get us, which means there's no way I'm going back to the house.

I back up and head for the library. I have to email Miles. He might not answer me immediately, but I at least have to tell him I'm in trouble.

"Fiona!" a familiar voice booms over the after-school noise.

Whirling around, I find Bea at the end of the hall. I almost consider continuing, but I turned too much. She had to have seen how my glasses moved to face her. I'll just have to deal with it.

"Please come to tutoring with me," she says when she catches up. "It won't be so bad if we do it together, I swear, and then maybe after we can—"

"I have to go to the library."

She lets out a long sigh. "Emailing your boyfriend back home or something?"

My jaw drops. What kind of guy would date an invisible girl? "No, I have . . . stuff to deal with. But speaking of boyfriends, where's yours? Shouldn't you be hanging out with him?"

One of her perfectly plucked eyebrows rises, and then her eyes go wide. "Oh, Brady? He's not my boyfriend, just a friend. My best friend, actually."

"Oh." I look at my sandals, even more confused about how nice he's been. I'd figured it was because his girlfriend wanted him to. "Well, I guess I'll see you later."

"Ugh!" Bea grabs my arm. I'm too shocked by the sensation to react. People don't touch me if they don't have to. I have this theory they're afraid their hands might go straight through. "What is your problem? I'm trying to be nice here, and I'm sick of you avoiding me!"

Her dark eyes search for mine. She seems genuinely hurt, but I've known a lot of great liars. Before I can think, one word escapes my lips: "Why?"

She tilts her head. "Huh?"

"Why are you being nice to me? Are you working for someone? Or do you want in with our syndicate? Either way, I'm not interested. Sorry." I turn to walk away, but she gets in my face.

"Are you freaking kidding me?" She's too close to me, so close I can smell her mint gum. "You didn't even consider that maybe I thought you needed a friend—that maybe *I* need a friend?"

My throat tightens, and I don't dare speak for fear I might sound more upset than I'd like.

She shakes her head. "You think you're the only person on the planet who gets shit for their abilities? Have you been paying attention to how people treat Brady? Haven't you noticed that all the open seats in class are around us? Why do you think that is?"

I hate admitting I've been more focused on how everyone treats me.

"We get it, too, Fiona. Maybe not like you, but people hate us, expect us to be bad, treat us like we're with Juan Torres when we're *not*." She looks me up and down, her lip curled. "I thought you'd be different. I thought you were more than a judgmental rich girl, but you're just like everyone else."

She steps back, waits for me to say something. I have nothing to say. She's right, and the truth of it hurts. She thought we'd have stuff in common. Maybe we actually do. That might have been my only chance to have a real friend, and I blew it.

She rolls her eyes. "Whatever. I get it. Have a nice life."

I watch her round the corner, already regretting not trusting her. But it's over now. She obviously doesn't want to be my friend anymore, so I head to the library. Emailing Miles is my first priority. Hiding from Graham is all that matters right now.

There are so many people waiting for computers that the librarian gives me a ten-minute limit. I barely have enough time to log in and type up an email to HotMulletMan1. I tell him I'll try to get another phone and call him if I'm in trouble. Then I get kicked off.

I can't go to the house. SuperMart is the only place in town that sells phones, but it's too far to walk in the Arizona afternoon inferno. I don't have anywhere to go. Except . . .

My chest tightens at the thought of going to tutoring. Bea's words come flooding back: *You're just like everyone else.* Well, that's a first. As much as I don't want to go, maybe Bea will give me another chance if I do. Besides, if I'm not going back to Dad, then I'll need any friends I can find.

I square my shoulders and head for the math room. But when I get to the door, a sudden wave of panic rushes in. What if Bea ignores me? I don't exactly want to spend the next hour doing more schoolwork, even if it could help take my mind off Graham. Maybe I should brave the trek to SuperMart and try to find a phone instead.

No. I can't let her think I'm that horrible, that judgmental. It's only one tutoring session. If she ignores me, then I won't come again. Taking a deep breath, I open the door and step into the cool room.

I'm surprised how many people are here, but relieved

to find Bea smiling. Only now do I notice how not a single person sits next to her, as if she's cursed. I'm such a jerk. I wave, the gold bangle around my wrist the only indication I moved at all. She pats the desk next to her, but before I head over I notice a guy coming from the front.

He must be the tutor, though I'm surprised he's not as old or geeky as I imagined a tutor to be. He's tall and thin, with strawberry-blond hair and a light dusting of freckles to match. His ears stick out, but he's actually pretty cute. Cute enough that I end up smiling a little as I wait for him.

Then his crystal-blue eyes meet mine directly, and I gasp.

A smirk crosses his lips. "You here for tutoring?"

"Uh." My heart flips, and I look down, unable to hold his gaze. Sometimes people hit dead-on like that—Miles more than anyone. It's unnerving, and yet comforting at the same time. I almost feel visible, just for the smallest moment.

He holds out his hand. "I'm Seth."

I stare at his palm. How strange that he would extend it to me. I take it reluctantly. "Fiona McClean."

His eyes go wide. "Oh! Right, yeah. Ms. Sorenson said you were supposed to be coming."

I purse my lips. "You . . . don't know who I am?"

"Not really." He scratches the back of his head. "I've heard things, but hearing and knowing aren't exactly the same thing, are they?"

"That's not what I meant."

He shrugs. "You here for tutoring or not?"

I watch him, trying to figure out why he's acting so . . . weird. Either he honestly doesn't care what my dad does, or he never watches the news and has no clue what's going on outside Madison, Arizona.

He waves his hand in front of my face. "Hello? Tutoring, yes or no?"

"Stop being a jerk, Seth," Bea calls. "Obviously she's here for tutoring."

He sighs. "I'll grab you some worksheets to do; that way I can gauge how far behind you are."

As he walks back to the front, I head over to Bea. "I thought you said he was really nice."

She chuckles. "No, I said he's helped me a lot—I never said anything about him being super-nice about it. Not that he's mean. He's just . . . Seth."

"Great. So no gold stars?" That gets a laugh.

"Unfortunately not. Seth's always been a little antisocial, but he's not so bad." She erases one of her answers and scribbles in something new. "He's like a math genius. He's a senior, but he's taken university-level courses for the last couple years. He tutors to pad his college applications."

"So is that his ability? Numbers?" Most everyone has some kind of mutation, though the change usually isn't more than a random hair color or other small alteration. It's the normal-*looking* people who are potentially dangerous, because their power lies somewhere else.

She opens her mouth to speak, but a stack of papers appears between us.

"Quit gossiping and get back to your graphs, Bea," Seth says.

She rolls her eyes. "Oh, c'mon, we both know I'm never gonna get this."

44

"You will. I'll make sure of that."

I raise an eyebrow, surprised by how cocky that sounded.

He turns to me. "Work through these. I'll check back in twenty minutes."

The worksheet starts out with basic algebra and geometry, but it quickly increases in complexity. By page three I can feel my brain seizing up. Before I know it, Seth pulls the paper out from under me. "Let's have a look."

I shrink in my chair, dreading his response.

As he flips the page, his brow furrows. It creases even more at the third page. He lowers the paper, staring at me for a moment. "Were you dropped on your head as a baby?"

I cram my lips together to stop them from quivering and push my tears into anger. "Actually, I was. I almost died, thank you very much."

He opens his mouth, but Bea speaks first. "Wow, Seth, can you be ruder? I don't think you've made her feel welcome enough yet."

He looks back and forth between us. "I—"

"Aren't you going to apologize?" Bea asks.

I can't express how grateful I am that she's defending me, because I can't seem to find any words. I never thought I was smart, but I didn't think I was stupid, either. Tons of people struggle with math. But Seth has probably tutored a lot of students. Am I really so dumb that he'd have to ask something like that?

Seth runs a hand over his face, letting out a long sigh. "Fiona, can I speak with you outside?"

"No," I barely squeak out.

He kneels by my desk, but I refuse to look at him. "I

need to talk with you about this worksheet, and I don't think you'd want everyone hearing."

I look around the classroom—everyone is listening, not even pretending to do something else. The last thing I need is more gossip fodder, so I reluctantly stand to face him. "Fine."

Chapter 7

I follow Seth outside, the hot air hitting me like a giant blow-dryer. My blue sundress flares up, but I don't bother pushing it down. Not like he can see. Besides, I wore underwear today, which I kind of regret now that Graham could be here. Sometimes underwear is the difference between getting away and getting caught. I scan the sky, the halls, even the tree branches for him. It looks safe. For now.

Seth sits under a tree in the courtyard, and I take a spot in the shade, plenty of distance between us.

He looks at my worksheets again, then directly at my frames. It freaks me out, how he doesn't search for my limbs or squint like that might help him see. He just picks a spot and stares. "I didn't intend to make fun of you. I meant that question literally. It seemed plausible, considering your ability."

I glare at him, the hairs on my neck prickling. Who does this guy think he is? "It doesn't matter what you intended, only how it's interpreted."

He raises an eyebrow. "Oh?"

"Yes." I force my mouth shut before I really go off on him. I shouldn't be this upset—I've been accused of far worse and it never hurt. A lump forms in my throat. The other accusations weren't true, but this one is.

Seth is quiet, watching me. I'm not sure if I prefer that to him talking or not, but it's easier to take in my surroundings, at least. Graham won't be able to sneak up on me—I already have every decent hiding spot in this courtyard mapped out. Seth finally says, "Would it have sounded better if I said I think you have a learning disability?"

Words won't form, and for a second all my other concerns disappear. When I said I want to figure out who I am, I wasn't asking to discover I'm an idiot. I finally compose myself enough to talk. "Barely. What makes you think that?"

"You missed simple questions, Fiona, and not on the algebra, but on the basic addition and subtraction within the algebra. See here?" He holds out the papers, and I force myself to look while he explains. "I can't believe no one has pointed this out to you before. Did your dad hire a bunch of fake tutors to give you a pretend education?"

I hate that I'm crying. Why am I crying over stupid math and this stupid boy who thinks he knows everything? Because he's right. That's exactly what Dad did—he put me in just enough school to keep me from noticing what I was missing. I didn't need a real education—not when I was his invisible henchman. I wrap my arms around my legs, wishing I had somewhere to run. If there wasn't a chance that Graham was at my house, I'd be gone.

"I need to recommend to Ms. Sorenson that you be moved to remedial courses ," Seth says.

That snaps me out of it. "What?"

"Your math comprehension isn't even at a seventh-grade

level, which means there's no way you can handle an eleventh-grade class. It would be better for you if you were moved. You aren't capable of passing."

"No." I can't seem to stop my head from shaking back and forth. I'm not doing that. Everyone will know. The teasing will never end. "No freaking way."

He rolls his eyes. "Calm down. It's not that bad. You're acting like I'm calling you stupid or something."

Finally I realize who he reminds me of—that attitude, playing down my feelings, belittling me constantly. He's just like Graham. Except he has no power over me, so I'm not putting up with this. "You aren't, genius boy? Maybe I'm too stupid to understand, but it sure sounds like you're calling me an idiot."

His eyes widen. "Hey, I'm not the bad guy here. I'm just telling it like it is."

I scoff.

"It's true. Having a learning disability doesn't mean you're stupid. It just means you need to learn in a different way."

"A slower, stupider way. Because I'm stupid."

He grips my worksheet, making it crinkle. "Will you quit it? I never said that—don't put words in my mouth."

I fold my arms, taking sick pleasure in seeing him squirm. "Why not? Maybe you should know how you sound to other people, because I have this feeling you don't realize what a jerk you are."

He opens his mouth, but then closes it again. The air goes silent. I can barely hear him breathe, and I refuse to look at him because all my anger seems to be pooling in my fists. If he flashes one more sneer, I might actually hit him.

49

"I'm not doing remedial courses," I say.

He sighs. "Then you'll fail, which would land you there anyway."

"I won't fail." I can't believe I'm saying it, but I don't have many other options. "You're gonna teach me."

His eyes go wide. "What?"

"Bea says you're the best, and it's not like everyone in that class is there for your charming personality."

His eyes narrow. "And why would I teach you?"

I smile. This is too easy. I already have Seth pegged. "I'd be a challenge, which you need because this whole place is too boring for your big brain. And it'd look good on your résumé, wouldn't it? If you could help me pass, you could teach anyone. Colleges would be impressed with that."

"Are you bribing me?"

"No." I smooth out my dress, confident he'll take me on no matter what. "I'm just pointing out the advantages, in case you don't see them. Bribing involves actual payment."

"Then extortion?"

I shake my head. "I'm not threatening you."

"So blackmailing."

"No!" I roll my eyes. "Blackmailing would be 'Teach me or I'll tell everyone you wear pink panties.' And besides, I don't have anything on you. Yet."

"Wow, you sure have your criminal terminology down." He sits back against the tree, smiling. "You really are Jonas O'Connell's daughter."

I about swallow my tongue. How did we get on this topic? "Don't say his name."

"Wh—"

"Just don't." I suppress a shiver. I am not like him. I'm not. "Will you help me or not?"

"Fine, but don't expect me to give you any special treatment. I'm not afraid of you like everyone else. I don't give a damn about abilities."

"Whatever. I could strip down, break into your house, and kill you before you even woke up." Not that I would, but I could.

Seth bursts out laughing. Not just a chuckle, but a full-on rolling-in-the-grass laugh. It doesn't sound right—too warm, kind. When he gets control of himself, his eyes run over my dress and back to my glasses, as if he's checking me out. "Are you saying you'll sneak into my room naked? Because that's what I heard."

My jaw drops, and my face burns way more than I want it to. I so regret thinking he was cute. "You're dead."

"Yeah, right." He stands, holds out a hand for me. "I have a feeling you wouldn't hurt a fly."

I get up on my own. "You have no idea."

His smile turns smug. "So you're saying you're a criminal and not some spoiled syndicate princess?"

I freeze.

"You know, I always wondered why people assumed Jonas wouldn't use such a valuable power, even if it meant manipulating his own daughter. Yet the way you avoided talking about him makes it seem like you're not exactly Daddy's little girl."

"That's not true," I say, though all I can think is, Crap, crap, crap.

"No?" He comes in too close, sending an unwanted tingle

down my spine. "You know what I think? You're on the run."

I can't seem to find air. How could he guess that? Was I that obvious? I've been working so hard to keep up appearances, but I was distracted with Graham and the learning disability stuff. I let my guard down. But I can recover—he can't see my face.

"Why would I run?"

He shrugs. "Maybe you're sick of doing your dad's dirty work?"

For a second I wonder if Seth's a mind reader, but then he would have known for sure I had a learning disability without the worksheet. "Look, I just hate the way people talk about my dad. You don't know him. You have no right to judge him or me. So if you start telling people—"

I go rigid when he puts a hand on my shoulder like it's no big deal. Maybe he really doesn't care about abilities. "Chill. No threats necessary. I'm not gonna spread rumors about you. But for what it's worth, if you were escaping, that'd be pretty amazing."

I can tell he means it, and that throws the entire horrible conversation on its head. It's official—Seth confuses the hell out of me. "Swear you won't."

"I swear it. Now let's get to work." He heads into the classroom, leaving my head spinning.

Chapter 8

Math tutoring may have been awful, but at least it was a decent distraction. As I pack up my things, all I can think about is Graham. I can't help but picture him at the house, perched somewhere high waiting to scare the crap out of me. His sick laugh plays in my head, and I shiver.

Maybe I should make for the desert now, except I don't have food, a way to contact Miles, or survival training. The little things.

"You didn't have to come just because I yelled at you," Bea says. "Not that I'm complaining."

A smile creeps onto my face. I still don't get why she wants me around, but maybe I shouldn't ask anymore. "Sorry. I'm not used to people being . . . nice."

She sighs like she knows what I mean. "What are you doing now? More library time, or you wanna hang out?"

"Oh, sure." I stuff my notebook in my bag, a flood of relief washing over me. This is perfect. I have a place to go, and I can at least stretch it out to the evening. Maybe I can form some kind of plan by then.

Bea's eyes narrow. "Are you sure? You sounded . . . hesitant."

"No! I want to." My face warms. People always have a

hard time interpreting my intentions without facial expressions to guide them, which is handy when I don't want them to. Not so much right now. "Um, I just need to go to SuperMart. You wouldn't mind going, would you? My mom took the car for the day."

She laughs. "That's fine! C'mon, I have a feeling you'll love Sexy Blue."

"Sexy Blue?"

She smiles wide. "You'll see."

Sexy Blue is a beat-up Bronco with no windows except the windshield, which is cracked. Bea is dressed well—cute, *short* shorts and a billowy teal tunic—so the dusty black seats and tacky giant dice on the rearview mirror surprise me. "My brothers totally beat her up, but she's still hot, huh?"

"Of course." I snap the tough, grimy seat belt over my waist. "So you have brothers?"

"Three older, one younger. My parents are hard-core Catholic, which means no birth control. Mom was basically pregnant for five years, had us all one after the other." She jams the key in the ignition, and Sexy Blue roars to life like a tiger.

"Wow, big family."

"Yeah, we're a regular litter." She laughs. "Actually, some people call us The Pack."

"Really?"

She nods. "We're really close, since a lot of kids in town weren't allowed to play with us. That's what happens when you come from a gifted family, right?"

"I guess so." Most of the people I knew in Vegas were

from gifted families, but I can understand a community of mostly normal people discriminating against the more gifted population.

"Anyway, what about you?"

I tense, unsure of what to say. It's not like I can tell her all about that time I went to California to help kidnap one of Valerie Sutton's brainwashers, just because Dad said we needed one and Val had too many. It's bad enough I'm a syndicate baby. She'd think I was horrible if she knew what I really did. "What do you want to know?"

She shrugs, a casual movement that makes it feel like we've known each other for more than a couple weeks. "Siblings?"

"Two older brothers. They're nineteen and twenty-two, so they don't live with us anymore." I neglect to mention the dozen or so half siblings I have. I try to pretend they don't exist, which is fairly easy because I rarely see them. Dad's smart enough to keep his women separated—heaven forbid they gang up on him. I accepted a long time ago that Mom and Dad would never get married, but it's still gross to think about how many other women and children he has, how he plays with their minds like he does with ours.

"Cool." Bea takes the turn sharp, and I grab the window-sill so I don't slam into her. She drives faster than a getaway man, but I don't complain. I don't want her thinking I'm a wuss or something. Besides, there's no air-conditioning and my butt is sweating way too much. The wind she generates barely takes the edge off the heat.

"So . . ." She grips the steering wheel tighter as she glances at me. "How's the invisible gig?"

55

I hold back my surprise. No one ever asks or points it out, just like they don't point out the blue people or the ones who smell like turpentine. "What do you mean, exactly?"

She scrunches her face. "My voice thing isn't so obvious. When we go to Tucson or something, no one knows and I can be normal for a while. I'm just curious what it's like not being able to hide it. I mean, you're *the* Invisible Girl. How does it all work?"

I watch her long hair fly in the wind. It's none of her business, but if I'm being honest I've always wanted someone to ask, to treat me like I'm normal. Miles is the only one who acts like it's no big deal, but Bea's trying.

I take a deep breath. "The doctors don't really know how it works, except that the mutation likely affects my pigment. They have a few theories, but they can't exactly study invisible blood or do surgery. They've tried dyeing me, but it disappears once I absorb it. All they know is everything my body makes is invisible—spit, blood, pee . . ."

"Wait, your spit is invisible?"

"Yeah."

"Spit on me! I want to see!" She bounces in her seat.

"You won't see; that's the point. I'm not spitting on you." I can't help but smile at the ridiculous request.

"C'mon! Do it! Would it look wet on my shirt? Or would I just feel it?"

"You wouldn't see it at all."

"I have to see! Please!" She shoves my arm. "I'm *asking* you to spit on me. How often are you allowed to use your invisible spit?"

"Fine." She has a point. I haven't spit on anyone since I

56

was a kid, and even then I only used it on Graham. I work up a good loogie and spit. She flinches, which is the only way I know I hit her. After touching the spot, she looks at her fingers with amused disgust.

"It doesn't even glisten, but it sure feels wet. Wow." She wipes my spit on the seat. "So what about eating? Could I see food in you?"

"No. Well . . ." I sigh, embarrassed. "If I ate with my mouth open you could see it for a second. Once it blends with my spit it goes invisible, and anything inside me can't be seen."

She laughs. "That's a relief. I was totally picturing this lump of mushy food under your shirt."

I snort. "Gross."

Her laughter dies out, and her eyebrows cinch together. "So no one has ever seen you?"

"No." It comes out harsher than I intended, but I didn't expect her to go that far.

She winces. "Sorry. I'm not good with boundaries."

"Don't worry about it. And no, no one has ever seen me. Not the real me, at least. I don't think X-rays and infrared count, because it's not my actual face, just a vague image."

She purses her lips. "Well, I bet you're banging hot. Your body is, from what I can tell of your clothes."

I stare at her, trying to convince myself I heard right. Then I laugh. Hard.

Her perfect eyebrows arch. "What?"

"That's the most ridiculous thing anyone has ever said to me." Bea is just plain crazy—that's why she's being so nice. Still, I like her.

"Whatever." She parks at SuperMart, and I can't believe we're already here. It doesn't seem like we drove all the way across town. "Let's get your crap. You better not expect me to pay for it, since I already gave you a ride."

I open my mouth, but nothing comes out. Her smile is different, this sly grin that says she's joking.

We head into the store, which is the only place in Madison to get anything from the outside world. The other businesses have been here for decades, like the old diner and bowling alley on Main Street, or the community pool I haven't had the guts to go to. SuperMart looks new. The red dust hasn't seeped into its facade yet.

I head straight for the electronics in search of a phone I can buy without too many strings. I find the perfect thing—thirty days, no contract, one-time fee.

Bea frowns. "That thing is a piece of junk." She holds up a flashy pink one I'd have picked myself. "What about this one?"

"I don't have a lot of cash." I only brought what I could find in my room when we escaped, and that was a few hundred.

She tilts her head. "You don't?"

I gulp. For a second I forgot she doesn't know why I'm here. She probably thinks I have all the money in the world. I would if I had Dad's credit card. I search for a good excuse, any excuse. "Uh, I didn't plan on being here so long."

"Right." The reality of this little friendship flits across her face—she's talking to syndicate royalty—but then it's gone again. She holds up the phone. "This is the one I'd get if I had the money. Mom and Dad can't afford five cells, and I'm not working at Taco Bell, you know?"

I laugh wryly. "Taco Bell doesn't sound so bad."

She bites her lip, and I fear I've said too much for us to ever really be friends. She has to know affiliating with me is dangerous. "Sorry. I must sound like a jerk."

"What?"

"It's just . . ." She shakes her head. "Never mind. I swear I'll figure out this friend-that's-a-girl thing. What else do you need?"

"Just some food and stuff." I pay for the phone there, since the salesperson won't let me leave the area otherwise. Then I head for the aisles, trying to figure out why Bea hasn't run for the hills yet. Whatever good vibe happened in the car seems to have died, and in its wake is some serious awkward silence. I grab a bunch of granola bars and Pop-Tarts, but not as many as I would have if Bea weren't there. I can feel her watching, thinking.

"Do you like movies?" she finally blurts out.

I try not to laugh. This could not get weirder. "Yeah, I do."

"We, uh, do a movie night at my house every Friday. I swear it's not as lame as it sounds. My parents usually duck out. Brady and—"

"Wait." I stop on my way to get water. "Is that why you stopped talking? You thought I'd think you weren't cool?"

She shrugs. "I don't know. There's probably a million exciting things to do in Las Vegas. Madison isn't exactly the center of awesome. Hell, it's not even the center of vaguely entertaining."

I can't help but smile. It's like we're both trying not to step on the other's feet. "You think I got to do anything fun with people always watching me? Of course I'll come."

She smiles. "Great. Except for the fact that Brady will so rub this in. He swore you'd say yes."

My cheeks warm. Brady wanted to invite me, too? Before I can reply, a guy floats into view and all the good feelings vanish. I shove Bea down the nearest aisle, abandoning the cart.

She stares at me. "What the hell?"

"I gotta go. Now." I can't seem to get air. This can't be happening.

"What? Why?"

My voice is a whisper, as if he'll hear me across the store. "Graham."

Chapter 9

"Who?" Bea searches between my rims, confused.

I regret bumming a ride off her. She shouldn't be involved, but she is and now I've put another person in harm's way. I take a deep breath. "He's my brother."

"I take it you guys don't get along," Bea says.

"Not exactly." I'm glad she can't see how I shake, because I'm seriously freaking out. Knees knocking, lip quivering, and all. Bea peeks around the corner, and I pull her back. "Don't!"

"Calm down, he's browsing for chips. He probably doesn't even know you're here." Her hands go to her hips. "Besides, he doesn't know who I am."

I stare at her, shocked by the fearlessness in her eyes. "Bea, I'm sorry I can't explain, but I have to go right now."

She nods. "I'll create a distraction, just in case."

For a second I'm speechless. She can't actually want to protect me. "No, you can't."

The grin on her face is positively impish. "Oh, yes, I can." Her voice sounds exactly like mine. "It's my specialty, actually."

I almost choke on my words. "You don't get it. Graham . . . he's not good, Bea. He'd kill you if he found out."

"He's not going to find out." Her eyes meet mine. "I knew it. You're trying to get out of your syndicate, huh."

First Seth and now Bea. "Is it that obvious?"

She shakes her head. "Not to people with average abilities. They don't know what it's like to be seen as a tool. How . . . hollow it makes you feel."

"And you do?"

She looks down. "We may not work for Juan's syndicate, but that doesn't mean he doesn't want us. You know how useful a voice contortionist can be; Juan could fabricate any sound with my voice, put out fake threats, trick people over the phone, whatever. He wants our whole family—my dad pays him off every year to keep him away. We may be poor, but it's worth it."

"It is," I whisper. Paying a syndicate to ignore you isn't new to me. Dad's brute squad collects dues every month.

"So I'm helping, no matter what you say."

I get this overwhelming urge to hug her, but I hold back. I never thought anyone else could relate. "Don't use my voice. He can't know you've seen me."

She nods. "Go. Tell me you're safe if you can?"

"Sure." I gulp down the lump in my throat. "Thanks, Bea. You are—"

She waves me off. "Just go! I get it."

I head for the exit, knowing I don't have time to buy food and water like I wanted. I have to get as much distance between Graham and me as possible. He flies fast, and he won't be at the store forever, no matter what Bea does to distract him.

As I reach the exit, a piercing scream comes from the

back. I don't turn to look, don't stop. I have to make Bea's risk worth it.

So I run. I run as hard as I can even though it feels like hell outside.

A few people stare. I hope they think I'm just in a hurry—at least the panic can't show on my face. I turn onto a quieter street, but keep heading for the desert. I need to get to that run-down group of buildings I saw last week. It's not much, but it's shelter and it's remote, which makes me feel safer.

I only stop when I find a green park, complete with shady trees and, most important of all, a water fountain. I drink until I can't anymore, and I'm so desperate I fill a crinkled bottle I find on the ground. It might be gross, but I'll be glad for it later.

Then I huddle under a bush and pull out my new phone. I curse when I realize my service hasn't been activated yet. I don't have time to wait around here, but who knows if I'll get service that far from town?

I make for the desert anyway. My sandals are so not meant for running; I can already feel blisters forming around the straps. Sweat runs down my back. I almost pull my dress off, but it would only help for a second. The sun would soak into my exposed skin, sucking the water out of me faster. I look to the sky every few minutes. Something flickers overhead, and I stop. Squinting into the sunlight, I catch the distinct flap of wings.

Stupid hawk.

But I can't help wondering if Graham will check the desert. When I don't show up tonight, will he suspect I've made a run for it? Probably. And he'll be pissed.

When I find the boulder from my first run, I plop down in the shade and pull out the phone, waiting for service. It kicks in just as I'm starting to cool off. Miles doesn't answer, so I leave a message. "This is Brittney. I need you."

My phone rings not a minute later.

"I think you should be in counseling, Brittney," Miles says.

Even his voice isn't enough to calm me. "Graham's here."

He curses. A lot. "Did he see you?"

"No. I ran—I'm out in the desert. I'm gonna stay in this old ghost town I found."

"I'm coming to get you. You're not allowed to argue."

"I wasn't going to. I called to tell you we're in Madison, Arizona." I give him our address and directions to where I'll be hiding. "I'm sorry I had to drag you into this, but I don't know what else to do."

"Don't be sorry. Let me look this up." The line goes quiet, save the faint tapping of keys. He lets out a soft whistle. "Jeez, Mom sure knows how to find the middle of nowhere, doesn't she?"

"And yet it's never far enough."

He sighs. "I'm sorry, Fi, but you could hop a plane to Mongolia and it still wouldn't be far enough."

His words hit me like a baseball bat. This will be my life, and whoever I let in will be dragged into this mess, too. It's a never-ending nightmare.

"Fiona?"

"How will I ever get away?" I choke back tears. "This is impossible, Miles."

"It's not." He says it so softly I can almost feel the hug

64

that goes with it. "We'll figure it out. I promise. You're about two and a half hours from me. That's pretty good luck, all things considered."

I let out a wry laugh. "Maybe Mom was trying to move closer to you."

"Hey, maybe. I'll just tell my boss I have a family emergency. She'll give me a few days—she totally loves me. I'll be there as fast as I can."

"Okay." The rock's shadow is getting longer, so I stand and prepare to go. "I need to run more before it gets dark."

"I'll find you, sis. I won't let Graham take you anywhere."

"Bye, Miles." I appreciate his words, but there's not much Miles can do against Graham. Even I have a better chance, since I can at least hide. Miles may be able to give off a nasty skunk scent, but that can only take him so far.

It's dusk when I reach what seems to be half of an old strip mall. The windows are broken, but it'll be decent shelter. I scan the horizon, surprised to find yet another structure in the distance. More like the skeleton of something. The desert is weird like that, with its cracked monuments to failed civilization. The call to explore it is strong, but it's too late today.

I hurry through the first window, hoping to find something comfortable to sleep on before the sun sets. The place is covered in fine red dust. Treading lightly, I keep my eyes on the floor in search of living creatures. The last thing I need is a scorpion friend visiting while I sleep.

It has to have been some kind of convenience store. There are a few intact shelves, sadly empty of Twinkies, which I hear last forever. The counter is still there, except half of it is missing, revealing a dark hole I don't dare investigate. Other than that, it's mostly broken plywood and twisted metal.

I brush off a few planks of wood, since that looks like my only option for sleeping, minus the floor. The dust sticks to my skin, giving a faint outline of where my arms are. Normally I wouldn't mind, but the idea of being seen right now is dangerous. I brush it off as best I can, leaving streaks thanks to my sweat. Hopefully it will absorb and become invisible soon.

My stomach growls, so I search my bag for any remnants of school lunches I might have missed. I manage to find a half-eaten bag of pretzels and a smooshed grape. Yum. I guess I can eat my math book if I get really desperate. I laugh a little—I'd love to explain that to Seth.

The desert is dark, but not pitch black. Starlight shines through the window, and I can't help but step outside and take a look. The canopy of lights takes my breath away. I've seen stars like this before, but the sight never stops making me feel small and unimportant. I like that feeling.

The stars twinkle like rhinestones, which reminds me of my mother. Will she worry when I don't come back? Or will she run to Dad without a thought? We used to be closer. We'd shop for hours at the most expensive places in Vegas. It's the only normal thing we've ever really done together.

I used to like it. I used to think we were bonding like moms and daughters do. She would clap or smile when I came out of the dressing room, and it made me feel beautiful. But then I started to notice something.

"Those clothes look great!" she'd say.

Not *you* look great. Not *you* look beautiful. The clothes did—I didn't look like anything. I was just the perfect mannequin.

"What about me?" I asked her once. "Do you think I'm beautiful?"

Mom froze, as if she didn't know what to say, which said everything. "I don't know, sweetie, but you shouldn't worry about it. You don't have to. Women everywhere would kill not to worry about that."

I nodded, wishing she'd lied and said I was the most beautiful girl in the world. It was then I realized even my own mother didn't quite see me as a real person. I was a doll, an empty canvas, something to play with when Dad wouldn't see her.

I started shopping on my own after that. At grungy places she'd never go to, wearing all sorts of strange things. It almost hurt more that she never got mad about it, never asked why I stopped going with her. She just complimented the clothes, like always.

A different light pulls my gaze from the sequined sky—a flashlight. My heart leaps. Miles! I can't believe he'd navigate the desert in the dark for me.

Then another light comes into view, and my stomach sinks. Miles wouldn't have brought anyone with him, but Graham might have enlisted backup. If he was at the store alone, then someone was probably watching Mom for him. What if they are coming to take me back?

I rush inside, stripping as I go.

Chapter 10

I have my clothes off in seconds. I'm not sure I should be proud of that skill, but it comes in handy when I need it. Searching for a place to hide my dress, I settle on stuffing it behind the counter. I mentally curse when I remember my bag is sprawled out on the floor. I creep toward it, trying not to disturb anything that could make noise or flare up dust. If I shove the bag under something, no one should know I'm here.

The flashlights cast two distinct beams outside, both growing wider as they approach. Though the light helps me navigate, it also makes my heart thump up my throat. I grab my things as the footsteps grow louder. I pause, confused. There's more than one pair, but Graham would never touch the ground if he didn't have to. It's "beneath him."

"Do you see anything?" a deep voice calls.

I gasp, dropping my bag in shock. I know that voice, though I can hardly believe it. What in the world is Brady doing out here?

"Uh . . . nope. Nothing," another familiar voice says. Seth.

It might not be Graham, but my pulse still hasn't slowed. I can barely wrap my mind around it. I had no idea they even knew each other, let alone knew each other well enough to run around in the desert together.

"Are you sure?" Brady says. "I thought I heard something."

I snap out of my daze, grabbing my bag and stuffing it under my plywood bed.

"There it is again. Coming from the building."

A light shines from the window, and I freeze. I may be invisible, but there's so much dust in here I have to be careful. I tiptoe to a corner, taking care to avoid leaving footprints, and huddle down just in case.

"It was probably a lizard or something," Seth says. "If Fiona was here, wouldn't she come out if she heard us?"

I can hardly believe it—they're looking for me. But Seth's wrong. I'm not coming out for anyone but Miles.

"I don't know." Brady steps through the broken window, shining his flashlight right over my concealed bag. He doesn't see it. "Trixy said she sounded terrified of her brother. Fiona didn't even want her helping because she'd get in trouble, so Fiona might think the same thing about us."

I smile because he's right. It's freaky how he seems to understand me.

"How considerate of her," Seth says. "Maybe she should have thought about that before coming here in the first place."

"It is considerate, since she's obviously trying to escape. There's no denying it now."

"You guys are so slow."

"Shut up, brainiac. You could have told us." Brady lifts things like they weigh nothing, checking for me. My heart warms at how concerned he seems. It's probably because Bea's worried, but it's still sweet.

69

"I promised her I wouldn't." Seth leans by the window, staring at the ground like he's completely bored.

Brady sighs. "Fine. I guess that's a good excuse, but from the way you were acting earlier I thought you'd be more—"

"Can we get going?" Seth stands away from the windowsill. "I don't run as fast as you."

Brady laughs as he shines the light on Mr. Cranky. "Changing the subject, huh? You must—"

"Will you quit it?" Seth holds up a hand to block the light. "We still have to check the factory, or we'll never get Bea off our backs. I don't know about you, but I'd like to get at least a little sleep tonight."

"You're not worried about her at all? It's not exactly safe out here, and Bea said she didn't have food."

"Fiona can take care of herself." Seth slips a backpack off his shoulders. "And that's what this is for. We'll leave half of it here and half of it at the factory. If she ran off this way at all, she's bound to see both."

Brady's shoulders slump. "I guess that's the best we can do."

"Yup." Seth unzips the bag, revealing several boxes of food, sports drinks, and even a blanket for the increasingly chilly night. "Let's get going."

Brady heads outside. "Do you want me to carry you?"

Seth scoffs. "I have some dignity, you know."

Brady laughs, and then their footsteps fade into the distance. I stay put for a few minutes, though the food and drink call to me. I don't want them to come back and see it gone. They probably don't realize I'm here, but it doesn't hurt to be extra cautious. When I can't take it anymore, I

70

rush to the window and look out. No flashlights. The other building's outline barely shows against the sky. They called it a factory, but it must be a ruin just like this. I'll have to check it out when I get the food they're apparently leaving there.

With the coast clear, I dig into some protein bars. I stuff one in my mouth, and I about die when I notice the box of blueberry Pop-Tarts, too. Bea must have seen them in my cart and figured I liked them. I pause midbite. I don't get it. I've never met people who'd risk themselves to help me escape, or who'd run around the desert all night leaving food just in case I was there.

I grab a drink, gulping it down as I think. They could be lying. Just because Bea said they weren't working for a syndicate doesn't mean it's true.

Bea's fearless eyes come back to me, then Brady's worried voice, and even Seth saying I'm amazing for trying to escape. They . . . might care about me. A chill runs down my spine.

Chapter 11

It's day three, and Miles hasn't come yet. He should have been here by now. As I stare out the window at the same tall cacti and mesa-lined horizon, I fear the worst. Graham found him. Graham knows there's only one reason Miles would be in Madison, Arizona. He's probably being tortured into giving them my location, except he never would.

If it were anyone else, I might be able to take it. But it's Miles, and it's my fault he's in this mess. The thought of him being beaten for me is too much.

I glance at my supplies. I went to the factory the first day, though it's so torn up you could hardly call it that. There's scrap metal everywhere, like a bomb went off. All that's left is half a building, gutted out. I stayed the night there, since I could see the stars through the holes in the remaining ceiling.

Brady and Seth left enough food to last a couple weeks, but I've already burned through most of the liquid. It's too hot out here. Just opening my mouth dries it out. I'll be dying for water before tomorrow night.

My legs ache as I pull myself up. There's not much choice—I have to get in cellphone range and at least try to call Miles before this phone dies. If Graham answers, I'll just hang up and get rid of it. I grab my things and head for my favorite boulder. The second I power it on, five frantic texts show up from Miles. Each one simply says **Where r u?** My hand shakes as I dial his number. It barely rings once before there's a voice.

"Fiona?" Miles asks.

Unexpected tears well up. "Are you okay?"

He laughs, though I don't think it's very funny. "Shouldn't I be asking you that? I went out there and couldn't find a thing—I thought you'd be dead by now. Mom's a mess."

I want to protest that I gave him good directions—at least as good as I could under the circumstances—but that doesn't matter once I realize the bigger issue. "Wait . . . Mom's still there?"

"Yeah." He doesn't say anything after that, and I can't seem to find words, either. Finally, he lets out a breath. "I'm not sure how to explain it, Fi."

"Is Graham there?"

"He left. Two days ago."

"What?" Too many questions run through my head, fighting for my mouth but failing to move it. Graham left *without* her?

"It'll be easier to explain if you come back to the house. It's safe, Fiona, for now. You know you can trust me."

I want to say it's some kind of trap, but Miles wouldn't do that. "You swear?"

"On my baseball-card collection—the whole thing." That's a serious oath. Miles is a baseball fanatic, both the normal and gifted leagues. If he could, he'd watch it all day and talk your ear off about stats. He knows I don't listen when he goes on his rants about batting average, but he does it anyway. He's determined to make me a fan.

"Okay. I'll see you soon." I close the phone and lean against the rock. There has to be some kind of catch. Graham couldn't have just left. Still, if he's gone, then we have time to plan. I don't know how much time, but it's better than hiding out in the desert and doing nothing but reading my math book. I was that bored.

I suck in a breath to calm my nerves and then head for town at an easy jog. By the time I reach the house, I'm drenched in sweat and sick to my stomach. I can't help thinking Graham's in there, waiting to trap me and take me back to Dad's casino. Now that he knows I tried to escape, I have this feeling we'll never leave Dad's watch again.

I almost turn back, but then Miles's warm laugh carries through the open window. My knees nearly buckle at the sound, and before I know it I've turned the doorknob.

There he is with Mom on the couch, all easygoing in his baseball tee and cut-off shorts. His hair is wild and wavy as usual, sun-kissed from the summer but still brown. He smiles at me, his eyes almost meeting mine. Then the room blossoms with the scent of blueberries. He knows how much I love them.

Scent imitation is a pretty useless gift, but in our family I consider that lucky for Miles. Dad hardly notices him, just remembers his ability is worthless. He made sure Miles knew that, too. I could never quite tell if it actually hurt Miles, but he's definitely no fan of Dad.

"I'd hug you, but I can smell you from here," he says.

"Thanks a lot." I shut the door, but stay where I am. "I'm surprised you're still here."

"I told you Graham wants to help us!" Mom's glare feels like a laser. "How could you run off like that? We thought you were dead! You can't just disappear on me!"

I scoff. "That's kind of hard to avoid, don't you think?"

"Don't use that attitude with me, Fiona Claire. I am trying to get us out, and every time you run off you risk ev—"

Miles puts his hand on her knee. "Mom, not exactly helping."

"I was just so . . . You shouldn't have done that." Her shoulders slump, and I stuff down the guilt. Let her be mad at me—I'm plenty mad at her for calling Graham. She deserves any worry I might have caused her.

I put my hands on my hips. "Is he waiting for me to show up?"

She purses her lips. "Graham is covering for us. He's making up fake leads, sending your father on a goose chase so we can live here in peace."

My jaw drops. "You're kidding." I look to Miles. "You can't actually believe this."

He shrugs. "I don't know, Fi. He seemed genuine. He didn't bring a team or even a phone. It's . . . possible."

"Possible?" This isn't happening. My family cannot be this stupid. After years of lies and manipulation, how can they not see through this? People don't change. Graham couldn't have woken up one day and decided he was going to be a good person again. "I need a shower."

"Hey, wait!" Miles calls, but I rush to my bathroom and lock the door.

I smell too awful to think clearly. So I pull off my clothes and let the warm water run over me until it gets cold, though it doesn't get *that* cold. Desert water only feels cool. I watch the water bead on my skin, try to hold perfectly still so I can see pieces of my fingers and arms. It's strangely beautiful, like dew on a spider web that reveals the shape.

My mind is surprisingly blank in comparison to the questions that pounded me before. I keep thinking about how thirsty I am, how much I want to sleep in my bed instead of on dusty plywood, how I should savor every day of freedom I have left.

When I shut the water off, Miles's voice comes from the hall. "You better wear something I can see you in. No shorts or stupid dresses."

"Fine." For some reason his joking never offends me. He's trying to tell me being invisible is no big deal, and it works with him. Mom could say the same thing and it'd piss me off. I dig out a pair of black jeans and a tight orange shirt, but then I feel like I'm dressing for Halloween. I slip the jeans off and grab some blue ones. Much better. Now I just have to accessorize. . . .

There's a knock at my door. "Are you decent?" Miles says.

I laugh. I once asked him why he doesn't barge in like everyone else does. He said it was awkward enough just thinking of me naked, and he'd prefer not to "see" it. "Yeah, come in."

He shuts the door behind him, a small grin on his face. "See enough of me?" I ask.

"Never enough." He holds out his hands, and I rush into him. His arms come around me firmly, and for a second I

76

feel safe. Miles's hugs always remind me how nice it is to be touched. "I'd go with your blue glasses. I always liked those."

I pull back, knowing he's trying to lighten the mood. But I can't let this one slide. "Why would Graham cover for us? He's never done it before—he has to be up to something."

Miles lets out a long sigh as he sinks onto my bed. "I don't know right now, Fi, but I'm gonna try and find out."

"Why did you believe him?"

He watches me put on my glasses, worry finally creasing his brow. "I only said that for Mom, since she believes it completely. I couldn't kill her hope—she's doing so much better than I've ever seen. She almost has a soul again."

I bite my lip. Mom has been more . . . *something*, lately. I'm not sure if it's better or not.

"She said he gave her the money to buy a place, told her to run when the time was right and call him when she felt like she had her head on straight. Or straighter, at least. He said he's coming every weekend to check on you guys, make sure you're 'safe.'" Miles makes air quotes, his skepticism completely apparent now.

I lean on my dresser, weak at the thought of Graham coming back. "You're kidding."

"I wish. Don't worry, though. I'll switch my work schedule around so I have weekends off. I promise I'll be here, too."

"But—"

He holds up a hand. "I know you want to keep me safe, sis, and I appreciate it. But you let me go to school without feeling guilty, so it's my turn to watch out for you. Whatever Graham's motive, this is seriously the best chance you've ever had to escape."

I know he's right, but it's still a huge risk. Miles will pay for this, one way or another. "Are you sure?"

He scratches his head. "Not really, but if we play along, maybe Graham will get careless."

I sit next to him. "Then we can find out why he's doing this."

"Precisely."

Chapter 12

After my stay in the desert, parking in front of the school is surreal. I didn't think I'd make it back, and I'm surprised by how nice it is to be here. As I walk though the halls, people stare like usual, but it doesn't bother me as much. They don't matter. I have to find Bea and tell her I'm okay.

"Fiona!" Before I turn around, Bea slams into my back, nearly knocking me over.

"Hi?"

"She might have been a little worried about you." Brady comes into view, as gorgeous as ever in a green T-shirt. He pulls at Bea's arms, grazing my skin in the process. "Trixy, let the girl breathe."

She lets go. "I was starting to think we'd never see you again, and after all that work just to get you to talk to me."

I turn the dial on my locker. "I'm guessing you guys were behind the food. It was a lifesaver, thanks."

"No problem," Brady says. "I run in the desert all the time."

I sigh. "So I figure you guys know I'm not with my dad?"
He nods.

"I know it's a lot to ask, but you have to keep quiet about it. If the wrong people found out . . ."

Bea smiles a Trixy grin, her eyes lighting up. Brady laughs as he puts one heavy hand on my shoulder, coming close to whisper. "Don't worry about that. We have it all taken care of."

I get fluttery all over being so close to him. "What?"

Bea shrugs. "We might have implied you were visiting your beloved father."

"We might have also implied that he'll visit if he hears about anyone being mean to you. That put the fear in everyone, so I think you'll be fine." Brady's smile dazzles me almost as much as his words.

I can't find a description for this feeling in my chest. The food was amazing enough, but putting together a cover for me? "I can't believe you guys would—"

"Believe it, chica." Bea punches my shoulder. "Don't think this got you out of movie night, either."

"Oh yeah, Friday's tomorrow, huh?" I'd forgotten with all the Graham drama. "Sure."

"I'll pick you up, if you want," Brady says as the bell rings.

"Okay. That'd be great." I'm glad neither of them can see how hard I blush. That's another great thing about being invisible: I can crush all I want and no one will ever notice. "I guess I'd better get to home ec."

"See you at lunch?" Bea asks.

I pause, the truth harder to say than I thought it'd be. But they've more than earned it by now. "Um, I email my brother Miles at lunch. It's the only time I have."

Brady nods. "Got it. We'll see you in class, then."

"Yeah." I practically skip to the home ec room. My limbs

feel lighter. I can't push back the smile. I'm . . . happy. No, more than that. It feels like the leash around my neck is gone. It feels like I can breathe for one second without having to worry about Graham or Dad or the next horrible job.

I can't remember ever feeling like this before, but I think this is what freedom feels like. This is what it must be like to be normal.

I could get used to it.

"Well, well, look who decided to show herself." Seth stands at the front in tutoring, arms folded. So much for good feelings.

"Shut it, Seth." Bea grabs my arm and plunks me down in a chair. "He has a weird way of showing worry, but I swear he was as scared as me and Brady."

"I don't care if he was worried or not," I say.

"Good." Seth's voice comes from behind, and I whirl around to find him standing right over me. "I take it you still can't figure out your math book?"

I glare at him. He knows I was out there in the desert hiding, and still no compassion. Too bad I didn't eat it. "I'm still putting up with you, aren't I?"

He holds back a smile. "Here's a worksheet. If you have questions . . . yeah."

He throws it on my desk and rushes to the next victim. Before I start in on my after-school torture, I notice Bea staring at me. "What?"

She leans in to whisper. "He *always* has a clever come-back. Did you perform some kind of voodoo?"

"Not that I know of. I just let him know what a jerk he is."

She laughs. "He's so not used to people calling him out. I know it doesn't look like it, but I think he respects you for standing up to him."

I shake my head. "No. He really doesn't. Trust me."

"Whatever. He so needs someone to put him in his—"

"Back to work," Seth barks.

Bea grumbles at her worksheet. I stare at my own, trying to remember what steps go into solving these problems. It's all a mess in my head, and soon I'm thinking more about what Bea said than numbers.

I'd have thought people would put Seth in his place all the time. He's not popular, at least from what I've gathered. He's not *that* hot. He doesn't even have a cool ability. He's just a glorified calculator. Why would anyone let him get away with that attitude?

The hour's almost up. Just when I hope Seth's too busy, he grabs my worksheet. He lets out a long, exasperated sigh. "It's like you went backward."

My fingers tighten around my pencil. I refuse to look at his face as he sits down next to me.

"Everything we went over the first day is completely gone, isn't it?"

I try to calm myself, knowing if I speak too quickly he'll sense my hurt. "Maybe you didn't teach me anything at all."

He leans forward, and I look away so I don't have to see his face. "Is that true?"

"You're not as good a teacher as you think."

He glares at me. "Everyone but Fiona can leave early. See you tomorrow."

I groan. I swear I was happy today, until he decided to remind me what an idiot I am.

"Don't make her stay forever, Seth," Bea says.

He rolls his eyes. "I just need to talk to her for a second."

She touches my shoulder lightly. "I'll wait, okay?"

"You don't have to. I have the car today."

"I will anyway. By your locker." She leaves, and I'm left to face Seth alone.

He stares at me like I'm supposed to talk first. I don't. Finally, he starts. "I need you to be honest, because I can't find what helps if you aren't telling me what doesn't work. Have I really not helped you?"

"Not really." I focus on my pencil, because his blue eyes are starting to freak me out. They're too intense, judgmental.

"Do you mind giving me more? If you really want me to help you pass, I have to know what's wrong. You . . . have to trust me."

"I don't."

"Why not?"

"Because you're a jerk."

"So?" He tilts his head, his smile smug. "I'm honest and you know it. I've kept your secrets—will keep them. It's not my problem if you can't handle someone who doesn't treat you like royalty."

"You have no clue how I've been treated."

"Then tell me."

"No."

"C'mon. Based on what you said the other day, I already

know you worked for him. It might help if you talked about it. What did he make you do? How were you treated?"

I squirm. Add a bright light and this could be an interrogation. "How does this help with math?"

"Understanding someone's background helps in any teaching situation. Knowing you had a head injury as a baby helps, and maybe there are other things I need to know."

"None of that other stuff has anything to do with math."

"What other stuff?" he presses.

Dad's image swirls in my head, his words and smile and love. All of which are lies. He comes when he needs me to do something for him, showers me with affection until I'd do anything just so he won't leave. So I rob a bank or destroy evidence. And he still leaves. "You wouldn't understand."

"You might be surprised," he says quietly.

I glance up at him. He looks upset, but I don't care.

"Forget it." Remedial math has to be better than this. I don't need therapy; I just need to pass my freaking class. I head for the door, but he beats me there. "Move!"

"Fiona, chill. I'm trying to help you, but I need your cooperation."

I fold my arms. "Then you have to stop treating me like an imbecile."

He rolls his eyes. "I'm n—"

"There!" I say, pointing. "Right there! You're doing it right now."

"What?"

"I don't care if you're not *trying* to make me feel stupid;

84

you are." I want to scream, but settle for a frustrated grunt. "You want me to tell you something? Fine! I have feelings, even if you can't see them. People have been treating me like an emotionless robot my whole life—people I *hate*. So stop."

His eyes run over me, but he says nothing for a while. Then he looks down. "S-sorry."

I blink. I have a feeling that word doesn't often escape Seth's lips. "Thank you."

"I get that you don't want to talk about your life." He kicks at the floor. "But I still need to know what, exactly, is making math so hard for you."

I decide to walk back to my desk, since I can't find the words to explain it immediately anyway. Seth follows, taking the seat next to me again.

"Numbers don't stick in my brain," I finally say.

Seth purses his lips, and I can tell he's trying not to be rude. "Can you be a little more specific? A lot of people say that."

I sigh. "It's like . . . I can't remember how things work, I guess. I can learn to add just fine, but then somehow I forget it. I have to constantly remind myself how to add and subtract—how to count, even."

"Hmm," is all he says.

"Hmm?"

He shakes his head. "I'm not trying to be mean, but it sounds like some kind of short-term memory loss, just more specific. It's only with numbers?"

"I guess. Not like I've been tested." I fiddle with my hands, trying not to get worked up over the idea that I

85

have brain damage. Of course I have brain damage—I was dropped into the world. Maybe I'm more upset that no one cared enough to find out earlier.

"How are you with mnemonic devices?"

I shrug. "I can remember them, but it doesn't help much with the actual numbers."

He nods. "True. Well, we'll figure it out. This helps a lot."

I search his face, surprised that he still looks as confident as ever. "You really think you can teach someone like me?"

He smiles. "I'm up for the challenge."

Cocky bastard. "Okay, well, can I go now?"

"Sure."

I don't waste a second getting out of there. Bea's at my locker just like she said she'd be. She winces when she sees me. "How'd it go?"

"Besides the giant fight? Great."

She runs a hand over her face. "I'm so sorry. Boys can be such idiots."

"Not your fault. Well, kind of." We both laugh as I shove all of my books in my locker; I'm too tired to think about homework tonight. I want to enjoy life a little for once. "It's burning up out here. Let's get an ice cream or something."

She smiles wide. "Excellent plan."

Chapter 13

It takes me forever to get ready for movie night. I go through every piece of clothing I brought. Nothing seems good enough. Brady's picking me up, and I can't help wondering if that means something. Bea could have gotten me. I could have come on my own. But he seemed like he *wanted* to.

Maybe I'm reading too much into it. It's not like I know him that well. I just think he's cute. But isn't that how relationships start? Not like I know, but from what I've seen in movies that seems to be the case. Bea said I have a hot body; maybe Brady noticed and that's enough.

I finally settle on a hot-pink tank top that shows off my boobs, or at least their outline. I grab a sheer black nylon shirt and slip that over the tank top. Since it has sleeves, it brings out the shape of my arms, even my collarbone, without making me too sweaty. I grab a gold headband to show where my head is, but forego glasses. With my tight black jeans and gold flats, I can't get much prettier.

Instead of waiting for Brady to ring the doorbell, I head downstairs a little before eight to wait outside. There is no way Mom is meeting him. She's in the living room doing yoga.

"I'm going out. I'll be back in a few hours," I say as she stretches out like a cat.

She looks up, her eyebrows arched. "Where? And with who?"

I sigh. "What's with all the questions?"

"I kind of need to know, since I'm your mother and all," she says, complete with eye roll like she's still a teenager. "This town seems pretty quiet, but I'd still like to make sure you're safe."

Where was this concern when we were sneaking into stores and spying on people? "Oh, because you cared so much before."

She frowns. "I cared. I always care about your safety."

"Sure." That is so not true, but whatever. "Why does it matter? We're probably going back home next week anyway."

Her mouth drops, and I immediately regret my sarcasm. I have to keep pretending everything is fine. I don't want her putting Graham on alert.

"We're not going back. I'm done with your father." She bites her lip and looks away. I don't believe her words any more than she does. So what if she's done better this time? Dad still has her on a leash, and it tugs at her neck even now.

I clamp my mouth shut, determined not to argue so I can leave. "Sorry."

She doesn't answer immediately, giving me this look like she expects answers and she expects them now. I'm not a fan of this newfound assertiveness. "Well, are you telling me or staying home tonight?"

"I'm hanging out with a girl from school, okay? We're watching a movie at her house." I'd rather not say Bea's name if I can help it. That will keep her safe.

Mom looks almost satisfied. "Any boys?"

"No. Can I go now?" It's ridiculously easy to lie when you're invisible.

"I guess this is real life, isn't it? Have fun." She goes back to her yoga, and I rush out the door.

Headlights shine in the dimming light. My heart speeds up, and I can't help but smile. I can make out Brady's silhouette in the driver's seat. Then my heart stops. There's not one figure in the old black truck—there's two. So much for this ride meaning something. He was just being nice, probably saving Bea the gas. I bet that's her in the passenger side.

The black truck slows in front of my house, and I briefly consider faking ill. Brady hops out, adorable smile pasted on his perfect face. "Hey, Fiona! You ready?"

"Yeah."

"Great. You get the middle." He moves to the side, searching in vain for my face, but then his eyes zone in on my chest. Maybe the night's not lost after all. "I think this is the most I've seen of you. You look nice."

I can't help but smile. Maybe it was just a slip of the tongue, but people usually don't say *I* look nice. "Thanks."

"You're welcome. Let's go."

I climb in the driver's side, but my stomach wants to climb back out when I see who's ruining my alone time with Brady. Seth. *Seth?* So the run through the desert wasn't just Bea gathering anyone who might help. They actually know each other, might even be friends, which sucks.

"What are you doing here?" I ask.

Seth raises an eyebrow. "I'm not allowed to take a ride with my brother?"

No. No no no. Brothers? I didn't think it was possible to feel stupider. Now that he said it, I can see the family resemblance. The same slightly wavy hair, though Brady's is redder. The freckles, the blue eyes, the smirk. Seth is like the grumpy, skinny version of Brady. How did I miss it?

"Wait," Seth says. "Bea didn't tell you we're brothers?"

"No."

He looks at Brady. "You didn't tell her?"

Brady holds up his hands. "I figured Trixy told her!"

Seth sighs. "And Bea probably assumed you told her." He glances at me, almost looking apologetic. "I thought you knew."

"It's not a big deal," I say, though it is. I didn't realize movie night meant spending more time with Seth. Not exactly what I signed up for.

"So now that you know us well enough to come to movie night, I figure it's time to decide on a nickname for you." Brady makes a tight U-turn and speeds down the quiet street. "'Fiona' is three whole syllables, after all."

I smile, searching for the seat belt as best I can without crossing personal boundaries. "Okay. What do you suggest?"

His grin turns mischievous. "How about Fifi?"

I'm glad he can't see me cringe. I hate, hate, *hate* that nickname. There's only one person who calls me that, and he does because he *knows* I hate it.

"She's not a poodle." Seth holds out the belt for me. "Here, *Fiona*."

I take it, not at all surprised that Brady isn't immune to Seth's rudeness. Of course he'd be like that to his own brother.

Brady pouts. "You don't like Fifi?"

I don't want him to feel bad, so I nudge him playfully. "It's okay. I don't mind."

Seth scoffs. I glare at him, but he's staring out the window, eyebrows pulled down, mouth pursed. He didn't have to come if he's going to sulk the whole time.

"You know," Brady says, "you don't look like a Fifi anyway. I think we'll just stick with Fi."

I laugh, hoping this is his way of flirting. "Sounds good."

"You'll love Trixy's family," he says as we head to the other, older side of town. The houses here don't look as uniform as in my neighborhood. There are real trees, with shade and everything. "We've been neighbors our whole lives."

"Wow." I had no idea they had such a history. It feels like I'm intruding on something special and reminds me that I don't know any of them that well. My heart beats against my ribcage. Maybe this wasn't such a good idea.

"Are you nervous?" Seth asks.

"What?" I realize I have my hand over my chest, giving me away. I put it back in my lap. "No. I'm fine."

Brady pats my knee. "Don't worry. They'll love you. Carlos maybe a little too much."

"Who?"

"Oh, you'll see. Carlos loves the ladies." Brady laughs.

Seth rolls his eyes. "She's invisible. He'll look right over her."

I bite my tongue. Maybe Seth has stopped treating me like an idiot, but he still finds plenty of ways to make me feel like crap. What can I say, though? He's right. I hate that he's right.

Brady shakes his head. "I don't know. I think you can tell Fiona's pretty, invisible or not. Ten bucks he'll be all over her."

My face warms. Brady actually noticed me. Not in an oh-she's-invisible way, but in a there's-something-underneath way. Maybe I'm not being crazy about him liking me. Maybe Seth decided to butt in and Brady couldn't say no.

"You're on," Seth says.

I'm lost for the rest of the conversation, which involves names of people I don't know and activities I had no clue they participated in. All I can gather is that Seth is on the soccer team with someone named Hector, who is trying to steal Seth's spot as forward, whatever that is.

Brady pulls into a cracked driveway in front of a modest, if not run-down, home. The paint probably used to be white, but now it's a dusty gray color. The blue shutters are cracked; one's even crooked. But for all its flaws, it has beautiful landscaping and a manicured lawn, almost as if someone's trying to hide the condition of the house.

"Home sweet home." Brady unbuckles his seat belt and motions for me to follow him. "Trixy's place is just over here."

"Okay." I walk with Brady and Seth to a neighboring house. The yard, with its rock lawn and cacti, is nothing like theirs. The house itself screams Southwest, complete with peach stucco and round terracotta tiles on the roof. An array of saints stand guard on the porch, and a large cross hangs on the door. A large cross that is also a doorknocker.

When Bea said her parents were devout Catholics, she wasn't kidding.

Brady ignores the knocker, walking into the house like he lives there. The place is messy, but not in a bad way, just in a five-kids-plus-parents kind of way. A pile of shoes partially blocks the hallway, stacks of paper cover the kitchen table, movies and game consoles litter the living room.

We walk past it all in silence. A place like this should be loud, but it sounds like no one's home. Brady stops at the back door, smiling. "You ready to meet the rest of the Navarros?"

I gulp, my hands suddenly sweatier than they should be. It's just Bea's family—what's the big deal? "Sure."

Brady opens the door, and I stifle a gasp. Maybe I'm not ready for this after all.

Chapter 14

The backyard is nothing like the rock front. A shaded patio stretches out across the back of the house, and past that lies a lawn almost the size of a soccer field, complete with goalie net. It's beautiful, but that's not the most breathtaking part.

I used to laugh at those old pictures of families around the dinner table, out camping, or in the backyard grilling. It seemed so over the top, unrealistic. Families aren't like that—most of them are messed up. Siblings fight. Parents say cruel things. Images like that were just as fantastical as dragons and unicorns. Maybe more.

But now I'm not so sure, because Bea's family looks like a moving version of one of those photos. Her mother, smiling and beautiful, sets plates around two picnic tables. Her father stands by a grill, spatula in hand, complete with chef's apron. And there's Bea, playing soccer with four black-haired boys. They're laughing, and I can feel their love from here.

I can't go out there. I don't belong in this perfect scene. A person like me is sure to ruin it. I back up, bumping into Seth.

He doesn't move out of my way. "I know Bea's brothers are butt-ugly, but you don't have to be scared."

Brady laughs. "They don't bite."

"It's not that." I wring my hands as I look for a way out, but Seth blocks the narrow hall.

He puts his hands on his hips. "Then what? Are they not good enough for you? I bet you're used to gold plates and fancy chefs."

I search his eyes, trying to understand what his problem is. I know I'm a horrible person, but I haven't done anything to him personally to deserve so much crap.

"Seth, you're being—" Brady starts.

I hold up my hand. "I can handle this." I take a deep breath. If telling him how rude he is hasn't worked, I'll have to try something new. "You know me so well, don't you? I never eat anything unless it costs more than a hundred dollars. That's why I request my Pop-Tarts dipped in caviar and wrapped in gold foil. And when I spent that time hiding in the desert, I had my masseuse fly in because I was so bored out there having my little-rich-girl tantrum."

He looks down, and I try to suppress my smile. Whether he respects me for it or not, I plan to put him in his place. I come in close, savoring his look of defeat. "Did you ever consider that maybe I don't want to bring my shit to that happy family out there? Do you think I don't know how much danger I've put them in just because they've shown me the smallest bit of kindness?"

Brady's heavy hand comes down on my shoulder. "Don't worry about that, Fi. Seth doesn't think you're spoiled or whatever; he thinks—"

"You just think *I'm* horrible," Seth says.

I roll my eyes. "I don't."

"Liar."

Before I can answer a knock comes from behind. It's a guy who isn't even close to butt-ugly, with his gorgeous brown skin and strong features. He reminds me of a panther, almost, with the sharp angles of his face and his knowing eyes. "There you are! I could hear you all the way across the field. Maybe you forgot, but the party's outside, guys."

"Hector." Seth scoots past me, and Hector gives him one of those guy hugs with the back pat. "This is Fiona."

He glances at me, seeming completely unfazed. "I gathered as much. Bea's out back."

I blink a few times as Hector and Seth head outside. I'm not sure what kind of reception I was expecting, but that certainly wasn't it. A lot more gawking and questions were involved in my version.

"Hector is Seth's best friend, and he happens to have extra sensitive hearing," Brady says.

I nod. It's not a particularly unique ability, but it's useful all the same. My dad has a whole squad of them for spying purposes. Then it clicks. "Ah, so he was saving Seth from me."

Brady smiles. "Something like that. Probably more like saving Seth from saying more stupid stuff. Sometimes he spits out clever comebacks before he realizes the consequences, but he doesn't mean it, Fiona. He doesn't hate you at all. I promise."

I lean against the wall, not sure I want to go out there yet. "I guess that's mildly comforting. Why is he like that? Did something happen to him?"

As Brady rubs the back of his neck, his whole

countenance changes, like I sucked the happiness right out of him. All that's left is pain—the deep kind that rips you apart. "I don't know. I guess everyone has different ways of dealing with crap, right? Let's go find Trixy."

He's out the door before I can get a word in, and I stay there a moment wondering if I should leave. This is already becoming complicated.

"Chica! C'mon!" I look out to find Bea waving, her smile calling to me. It's real, this genuine happiness I've never felt. So I step across the threshold and into the backyard.

But as I walk through the cool grass toward her, an unexpected pang of frustration hits. "Why didn't you tell me they were brothers?"

She sighs. "Would you have come if I did?"

"I . . ."

"Exactly." She hooks her arms with mine. "Seth's always been a bit blunt, but you can't judge the whole group on one bad apple, can you?"

"I guess that's—"

"Well, well, is this fine thing Fiona?" A voice comes from behind. I turn to find a guy about my height and just as good-looking as Hector, except his eyes are yellow like a cat's, complete with diamond pupils. "No wonder you kept her from me, Trixy."

Bea groans. "Make that two bad apples. This is Carlos."

"Bad is right, baby." Carlos comes in closer, and I shudder. "It's so nice to have a beautiful girl in the house for once."

Brady laughs. "Seth, you owe me ten bucks!"

Bea punches Carlos. "Cut it out. This is exactly why you'll never have a girlfriend."

Carlos grabs me around the waist. "I don't know what you're talking about. Fiona and I look good together, don't you think?" His arm slides down a little. "Wow, you're toned, chica."

I grit my teeth. Usually I savor every touch I get, but there's something I don't like about his. "Please don't make me kick you in the balls."

"Aww, don't be li—" A soccer ball smacks Carlos right in the head, and he loosens his grip enough for me to get away.

Hector, Seth, and Bea's other brothers are practically rolling on the grass in a fit of laughter. Bea and Brady join in, and even I can't keep the smile off my face. That was some good aim and seriously perfect timing.

Carlos grabs the ball. "Okay, who ruined my moment?"

Without a hint of apology, Seth raises his hand. "Keep your hands off her. She's nervous enough without you mauling her."

Maybe I don't mind his jerkiness as much when it's used for my protection.

"You'll pay for that!" Carlos drop-kicks the ball at them, and then charges. They pile on him, wrestling in a brotherly display of affection.

Bea sighs. "Boys."

"Yeah. We suck." Brady smiles, which is when I realize he's not over there with them. He can't be—he'd smash them all to bits. I ache for him, knowing how much it sucks to be on the outside even among powerful people.

"At least we're in agreement." Bea points out her other brothers, José and Antonio, who I'm told won't answer if

I call them that. It's Joey and Tony, and they have a perfect sense of direction and the ability to "speak in tongues," respectively. Very handy skills. They're both in college, but they always drive home for the weekend family stuff. Then Bea introduces me to her parents, who seem too nice to be real.

"You'd better eat four burgers," her dad says. "You're too thin; I can hardly see you."

"Alejandro, save your jokes. Start her out easy; tell her about your glory days in the National Soccer League instead." Her mother, Rosa, turns to me. "He was one of the best in the Gifted Division."

So that's how he paid off Juan.

He nods. "Excellent idea."

And with that, her dad regales us with tales from his more athletic days. Apparently he made the National Gifted Team because of his extralight body tissue and resulting speed. The year before the Olympics, he took a cleat to the knee and hasn't been able to run the same since. "That's when we moved here, and I started working for John as his second-in-command."

"My dad," Brady whispers to me. "Runs a construction company."

"Oh. He doesn't come to these?"

Brady's Adam's apple bobs. His hesitation tells me I've crossed into forbidden territory.

"Okay, boys!" Bea's dad waves the spatula. "Come and get your buns ready!"

Bea hangs her head. "I forgot how embarrassing it is to bring people over here."

99

"Don't be embarrassed; your family's cool. Minus Carlos."
I leave out the part where I'd kill to have a family this close to normal. This happy.

She laughs. "Don't you want to spit on him?"

"Fiona can spit on me as much as she wants." Carlos sits next to me. "Anywhere she wants."

Almost everyone at the table smacks him across the head. His mother glares at him. "You are going to confession twice next week."

His shoulders slump. "Fine."

"You count those stupid comments up, Fiona," Joey says through his food. I can tell he's just what an older brother should be. "Give me the numbers each week, and I'll make sure he pays for them."

"You say that as if you expect there will be a lot," I say.

"Because there will be," Hector says. "Carlos practically has a degree in douchebaggery."

Carlos straightens proudly. "I could be a professor of douchebaggery. Fiona can be my teacher's aid."

Tony, who hasn't said a word, grabs Carlos's exposed boxers and pulls. Carlos lets out a yelp, and everyone laughs save Bea's mom, who shakes her head. "I'm so sorry, Fiona," she says. "I tried to teach them manners."

I smile. "I have two brothers. Don't worry about it."

"Then you'll fit right in." Bea's dad smiles as he raises his glass to me. I raise mine to him, touched that he could be so kind and welcoming to someone like me.

"Come sit over here, Fi, before Carlos gets sent to confession all week." Brady scoots over, giving me just enough room between him and Seth. It's scary that sitting by Seth

100

is the better option, but being next to Brady makes up for it.

After the first prayer of my life, we dig in. The burgers are amazing, mostly because Bea's mom prepared a full spread of toppings. Everyone likes theirs differently. Carlos piles his with salsa, while Hector tops his with more bacon than patty. Seth adds a mound of pickles and peppers. Brady just puts cheese and ketchup on his.

I opt for a BLT style for my first one, with ranch dressing. Then something more traditional for my second. Bea gets me to try my last one with a cheese called *cotija*. It's salty and strong, almost like feta or goat cheese but not quite so soft. I wish I had room for more.

After dinner, her parents disappear into the house, and the guys set up a projector and screen on the lawn. We spread out blankets while Joey and Hector fight over which movie to watch. Carlos tries to sit next to me again, but Brady picks him up and moves him. My heart jumps as he takes Carlos's spot.

He smiles, almost catching my eyes. "Having fun?"

"Yeah. I really am." I'm surprised how much truth there is in my words. Not much has happened, but maybe that's why it's so nice. For a while I forgot I don't belong here.

"Good." Brady leans back on one arm, facing me. His face is serious, though the smile is still there. "It's hard being on the outside, isn't it?"

I bite my lip. "Yeah, it is. I'm a freak among freaks."

"Even your friends are afraid of you."

I sigh. "You mean if you have any."

"Right." He smiles wider, and I know he understands

how I feel better than anyone else could. "I've been there. As a kid, I couldn't control my power like I can now. My tantrums were more like war zones. I once threw a beanbag in kindergarten and it went straight through the wall and knocked out the teacher in the other room. Everyone has always been afraid that I'd snap them in half—everyone but Trixy."

Bea sits on my other side. "I sure put up with a lot of bruises, though, to earn his trust."

Brady winces. "It's hard to believe that anyone could actually want you around."

I know he can't read my mind, but sometimes it feels like it. "You guys have so much history. I wasn't sure if I belonged here."

"Well, stop worrying," Bea says. "You're stuck with us."

Brady nudges me. "We need a new chapter anyway."

I smile, a wave of flutters rushing through me, and I force myself to watch the movie instead of Brady's face.

Chapter 15

It's warm, almost too hot with his arms around me from behind, but I don't want to move. I want to stay right here forever, watching the sunrise. It glows pink and orange as it hits the spattered desert clouds. I lean into him, sighing at the beauty. I've never felt like this before, and yet I recognize it all the same.

I'm visible. If I look down I'll see my skin, but I don't because I feel real already. I am myself—the one I want to be.

"You're beautiful," he says.

I smile as his lips touch my ear. "How do you know?"

"Because I can see you, inside and out."

My heart warms. As hard as it is for me to believe, it's true. I can feel it in every cell of my body. "What do you see?"

Instead of answering, he shakes me. Then the sunrise fades to blackness, and I shoot up from bed, gasping. I've had dreams like that before—almost looking in a mirror, seeing a blurry reflection in water, someone just about to tell me. The ones with boys are always the best. I'll take it over the usual repertoire of nightmares, which always have something to do with Graham dropping me from thousands of feet up. Or Dad leaving. Or getting shot and no one being able to fix it because of my stupid ability.

"Morning, sleepyhead," Miles says.

"Come back in an hour." I pull my covers over my head, trying to hang on to the last shreds of my dream. I imagine Brady as that boy, would have daydreamed about him all morning if Miles weren't still shoving me.

"Fiona, I can't spend one more second alone down there with *them*. Don't be so cruel."

I groan. The thought of Graham at my kitchen table replaces all the happy feelings with dread. Seeing him will make the danger real again, and after yesterday's movie night I really don't want it to be. I want to pretend that I'm a normal girl in a small town with crazy friends and too much homework.

"Please." Miles draws out the word, like I'm killing him by not coming. I glance up, not surprised to see The Pout, complete with lip curled under so his chin looks like a prune. Kills me every time.

I push the covers down. "Fine. Just let me get dressed."

"Of course." Miles heads for the door. "Let's go somewhere if we can. I'd rather avoid him when possible."

"Definitely."

I rummage through my dresser for something easy to take off. This could be a trap. Graham could have backup or surveillance this time. He could be messing with us, and Mom would never recover from that kind of betrayal. She'd never try again.

I settle on a bright purple halter dress. It has built-in support, so I don't have to worry about a bra. I grab a pair of flip-flops and leave the rest, though the impulse to accessorize is strong.

Taking a deep breath, I head downstairs. Noise comes from the kitchen, and I pause a moment before interrupting the conversation.

"I don't see what the big deal is." Graham's deep voice sends a shiver down my back. It's all I can do not to run.

"You don't exactly have the best track record with Fiona," Miles says. "Do you honestly expect her to trust you after everything you've done?"

He doesn't like how Graham treats me, but he can't change it any more than I can. Graham got away with everything growing up. When Miles tried to stand up for me, he'd get my "flight lesson" instead. That is Graham's favorite scare tactic—fly a person thousands of feet up, dangle or drop them, and wait until they do what he wants, or splat.

It wasn't as bad for Miles, since he's not afraid of heights, but I hated watching him fall because he tried to protect me. Even if Graham always caught him at the last second, Miles would have bruises from smacking into him at that speed. Sometimes they'd throw punches over it, but Graham always won because he's bulkier. Miles isn't a wimp, but he's thin and agile like Dad.

Graham laughs. "You two are both acting like babies. If I really wanted them with Dad, they'd have been back a month ago. Isn't that proof enough?"

"No. It's not." I step onto the gray tile, eyeing Graham.

Like always, he floats a few inches above the floor. He only touches the ground when he lifts weights, which he

105

has to do to maintain bone mass. Graham has a cellular mutation that makes it so his body can run on hydrogen instead of oxygen. He could only float when he was little, but over time he figured out he could go back and forth between the two elements and manipulate them so he could get speed.

He's one of nine in the world with such advanced flying.

He smiles his trademark smug grin, eyes dark and intense. He looks like Dad with his strong jaw, square shoulders, and an air reeking of confidence. But he has Mom's auburn hair. "Did you miss me?"

"Terribly." I head for the Pop-Tarts in the cupboard, feigning as much indifference as possible.

He snorts. "You haven't changed at all."

I bite into the sugary blueberry pastry. He has no idea who I am. "Neither have you."

"Hey now." His face softens, but I don't let if fool me. "I know things have been rough between us, but I mean it when I say I want to help. I have a plan to make it so Dad will never find you, and you'll be free to live here forever."

It sounds too good to be true, and yet part of me wants to believe it. "And what plan is that?"

"Can't tell you, just in case the syndicate does find you."

"You just said they wouldn't."

His face tightens. "I really think we can do this, if no one gets too careless."

I put my hands on my hips. "You're talking about me, aren't you? Well, if you think I'm going to ruin it, you better just tell me what it is now."

His smile disappears. So much for his attempts at

niceness. "Do yourself a favor, Fifi. Take my charity and don't ask questions, okay?"

"You can't possibly expect me to believe you have a charitable bone in your body. After the trailer park? The campsite in Yellowstone? Portland? C'mon." I look for the closest exit, knowing I'm already pushing it. "No matter what you think, I'm not that stupid."

His eyes flicker with anger. "Yes you are. Don't make me have to do things the hard way."

"Just tell me why you're doing this! Is it that hard? Give me one good reason—and not some sob story about you caring for us. That didn't stop you before."

His whole body flexes, and he flies in closer. Miles stands between us. "You think taking her flying will help?"

I try to stop shaking, but it doesn't work. "I'll run, and I'll never come back."

"Fiona." Mom sits at the table, looking frustrated with me, even though Graham's the one threatening us. "Please, listen. I know it's hard, but he means well."

"They won't believe anything I say—they're too stupid to see what's right in front of them," Graham says.

Miles rolls his eyes. "Here's what I think of that."

A rotten-egg scent saturates the kitchen. I cover my nose, which makes my laugh sound funny. Then that makes me laugh harder. Miles has quite the list of awful smells, from skunk to outhouse to grandma perfume. Graham has a tendency to get the worst ones out of him.

"Turn it off!" Graham waves his hand like that will help.

"I can't; I'm too stupid." Miles folds his arms, an impish grin on his lips.

107

"Fine, you're brilliant. Smarter than all the savants combined!"

"Don't forget it." The room blossoms into a rose garden, then morphs into vanilla, one of his favorite scents to give off. "Fiona's right. If you want our trust, we deserve a reason at the very least. Especially if you won't tell us the plan."

Graham folds his arms, glancing at Mom before his eyes turn hard. "I can't give you one. It could risk everything. I don't care if you trust me—just lay low and don't mess anything up."

Mom stands from the table. "It's been so long since we've all been together. Can't we just get along? Maybe go out to lunch?"

We stare at her, Miles with his mouth gaping and Graham with an eyebrow raised. I cram my lips together, trying not to laugh. She has to be kidding, but she's not cracking a smile. She's gotten so parental since we left, and it seems to be getting worse.

"Fiona's taking me to meet her friends. Maybe some other time, Mom," Miles says. I flick his arm, grateful for the save, at least until I catch Graham's expression.

"Friends? What kind of friends?"

I force down the lump in my throat. Maybe that wasn't such a good save after all. The last thing I need is Graham finding Bea and Brady. "None of your business."

He flies above Miles and me, proving how easy it would be for him to pluck me off the ground. "What did I just say about laying low? Everything here is my business."

"You sound a lot like Dad, you know." I cover my mouth

as I realize what I've done. I'm not goading Seth—this is Graham. He won't just roll his eyes.

"You want to do this the hard way? Fine." He grabs my neck, right where the halter ties. I work at his strong fingers in a futile attempt to pry them off. Miles's yells barely register against my pounding heart and burning lungs. It hurts so much I wonder if Graham's nails have broken through my skin, but I don't feel blood. At least not yet.

I can't get air, and when I try it seems to make his grip more painful.

His eyes somehow find mine, and he smiles. "Look at you, Fifi, standing up for yourself." My feet leave the ground. I can't scream, can't do anything to save myself. "Here's a tip: Don't get mouthy until you can fight back."

Just when I think I'll be taking yet another flight lesson, Graham drops me on the floor. Miles rushes over, wrapping around me as I gasp and cough. "Yeah, real trustworthy, jackass."

Graham shrugs. "I tried to be nice. I will have your cooperation, one way or another." He nods to Mom. "Let's go find you a real job."

She throws me a glance of regret before she says, "Okay, but you have to promise me one thing."

"What?" he asks.

"Don't hurt Fiona like that again. This is hard on all of us, especially her, and that was way out of line, Graham."

"Fine," he says reluctantly.

Sure, right. Unless I say the wrong thing again.

He picks her up gently, and she wraps her arms around his neck. I'll never understand how she can trust him like that, even after all this. Though I can't ignore that she kind of defended me. It was a weak attempt, sure, but it was the first time I can remember her ever telling Graham what to do.

Miles and I sit on the floor for a moment without speaking. "You okay?"

I rub my neck, which burns and throbs. I take in a deep breath. "I don't think he did permanent damage."

He lets out a long sigh. "Someday, we're gonna get him back, Fi. Him, Dad, the whole syndicate. I promise."

Miles always talks big, but I don't feel like entertaining the dreams right now. "How will we do all that? He could have killed me right there, you know."

"I know." He stands up, and I follow. "He might be an evil syndicate boss in the making, but he has a point. You need to learn how to fight."

"You really think karate lessons will stop him from tossing me off a cliff?"

He shakes his head, a wry smile appearing. "Couldn't hurt. You could at least kick him in the balls before you go."

I shove him. "Thanks."

"That wasn't exactly the kind of fighting I meant, though."

"Then what? Fencing?"

He rolls his eyes. "I think you need to figure it out yourself. In fact, you already are." He grabs Mom's keys off the hook on the refrigerator. "C'mon, take me to the coolest place in this sorry excuse for a town."

Chapter 16

There's not much to do in Madison, but we settle on the community pool. It's crowded, or at least as crowded as this town gets. Children and parents huddle around the kiddie pool, while teens and adults mob the bigger one. They swim laps, dive from the springboards, and lounge in the water. With the temperature rising every second, I'm more than ready to join them.

"So how hot is this Bea girl you've been hanging out with?" Miles says as we walk to the entrance.

"She's my age, you perv."

"Psh, that's only two years' difference, and she must be smoking if that's all you have to say."

I roll my eyes. Miles has always been popular, almost like he inherited some of Dad's charm. He was never short on girls in high school, though he's never been in a serious relationship.

"Yeah, she's disgustingly gorgeous, actually."

"Excellent. You think she'll be here?"

"I have no idea."

"I guess I'll have to hang out with you then."

"Oh, you poor thing." It's like he never left, and the thought brings me home in a way. We pay at the gate and head in. "I just need to put on some sunscreen. I'll be right back."

"Sure, I'll see if I can stake out a spot on the grass. I know how you like to keep your tan nice and golden." His eyes glint with mischief.

"I am pretty vain." I head to the bathroom, which is beyond disgusting. The entire floor is wet, and wads of spitball spatter the ceiling. It smells about as bad as Miles's fart-bomb attack.

I apply the sunscreen liberally, knowing how bad sunburn hurts even if I can't see it. When I was little, I'd get it in hopes that it would burn off the invisibility. After the third time I got blisters the size of lemons on my shoulders, I gave up on that. I settled for the knowledge that there's at least pigment underneath to burn.

I put it on in the bathroom because I tend to draw attention. For a moment the white coats my body like paint, and people try to catch a glimpse of what's there. I imagine it's the closest I could ever feel to naked. The sunscreen absorbs, and I'm left as a cute red-and-white polka-dot one-piece with a little skirt. I would love to wear a bikini, but I've learned that's the best way to get accidentally pummeled in the water. The casino pool was a battlefield filled with kids hopped up on buffet desserts.

When I get back outside, I can't find Miles. He couldn't have picked up a girl that fast. Well, maybe he could. I push through a group of purple people, trying to get up to the hill for a better view. Still no sign of him.

Then I notice four boys with black hair who couldn't be anyone but Bea's brothers. I spot Bea right after, though

I hardly recognize her with flat, wet hair. She totally pulls off the skimpy white bikini, which makes me a little jealous.

Miles is nowhere, so I head toward Bea. She spots me and waves. "Fiona! Wow, that suit is adorable!"

"Thanks." Adorable is sad in comparison to her, but I guess I should take what I can get. "I didn't realize you'd be here."

"Oh yeah, we come here all the time. 'Cept Sundays— Mom would never let us break the Sabbath." She points to her brothers, who are huddled around someone, as she talks.

"So you weren't looking at our sister?" Joey says.

"Poor soul." Bea sighs. "He just said hi to me, but that's all it takes to get them going."

"I . . . uh . . . yeah I was, but I didn't mean . . ."

I know that voice.

"Wait! That's my brother. Don't hurt him!" I push through The Pack and take Miles by the hand. He lets out a relieved breath, probably one second from releasing some nasty smell. "I'm sure he just recognized Bea—I told him about the friends I made. That's all."

"I don't know," Carlos says, eyeing him. "He had that look. I know that look well."

"Tell them you didn't mean anything, Miles."

"I just said hi." He shrugs, and I hold in my groan. Of course he was hitting on her. "It's not every day my sister makes friends, if you know what I mean."

"Are you gonna be trouble?" Hector asks. It's then I realize they think he's in the O'Connell syndicate. Of course they think that—he's related to me. I wish I could blame them, but I'm honestly glad they're watching their backs.

"No. I'm basically disowned." Miles releases a sweet cinnamon scent. "You think my dad has any use for a guy who can smell like a bakery?" He switches to a sticky-mango smell. "Or perhaps a fruit stand? Maybe if he owned a smoothie store."

The guys try to restrain their smiles, but eventually they laugh. "Well, if you're not gonna scandalize Trixy, I guess you can hang with us." Joey holds out his hand.

"Deal." Miles shakes it. "And you are?"

Bea points to each as she talks. "Joey, Tony, Hector, and Carlos, but you don't need to remember their names—they all answer to 'dumbass.'"

"Funny, funny. At least we don't answer to 'screaming banshee.'" Carlos ruffles her hair, and then runs when she tries to swat him.

We decide to play Marco Polo, and I never get tagged, even when Carlos opens his eyes just to go after me. Miles slips into the group easily, like he does with most people. All he has to do is flash a smile, drop a clever joke about his lame ability, and everyone seems to trust him. I might be jealous if he were anyone else.

Once the boys suggest racing laps, Bea groans. "You're wearing me out. Fiona, let's get a drink or something."

"Sure." I hate getting out of the pool, since the water sticks to my skin just enough to give me a glistening outline. People stare as I pass, and even Bea sneaks a few glances. I follow her to the small concession stand, and she buys me a grape slushie though I tell her she doesn't have to. Then we lie on our towels and dry out in the sun.

"Miles is a cutie," Bea says. "I almost wish my brothers hadn't interrupted."

I sigh. "He's subtler than Carlos, but he's still a total flirt."

She laughs. "In the right way, though. Carlos has no filter at all."

I've never talked about my brother like this, and I'm not sure how I'm supposed to feel about Bea eyeing him. She's already tangled up in this enough. "So . . . where are Brady and Seth? I thought you guys were joined at the hip or something."

She rolls her eyes. "Seth decided to gut their house and renovate it this summer. They work on it most of the weekend, unless Brady can talk Seth into taking breaks."

I sip my slushie, confused. "You make it sound like Seth is in charge or something."

Bea chews her lip. "They're really private about their family. They wouldn't want me to tell you."

"Tell me what?"

She shakes her head. "Look, Seth does kind of run the show, but it's not what you think. You can't ask, okay? If you ask them, they'll probably just freak out on you and run away. They'll tell you when they trust you."

"Okay . . ." I sip at my drink, surprised by Bea's words. She makes it sound like something horrible. Sure, Seth acts like his life sucks, but I've never seen Brady without that adorable one-dimple smile. Except for yesterday when I asked him about Seth. It was like his whole being changed. He was avoiding something.

My mind runs through the possibilities. I have a feeling

it's about their dad, maybe just because mine sucks so much. But there are a lot of crap dads out there. "I really can't ask?"

"Trust me, it'd be faster to wait. They like you. It's only a matter of time."

I sigh. "Fine."

She rolls onto her back, I guess to even her perfect tan. "They're meeting us at Taco Bell for dinner, if you and Miles want to come. We might mess around after that."

I'm already so tired from swimming that I almost say no, but then a bird crosses the blue sky and I flinch. Better to be out than spend the evening with Graham. "Sure, I bet Miles would be all over it. He seems to like your brothers."

"Yeah, weird. Most people can't stand them. Of course, Miles is used to ultragifted people, huh. They must not be scary to him at all."

"Nope."

Miles's laugh carries over all the pool noise. I'd know it anywhere. He's having so much . . . fun. Sometimes I don't understand how he can let go like that. He barely knows them, and they look like old friends. He knows Graham's here, that the Navarros are at risk being with us, that there's more going on than people are telling us. And yet you'd never guess he had a care in the world.

I wish I could be more like that. I want to put my problems in little boxes and only deal with them when I need to. I want to live like Miles.

I just don't know if I can.

Chapter 17

Dinner at Taco Bell is actually a who-can-eat-the-most-burritos contest. I'm starting to wonder where all the food is going, because it can't be possible to hold eight burritos in your stomach and not puke. Yet Hector opens a ninth without hesitation.

"Your record is going down tonight, bro," he says to Tony.

Tony just grabs another one. For a guy who supposedly knows every language in common use, he sure is quiet. He hasn't said a word since I've met him, but he doesn't look sulky like Seth. I figure everyone says plenty, so he doesn't see the need. Maybe language is as dull to him as invisibility is to me. I like him for it.

Miles throws down his fifth burrito, half-eaten. "Dude, I don't know how you do that. I'm out."

"Wuss." Bea licks her fingers, finishing off number six. Somehow she still looks good, even with hot sauce on her face.

"Oh, you'll regret that, Trixy." Miles takes another bite.

"We put off tiling the bathroom for this?" Seth grumbles.

Brady hands him a burrito from the pile in the middle of the table. "Loosen up. Sitting between you and Miss Tense Invisible Girl is giving me ulcers."

"What?" I say. "I'm not tense!"

"Oh?" I swear his smile has some weird power to melt my insides. "You've barely said a word tonight. What's up?"

I bite my lip. It's sweet that he's worried, but I can't tell him what's really bothering me. When Miles and I went to change clothes, Mom and Graham weren't back from the supposed job hunt. I hate that I'm worried about her—she was asking for it—but I keep picturing her back in Las Vegas tied to a chair. "I'm just tired from swimming earlier, that's all. And I'm trying to keep score on this riveting burrito competition."

Brady laughs. "I'll get you some more caffeine, then."

Before I can protest, he takes my cup and makes Seth move so he can slide out. I watch him go, wondering how someone so kind could have any problems. And maybe I'm a little distracted by how much his muscles stretch out his shirt.

When he gets back, Seth doesn't move; he just slides over so he's next to me. Brady sits on the end like it doesn't bother him, and I feel silly for thinking he sat next to me because he likes me. I'm reading way too much into everything, and yet I can't stop myself. If anyone could deal with my invisibility, it's him.

Brady slides my cup over. "Drink up."

"Thanks." I grab the soda, but miss the straw because Seth's shoulder slams into mine, almost spilling the drink over the burrito pyramid. "Ow!"

"Sorry!" Brady says. "My bad."

Seth rubs his arm, which is when I realize Brady probably bumped him too hard. Seth gives me the saddest, most

118

sympathetic expression. I had no idea he even possessed the ability to look like that. "You okay, Fiona?"

"Yes." My fingers go to my neck. It's still sore from Graham, and the jostling made it worse.

"You sure?"

I pause, surprised by his concern. "Uh . . . yeah."

"What?"

Maybe he didn't notice he actually sounds nice for once. It could have been a fluke, and I probably shouldn't point it out. He might never make that mistake again. "It's nothing."

He sighs, and I expect him to grumble about my answer. He doesn't.

"Hey, Fiona, mark me down for another!" Carlos puffs out his chest. "I'm gonna break the record in your honor tonight."

Seth scoffs. "You've never even gotten close."

"I didn't have my muse!" Carlos grabs another burrito and then blows me a kiss. "For you, baby."

I'm not sure if I should gag or laugh, so this embarrassing half snort comes out instead. "I think I just threw up in my mouth a little."

Everyone bursts into laughter, and even Seth manages a little grin. He finally unwraps his first burrito and eats. I take a deep breath, hoping he doesn't bite my head off for talking to him. "Are you in for the contest?"

He shakes his head and takes another bite.

I sip my drink. I guess that was the end of that conversation. There's something off with him tonight. This isn't his usual negativity.

After Hector and Tony both finish their tenth, Seth clears his throat. "Would you hand me another one, please?"

He's not exactly out of reach, but I'm so taken back by the softness in his voice that I comply.

"Thanks." He glances at me, almost meeting my eyes. "Aren't you going to eat?"

I bite my lip, wondering if this is some kind of joke. "I had a couple tacos before you guys got here. The burritos gross me out."

"They are kind of gross." He takes another bite.

I hold in my laugh. "Then why are you eating them?"

He shrugs, and it's so chill I'm temporarily thrown off-balance. "I'm starving. Free food."

"True." I take another long sip of my drink, grateful for something to fill the awkward pauses with. What the hell is up with him? This is the first normal conversation I've had with Seth, and it's so . . . well, normal. I glance at him, and for a second it seems like all the tension in his face is gone, just like Brady changed yesterday. I don't understand, but it's strange how they both have two completely different sides.

"Hey." Miles snaps me out of my daze, but when I look up I realize he's not talking to me. He's looking at Bea and Brady, who're whispering to each other. "You guys look like you're plotting."

Bea laughs, her Trixy grin firmly in place. "Oh, we are. We thought some night games were in order after dinner."

"Night games?" I say.

Brady's face lights up like a five-year-old about to tell a cool story. "Yeah, you go to a park after dark and play. I call you for my team."

"Hey!" Carlos cries. "No fair! She has way too much advantage."

"You're the one with night vision!" Hector says.

"That doesn't mean I can see past invisibility, stupid."

They fight over whose team I'm on through the rest of dinner, then all the way to the park, and for a good ten minutes after that. I'm not sure whether to feel flattered or just exhausted. They'll see my clothes, so I don't know what the big deal is.

Bea groans. "Joey, just pick! If I hear any more of this I'll make Fiona go home right now and keep her to myself."

"We'll play sardines, okay? Then no one can have Fiona," Joey says. "Everyone happy with that?" They all agree. "Fiona, you get to hide; last one to find her has to do whatever she dares them to do."

"Okay." I smile at the possibilities, hoping Brady will find me first.

To add difficulty, I pull off my sheer peasant shirt, leaving just my black tank top and dark jeans. Off go my glasses and my shoes, too. Then I notice all the boys minus Miles gaping at me. "What?"

Carlos shakes his head, smiling slightly. "Invisibility doesn't exempt you from our imaginations. You just took off half your clothes."

Seth smacks his arm, but the others laugh. I'm confused. Did they find that . . . sexy? They can't see anything. It's not like I'm naked, yet they look at me like I'm some kind of supermodel.

"Dude, she's my sister. Don't make me skunk it up," Miles says.

121

They shut up.

"Cover your eyes, sickos," Bea says. "I'm counting. You got sixty seconds, Fiona."

When they close their eyes, I run. I've never been to this park, so I have no idea where a good hiding spot would be. There are lots of trees, but not so many bushes, and even being invisible, they'd still find me under the picnic benches or behind the trash can.

"Thirty-six!" Bea yells.

After forgoing the trees and bathrooms, I sprint for the playground. It's actually huge now that I take it in. A large central tower is lit in the moonlight, surrounded by slides and ramps and tunnels. Perfect. There has to be a good hiding place around here somewhere.

"Forty-nine!" Bea's megaphone voice is so loud she may as well be next to me. I'm positive the whole neighborhood can hear.

I jump into the first tunnel slide and climb halfway up. I have no clue if I've picked an easy spot or not, but I guess it doesn't matter since they're supposed to find me.

"Sixty!"

I hold my breath. My heart pounds as I listen for them. They whoop and holler like they're on some treasure hunt. Some of their voices get quieter as they go the wrong direction, but there's a set of feet approaching. They circle around me for a minute. I hope like a dork that it might be Brady.

The footsteps are close, just above me on the ramp. My skin tingles with anticipation. I look up as a pair of skinny legs comes into view.

Seth. Of course. Just my luck.

"There you are." Seth's voice is a whisper. He crouches down and carefully makes his way toward me. "Tell me if I almost smack your head or something. I don't want to hurt you."

"Why are you being so nice?" I snap.

"Weren't you the one who said I should be nicer? Now you have a problem with it?" Seth holds out a hand like he's blind.

"No! I . . ." Sighing, I grab his hand to guide him, so he doesn't have to look so silly.

"Thanks." He settles right next to me, our legs touching since there's not much room. "What were you saying?"

I keep to my own space as much as possible. "I guess I didn't expect you to actually listen."

"You really think I'm horrible, don't you?"

I grit my teeth, trying not to get upset. If he's being nice, then I should try, too. "I don't. How could I think that, growing up like I did?"

He's silent.

I put my head to my knees. "I can't blame you if you think I'm horrible, though. I am. There's no avoiding it when you're syndicate-born."

"That's not your fault. Being syndicate-born doesn't make *you* horrible. You can't control that."

I laugh bitterly; the thought of Dad's last order still makes me sick. I wonder if he went through with killing those girls without me. It still feels like my fault. If I hadn't spied on those men or brought back the Radiasure . . . I may not have killed anyone with my own hands, but how

123

many people have died as a result of information I supplied? I don't know. I don't *want* to know. "You're so naive. You don't even know what horrible is, Seth."

I can feel his shoulder tense. "I wouldn't say that."

A lump forms in my throat, remembering what Bea said earlier. "Sorry. I guess I don't know enough, do I?"

"Not yet." His voice is a whisper.

My skin tingles with curiosity. Will he tell me now? I want to ask, but I keep my mouth shut. It took me so long just to get Seth to be nice to me. I can't risk going backward now.

"She's over here!" I jump at Seth's voice, then realize he didn't say anything. It's Bea messing with everyone. I cover my mouth to muffle my laugh, and Seth actually smiles.

"The sad thing is they always fall for it," he says.

"That is kinda sad."

Cursing breaks out when they realize it's not me, and I can barely keep it together. I can't believe no one else has found us yet.

"Shh. You'll give us away before it gets really hilarious." Seth's face is close, so close that I can feel his breath though he doesn't know it. The sensation brings an unexpected shiver, and I look away.

Footsteps finally come near. It sounds like two pairs. I hold my breath.

"Damn, that Fiona is hot," Carlos says. "And she's way too good at this."

I hear Brady laugh. "You don't even know what she looks like."

My chest tightens. Why do I keep hoping my invisibility

doesn't matter to him? Of course it does. He's just a nice guy. That's all.

"That's the thing, though—she could look however you want," Carlos says. "I could picture her different every day." The way his voice sounds makes me sick. I pull my knees in closer, hoping they don't find us. I don't want to be anywhere near him. I tense when Seth's arm comes around my shoulder, but I don't move. Surprisingly, it's not so bad. Maybe Brady and Bea were right—Seth doesn't hate me; he just sucks at expressing himself. I lean my head on his shoulder, wishing I could run far enough to block out the rest.

"Jeez, she's not a shape-shifter, Carlos." Brady sounds angry. "Don't talk about her like that. Besides . . ." I don't hear the rest. They must have gone to whispers.

"Ah, gotcha." Carlos laughs. "Fine. I won't ask her out."

"Like she'd say yes."

"Ouch, man!"

As relieved as I am that Carlos isn't going to make a move, my mind reels over what Brady could have said to make that happen.

"Only two people haven't found me!" My voice comes from behind, startling me out of thought. Brady and Carlos run for it, Brady's feet pounding the ground hard enough to make a mini earthquake.

"Carlos is a horndog. Ignore him," Seth says.

My stomach turns. "Is that what all you guys think? Do you just imagine me as whatever you want?" I should probably see it as a good thing—as far as I know that was the first time any guy said I was hot.

125

"No." He squeezes my shoulder, which is when I realize he hasn't let go yet. Somewhere in the back of my head I know it should bother me, but it doesn't. "Like I said, Carlos has always been a perv. I know you have a face, your own face that's unlike anyone else's."

"Really?" My voice squeaks, and I shove the tears back inside. No one has ever said there's something under my invisibility. It's always been *maybe*. Knowing someone might actually believe it means more than Seth can understand.

"Really. Brady knows, too—same with everyone else. And if they don't, Brady will squash them."

I nod into his shoulder, unable to say words without betraying my feelings. *I have a face. Other people believe it, too.*

There are footsteps on the ramp, and I realize it's been a long time for a game of sardines. Bea's perfect legs appear. "Well, well, am I interrupting?"

"No." I smile as she scoots into the slide just above us. "You're hilarious, by the way."

She shakes her head. "I know. Total dumbasses, huh?"

It doesn't take too long for Hector to show up after that. Then Miles, Tony, and Joey come a minute or two behind. It's between Brady and Carlos for the dare, and I start planning what I'll do to the one who loses. It has to be good.

"Noooo!" Carlos yells as the ground rumbles. Brady must be running, which means he must have seen Joey climb into the bottom of the slide. It feels like an earthquake as we laugh and hold on. We still slide down the tube and fall into a dog pile.

"Yes!" Brady pumps his fist. "Carlos, I have a feeling you're in *big* trouble."

I stand, looking forward to inflicting punishment on Carlos. He breathes hard, his eyes glowing like a cat's. "Okay, baby, give it to me. I deserve it."

"Hmm." I want it to be mortifying, something to get him back for what he said. "I dare you to streak down Main Street. It's only fair."

Everyone breaks out in howls of laughter, but Carlos's face turns cunning. "You just wanna see me naked."

"Oh, I'm not coming—that's the last thing I want to see. I need to get home." It's past midnight, and my body begs for sleep. That, and I have to know if Mom's still here or not. Even if she isn't the perfect mother, we've always been together.

"Sounds good," Miles says.

"Don't worry, Fiona." Joey gives Carlos a noogie. "We'll make sure he goes through with it."

"Awesome." Before I chicken out, I touch Brady's arm. He flinches, probably because I don't have sleeves and he didn't see it coming. But he doesn't pull back. I lean in to whisper. "I just wanted to say thanks, for what you said."

He smiles. "No prob. Gotta protect you."

If The Pack and my brother weren't there, I would kiss him right now.

After saying good-bye, Miles drives us back to the house. We're quiet at first, but then his mouth breaks into a huge smile.

"What?" I ask.

"I like seeing you act like yourself in front of other

people." The light from a streetlamp shines on his face for a moment, and then it's back to the green glow from the dashboard. "They're good for you. I'm gonna make sure you can stay here with them as long as you want."

I laugh, wishing it were that easy. "They must have put something in those burritos."

He punches my arm. "I'm serious!"

"Fine, fine. I won't complain."

When we get home, Miles collapses on the couch. I tiptoe upstairs to Mom's door. I'm not sure what I expect to see when I open it, but I hope like I've never hoped before that she's there. I turn the knob slowly and peek in. Mom's figure rests under the covers, her chest moving up and down. I watch for a moment, just because it's so surprising to see her safe. Graham really didn't take her.

I shut the door, deciding I better enjoy my luck while it lasts.

Chapter 18

Mom and I don't speak much at breakfast, not that it's new. Her drinking a half pot of coffee isn't new, either, but something else is. I stare at her blue-and-white uniform, "Lauren" neatly carved into a plastic name tag. Graham's taken her "job hunting" twice in the past two weeks, but I didn't believe that's what they were really doing. I imagined something more along the lines of telekinetically lock picking bank vaults.

"Y-you actually got a job," I finally get out.

She nods. "At the bowling alley. Not exactly glamorous, but we'll be able to buy food. Thank goodness the house is paid for."

I take another bite of my Pop-Tart, too shocked to say more. Is Graham actually protecting us? It's too good to be true, and I know what that means: There's a catch. I just don't know what it is yet.

"I'll need the car. Do you have a ride? Or should I take you to school?"

She's not taking me to school. I'm still trying to forget the day she registered me. Pulling out my cell, I say, "I'll find a ride."

I head outside after I get off the phone, and Bea, Carlos,

and Hector pick me up in Sexy Blue five minutes later. "Hey, chica! Hop in!"

I slide in next to Bea. "Thanks. Sorry for the short notice. My mom decided not to mention she got a job. At the bowling alley."

"So she'll be waxing balls all day?" Carlos asks.

Hector punches his shoulder, looking crankier than I've ever seen him. "What did I say about idiocy before school?"

Carlos smiles. "Remind me."

Hector grabs Carlos's bag and throws it out the window. He pulls up on the side of the curb. "You piss me off, you walk."

"Fine." Carlos opens the door. "Then I won't have to be seen with you."

Hector floors it once Carlos is out. He parks a few minutes later. Bea and I watch Hector storm off, and I can't help thinking he's the perfect best friend for Seth.

"Note to self," I say. "Hector is not a morning person."

Bea looks embarrassed. "You noticed?"

We laugh as we head to our lockers. I don't mind school so much now. Hanging out with The Pack gives me a place, and I never realized how nice it would be to have one. Math still sucks, but my other classes aren't too bad. My favorite, to my surprise, is PE. I can barely contain my excitement as I change into my uniform.

"Man, I hope we're done with basketball soon. It's so boring." Bea pushes the locker room door open, and we head out to the gym to meet up with Brady.

"I don't know, basketball's kind of fun." I like playing sports. It takes my mind off things, forces me to concentrate on the moment instead of my problems. There's one goal—win. I like winning.

Bea rolls her eyes. "Maybe when you're good it's fun. It probably helps that you're tall, too, punk."

"Hey," Brady says when we sit next to him on the bleachers.

"Mile run today! Everyone under seven minutes gets a break after," Coach Ford calls. She's not quite as loud as Bea, but the strange deepness of her voice makes up for it.

"Yes!" I pump my fist.

"You're a freak, you know that?" Bea says.

I laugh. "Don't tell me you just figured that out."

"Don't listen to her. It's cool that you like to run," Brady says.

If only he could see my smile. "I just want to see if I can get a faster time."

Bea shakes her head. "Like I said, freak."

"Whatever, wuss." I love that we've gotten to this joking level, where I know she's teasing me and I can tease back.

After we line up, the coach blows her whistle and off we go. Half the class is already walking around the track, not even trying. I don't care if I look like an overachiever. I want to be the first girl across the finish line. I bet I can beat at least half the guys, too.

I push myself hard, though it's still hot outside. The end of October doesn't seem to matter to Arizona. Sweat drenches my back, under my arms, and even between my boobs, but I don't care because no one can see anyway.

Halfway done.

The heat radiates off the track, burning at my legs. My

lungs beg me to slow down, but I know from experience that'll wane if I just keep going. I could use a drink of water, though. Or maybe like a gallon of water. The girl keeping pace with me finally slows a little. I smile and run harder. I feel even better when I catch up with a few boys. They struggle to keep my speed as I pass, but eventually give up and fall behind.

With the finish line in sight, I give it every last bit of effort I have, though my whole body burns.

"Five-forty-three!" Coach Ford cries. "Great time, McClean!"

I smile wide—five seconds off my last time. That's probably the best mile I've ever run, though I've done far too many without a timer to know for sure.

I jog to the drinking fountain, breathing deeply to slow my heart rate. Then I proceed to try to run the fountain dry.

"I hate you!" Bea calls as she passes. I'm pretty sure she just finished her second lap.

When I'm done rehydrating, Brady waves to me from the bleachers. He finished probably a minute before me, and I have a feeling he could go faster if it didn't risk destroying the track.

"Awesome time, Fi," he says when I sit next to him. "You're the fastest girl in school."

I try not to stare at him too much, but he even looks good sweaty. It's bad enough he's hot, what with the freckles and perfect smile. Oh, and the cut muscles. Does he have to be so freaking nice, too? "Yeah, right."

"I mean it. You should go out for track this spring with

me. I'm not sure if they'd put you on the gifted team or not, since invisibility doesn't help much with running, but either way you're fast."

"Really?" I can't help but grin. It feels nice to be good at something, especially when that something isn't illegal.

He smiles. "Yeah, really. Or you could try soccer. Oh! I bet you'd make an awesome running back—Seth could give you pointers. He and Hector are co-captains this year, so he would know exactly how to train you."

Because I need more of Seth telling me what to do. "Maybe. I'll think about it. Track sounds fun."

He leans forward, looking over the remaining runners, or rather, walkers. "Well, either way, you should come running with me this weekend. I go out in the desert so I can run full speed. There's some pretty cool stuff out there."

My heart skips. I repeat his words in my head to make sure he really asked what I think he asked. "Yeah, I'd love to go."

"Great. Saturday? At like eight?"

"Perfect."

I float through the rest of school, replaying the conversation in my head to make sure it actually happened. I've been trying to resist my crush, but maybe I don't have to. Brady asked me out. He likes . . . me, my personality, I guess. That had to be why he told Carlos to back off. He was planning on making a move.

This is the best day of my life.

Chapter 19

When I walk into tutoring, the Brady-asked-me-out high dissolves. Not like Seth looks pleasant often, but today he's beyond stressed. And he won't look at me. Bea glances my way several times, then finally leans over. "Do you know what's up with him?"

"How would I?"

She shrugs. "He seems to be avoiding you. Wondered if maybe you guys got in another fight or something."

"Not really." I thought Seth and I had reached some tentative truce since that game of sardines. Not that he's been chummy, but he certainly hasn't been as jerky as before. He even talks to me sometimes at lunch, though he mostly studies with Hector. We're kind of friends, I think.

"You should talk to him and see what's up," Bea says. "He seems to open up around you, and he listens to you."

"What?" I try not to laugh. "He does not."

Her look is flat. "He does. Trust me."

"Whatever." I focus on my homework, sure we're reading into it too much. Seth is always stressed over something.

But then the entire hour passes without Seth checking on us once. In fact, he stays as far away from me as possible. Maybe his furrowed brow does have something to do with me. Every minute he avoids me makes my heart beat faster, and I go into panic mode.

He let my secret slip.

My mind races through the possibilities. Maybe he was talking to Hector about me and someone overheard. They figured out I'm not hiding from my dad. He's probably scared to tell me. And he should be, because I'll never forgive him if he ruined everything.

As I pack my stuff, his feet come into view. "Fiona?"

"Yeah?" I look up; he stares at the floor.

"I need to talk to you."

"You could have done that during class—Bea's my ride. My mom actually got a job. . ."

"I can take you home. This is really important and . . . private."

My throat closes. Crap. Someone *does* know I'm on the run. They told my dad. He showed up and seduced the school secretary into telling him where we live. He's probably there waiting for Mom and me to come home.

I'm such an idiot. I'll never have a normal life, and now that I'm losing this one I know what I'm missing.

"Fine. See you, Bea."

She nods. "It'll be okay."

I wish she was right.

After the door closes, Seth takes the seat next to me. He chews the inside of his lip, and his blue eyes turn sad. "I have some bad news."

My hands won't stop shaking. "Who'd you tell?"

His brow furrows. "What?"

"C'mon. You look like you're being followed by the Grim

135

Reaper. You must have let my secret slip. Who'd you tell?"

"I didn't tell anyone. She figured it out on her own and came to ask me about it."

My jaw drops. It was probably one of my dad's spies, following a lead. I thought Seth would be a lot smarter than that. "And you just *told* her? I thought you said you were good at keeping secrets!"

His eyes turn angry. "I didn't tell her anything! I lied to her for you, but she's not happy with your performance either way."

I pause. "Wait . . . what?"

He sighs. "You failed your test again. Ms. Sorenson wants to put you in remedial classes like I told you she would."

"Oh." I put my hand to my heart, noticing how fast it's beating. As I realize how wrong my assumption was, I sink in my seat.

"What did you think I was talking about?"

"You kept avoiding me, so I was worried you were going to say you let my *other* secret slip. I thought I was about to see my dad walk through the door or something." I squeeze back the tears. So much for feeling safe under Graham's supposed protection. Try as I might, his words aren't enough to keep me from constantly looking over my shoulder.

"Bea and Brady know, even the rest of The Pack—you trust them. Why don't you trust me?" His voice is indignant, and I open my eyes to find his face the same way.

"They earned it."

"And I haven't? If anything, I've done *more* than them!" He puts a fist to his mouth, as if he's trying to stop the words from coming out wrong. "I thought . . . we were friends now. I thought you trusted me. I know way more than they do."

"That's the problem! Yes, we're friends, but you could ruin me in one breath, accident or not. You know way too much for your own good—and you keep prying."

"I'm not prying."

"You're always asking if I'm okay and trying to get me to tell you about my past. And you won't breathe a word about your own! Not exactly fair." The words feel like a cheap shot now that they're out, and I wish I could take them back.

He glares at me, like he's trying to push away whatever he feels. "I'm just trying to help."

"What do you expect from me, Seth? You think it's easy for me to believe people when I've lived one giant lie of a life?" I try to force down the guilt, but it doesn't go away. "Under my dad's control, I couldn't even trust myself, my own feelings. I want to trust you, I really do, but . . ."

"But what?"

I'm scared. "Cut me some slack. Please."

He folds his arms. "Then do the same for me and stop worrying about if I'll tell. I won't."

I nod. "Fine. Whatever."

We're silent for what seems like ages. I almost get up to leave, but then I remember he's my ride. Why did I agree to this again? I just want to run away. I can't seem to get enough air when he gets worked up. It stresses me out.

"Can I say what I was going to say without you getting mad at me?" he asks.

"Go for it." The sooner this is over, the better.

"I told Ms. Sorenson I'm still helping you catch up, since your tutors were neglectful. She agreed to give you one more chance—if you pass the next test you can stay in the class."

A lump forms in my throat. I'm not sure I've ever felt like such a jerk. "Thanks."

He glances at me, his eyes meeting mine just briefly before he looks down again. "I think you'll need more personalized tutoring to pass. I know it's probably the last thing in the world you want to do, but we could figure this out if you stayed after every day. You're getting better; you'll keep getting better."

I stare at him, unable to speak. "You'd still help me, even after I treated you like that?"

He nods. "I'm kind of used to it by now."

My eyes narrow, and I have to hold back a smile. "Okay. May as well give it another shot."

A small grin crosses his lips. "I won't give up if you don't."

"Deal." I swallow the lump of pride in my throat. "Sorry. I'm a little on edge about stuff."

He shakes his head. "Don't worry about it. I'm dealing with crap, too. Maybe I've been taking it out on you, since everyone else gave up on my attitude problem a long time ago. They don't even bother fighting back."

I almost ask what that means, but I don't. I have a feeling it's been a while since Seth's said something like that to anyone. "So, are you gonna make me start working today? Or do I get a break?"

138

His smile breaks into a full-on grin. "I'll take you home."

I can't help smiling back. "Wow, so you do have a heart in there somewhere."

"Shut up."

My laugh surprises me, as does Seth's.

Chapter 20

Miles and I sit under the tree out front, savoring the shade in the fading light. He leans on the trunk, pouting.

"Stop it." I close my eyes, unable to look at him any longer. It kills me every time, but I am not giving up my date with Brady no matter how watery my brother's eyes get.

"I can't believe you're ditching me for a guy."

"It's just one night, and it's not like this happens every day."

"I guess that's true," he grumbles.

I venture a peek; he doesn't look happy, but the pout's gone. "You know Brady. How could you not approve?"

He shrugs. "Yeah, he's nice, but I guess I never pictured you with someone like him."

I scoff. "You probably never pictured me with anyone."

"No!" He smiles. "Well, not like I sit and think about it all the time. I just imagined someone . . . less huge."

I laugh. "You have a problem with his muscles?"

"He could hurt you! Not that he would, but that kind of strength . . . Fi, it's not something that's easy to deal with." He bites his lip. "I always hoped you'd find a guy who wouldn't make your life any more complicated than it is, you know? Someone safe."

As I look at the ground, this ache forms in my chest. I'd never thought about it, really. Brady's strong. He could easily demolish a house with his fist, never mind a person. And yet . . . "He's so gentle. He controls it really well. You can't say he's not one of the nicest people you've ever met."

"He is." Miles puts his arm around me, squeezes tight. "But people are like paper to him. Don't forget that. Of course he'd never do anything intentionally—that doesn't stop accidents, though."

I push his arm off. He should be happy for me. He has to know it's a miracle anyone would ask me out, especially someone like Brady. "You're judging him."

"Fi, calm down. That's not what I'm saying."

"Then what?"

He takes a deep breath. "I'm just making sure you don't forget what kind of sacrifice you'd be making, if this does go further. I mean, look at Mom. She resisted Dad at first, and he was so crazy about getting her because of it. Then things changed. She thought she could deal with it. She wanted to love him for real, and she paid the price."

My eyes go wide. "What?"

Miles tilts his head. "Didn't you know?"

"She never told me that." I try to picture Mom *choosing* to love Dad, instead of falling prey to his unrelenting charm drug. I had no idea she was that crazy. "How could she do that?"

"Why don't you ask her?"

I don't answer. Lately, talking to Mom leaves me feeling like I'm the one to blame.

Miles picks at the grass, and I know he's trying to find

the words that will keep me from yelling at him. "There are always sacrifices when you get involved with someone, sis. Ignoring them and their consequences can really screw you over. As long as you know what you're getting into and are honestly willing to deal with it, then I'll back you up."

I roll my eyes. "With such good advice, you'd think you could keep a girlfriend for more than two wee—"

"You don't need to come." Graham's voice comes from above. Miles and I freeze. For a second I think he's talking to me, but I can't see past the branches so he can't possibly see me.

I check the clock on my phone. Five to eight. If he doesn't go into the house soon, Brady will show up. Then Graham will know we heard.

"Dad, trust me. They're fine."

My heart stops. Dad's on the phone. Dad. And he wants to come *here*? Miles wraps an arm around me, and I nearly scream in surprise but cover my mouth.

"About that. I really think it'd be better if you held back for a second. I still have to make sure."

Tears well up. I hate Graham. I knew he was lying. He should have taken us back before we had a chance to hope. Dad knows. He *has* to know where we are if he's talking to Graham. That stupid cell phone is like a GPS pin right over our house.

Graham swoops down in front of the door, not even looking back. For once I'm glad he's too self-absorbed to notice we're right there. It slams behind him, at which point Miles grabs my shoulders and turns me to him.

"Fiona, don't come home tonight, okay?"

I can't seem to stop shaking, even under his firm grip. "B-but what about you?"

"I'll see if I can get anything out of him and call you when I know it's safe. Mom might need me to get her out, too."

"But what if—?"

He shakes his head. "Don't start that. Go with Brady; tell him what's going on if you want, or run out to the desert again. Whatever. Promise me."

"Miles . . ." I can't leave him. He'll get hurt. Graham will figure out that we heard, and then it'll be over. I don't want this to be over.

The black truck pulls up front. Miles pushes me away, but his eyes lock with mine. "This is not the time to worry about me. I'm worthless to Dad, which means I'll be fine. I'm dead serious. I don't want to see you back here until I say so."

"Okay." I force myself to stand. It takes all my strength to leave my brother and run for Brady's truck.

Chapter 21

I hear Brady say hi as I slide into the truck, but I'm not sure if I say it back. I don't even care that Seth's there in the passenger seat, which is saying something. There's just one thing on my mind:

Dad.

Some criminals are easy to root out. Not Jonas O'Connell. Dad's the untouchable kind. The kind who does horrible things and gets away with it, even though everyone knows how bad he is.

I can't stop thinking about that last night, the fury on his face, his final command. I know without a doubt he meant for me to kill Juan's little girls. He didn't care how I felt about it. I was a tool to him, and the sad thing is that I acted that way, too. Now that I've been without him so long, the fear of going back is paralyzing.

A hand waves in front of my face. "Fiona?"

I jump, realizing it's Brady. "Huh?"

"Are you okay?"

"I told you she'd be pissed that I came," Seth says.

Brady bites his lip. "This is your first time out, and I didn't want you to get lost when I run off fast on my own. Seth knows the desert like the back of his hand."

"It's not that. I'm not mad. It has nothing to do with you guys." Tears prick at my eyes. Ten minutes ago I'd have been excited to hear him say "first time"; now all I can think is that it'll be my last, too.

"Do you want to talk about it?" Brady asks.

I stare at my hands, unsure. It's not that I don't trust them—they probably already have their guesses—I'm just not sure I want to get them so involved. But then again, Brady is good protection, and Seth is smart enough to come up with a plan. Except can I really be that selfish, using them like I've been used?

"No." I take a deep breath. "I just want to run."

Brady smiles. "We'll do plenty of that; don't worry. Running always takes my mind off crap, better than any medicine. I bet you'll feel great by the end of tonight."

"I hope."

"You will. We're taking you somewhere special."

My ears perk up. "Special?"

His smile breaks into a full-on grin. "You'll love it. It's impossible to feel bad there. Trust me."

Brady turns off the road and keeps heading into the desert. I bounce between them as we go over uneven ground. It's dark before we stop, and when the headlights go out I can barely see. This area isn't anywhere near the run-down buildings I stayed in, and I can't see the town lights, either. With Brady going off by himself, I'm actually relieved to have Seth and his flashlight. It was considerate of him to think of that.

After a few stretches, we start at an easy pace to warm up. The air has cooled enough to make running nice, almost relaxing if I didn't have to dodge a pothole every few seconds.

"What are these holes?" I ask through my breaths.

Brady laughs. "My fault."

My eyes widen. "Really?"

"You'll see," Seth says.

"That's why I don't run in town. Even as a kid I'd make little divots. But I have to release all this energy sometimes, and out here I can lose control." Brady's smile looks sinister in the flashlight's sparse beam. "Seth, you know where to meet."

"Yup."

The ground cracks when Brady takes off. I skid to a stop, barely able to believe my eyes. Brady is a force, like a mobile earthquake crashing its way through the desert. The earth still shakes beneath me, though his flashlight's beam is already a ways off. I look down at the sizable pothole he just made, and Miles's advice comes to mind. What would it be like to live with such a dangerous ability? Mine may feel awful, but at least I never have to worry about accidentally hurting someone.

"Pretty crazy, huh," Seth says.

"Yeah." It comes out as a whisper.

"Ready? Or do you need more of a break?"

I shoot him a glare I wish he could see. "I'm fine. Do *you*?"

He smirks, then breaks out running full speed. I follow his pace easily, and we run in silence for a long time. I stay behind Seth to avoid the potholes, trusting his swerves and directional changes.

Every now and then, the sound of Brady's own personal thunder grows louder, but I can't see his light. I wonder how far he's gone, where he's gone. He must know this desert better than anyone if he's out here so much. No wonder they knew where to look when I hid from Graham.

My lungs burn, but I keep pushing hard. It feels good to get distance from the house, from what might be happening there. I feel like I can finally think clearly, maybe even form a plan. I'm safe for now, and Miles will be okay. I hope.

Suddenly I notice I'm next to Seth instead of behind him. Sweat beads at his forehead and around his neck, making the ends of his hair curl. He glances over. "Need a break?"

"Why do you keep asking that?"

He stops and leans one hand on his knee. "Maybe because you're killing me, and I don't want to admit it."

"Oh." I walk back to him. Now that I've stopped, I realize how hard I was running. "We can rest. I guess I have a lot of steam to burn off."

"This is where Brady will meet us anyway." He sits on the ground and pulls off the CamelBak, and I sit next to him. After a long drink he tosses it to me. "Man, Brady said you were fast, but I didn't think he meant *that* fast."

I smile. "He said that?"

Seth nods. "Girls' soccer team could use a runner like you. You'd be a star."

I take a long drink. "Maybe."

"Why maybe?"

I shrug, hoping my wide tank top straps will be enough

to show it. Tears come out of nowhere. This could be my last weekend here. My last day, even, depending on how much Dad knows. I look up at the stars, hoping the water will sink back into my eyes. Some people don't like the desert, since it's so hot and dry and lifeless or whatever. I love it. Any time I want to feel alone, all I have to do is find a desert. No one for miles. Endless stars to remind me how small I am. Hidden beauties for those who look hard enough.

I like *this* desert.

I want to stay here.

I won't give up. Not yet.

"Fiona?" Seth's voice cuts through the quiet. "Are you okay?"

"Yeah." I run my finger over the dust, making circles and swirls appear from what looks like nowhere.

"You're lying."

I glare at him. "And?"

He looks away. "Can't you just tell me?"

"No."

He tenses. "If this is because you still don't trust me, I might have to—"

"It's not!" It comes out angrier than it should, and I have to take a moment to compose myself again. "It's not that at all, Seth. It's just . . . for your own good."

"What's that supposed to mean?"

I can't get my mouth to move, and then I can't hear myself think over Brady's pounding feet. The light comes closer and closer until a cloud of dust and dirt hits me.

"Whoa! I can kind of see you, Fi!" Brady says as I attempt to brush myself off.

"Yeah, *kind of.*"

"Are you ready for the coolest thing in the world?" Brady sounds like a little kid, and his grin matches.

I laugh at his excitement. "Yes. I'm pumped."

"Over here."

I follow them to the base of a small mountain. Brady pushes a massive boulder aside, revealing an opening to a cave. I peer through the darkness and gasp.

Chapter 22

I take a few steps closer. The cave isn't entirely dark—the faintest blue light shines from below. "What is that?"

"You'll see." Brady steps into the cave and holds out his hand for me. "It's really steep here. If your legs are weak from running, just let me know and I'll carry you."

"I think I can manage." My face burns as I take his hand. I'm tempted to trip and take him up on being carried.

His hand is softer than I expected, though his grip is strong. It's strange how his skin can be so normal when there's so much power underneath.

Brady wasn't kidding when he said steep. The cave may be tall enough to fit us standing, but it's narrow and so vertical I worry I might slip and tumble all the way to the bottom. My legs burn at each step. I don't even want to think about climbing out of it. The blue light grows brighter as we descend, and it reflects off the rock like sunbeams at the bottom of a swimming pool. There must be water down here, but I still don't understand the light. It's not possible.

After what seems like forever, the cave slowly opens up. The ceiling gets higher, the walls farther apart, the ground flatter. I stare at the source of the light—three pools of water. As we get closer, I search for the bulb at the bottom, as if for some weird reason these were built here. Maybe it was an old spa location, just like that run-down building and factory.

No lights.

"What do you think?" Brady asks as he lets go of my hand.

"It's . . . amazing." I kneel down to get a closer look, just in case I missed something. "Why do they glow?"

"Not sure," Seth says. "We found them a long time ago, and the glow never fades; the temperature of the water never changes. I tried to do research, but I couldn't find a thing like this. The closest were the New Zealand glow-worm caves, but that light comes from the worms in the rocks, not the water."

"Weird." I touch the water, surprised to find it warm. "Maybe it's just a special hot spring."

"Who cares how it got here? It's time for a swim!" Brady takes off his shirt, at which point my heart stops. Then he does a cannonball right in front of me.

I wipe the water from my face, smiling. Dad might be out there hunting me, but I'm here now and it'd be a waste to spend my time worrying. This place is cool. I can't believe Brady decided to share this secret with me. I slip my shoes and socks off and jump in.

The water is just right, not a hot tub but not a pool. My feet barely graze the bottom near the edge, but in the center it's deeper. After a few small laps to explore, I settle into a ledge I found and try to chill out. My eyes close, and I focus on the comforting feel of the water running over my

151

skin. I am miles from Madison. In a secret underground cave. Dad can't find me here.

When I open them again, I jump. Brady's not a foot from me, his smile wide and his hair dripping water down his face. "Feeling better?"

"Yeah." I smile, surprised at how relaxed I am.

"Good." He leans on the ledge next to me. "Sometimes I swear this place is magic. It sucks out all the bad feelings or something."

"I could see that." I lean my head back, watching him stare into space. He's just so . . . beautiful. I could look at him forever and not get bored. "None of my problems seem to matter here."

He smiles. "Yeah. No school."

"Or people acting like you're going to kill them."

"I hate that."

I scoot a little closer, whisper so Seth doesn't hear. "No math."

He laughs. "Or dads."

"No kidding. Though my mom is a piece of work, too. What about yours?"

His smile fades, and just like that the energy between us is gone. Without a word, he pushes himself out of the pool and runs to another one, disappearing with a huge splash. I frown. What did I do wrong? It was going so perfectly, and then . . . Seth swims up to me.

"Sorry, Brady's sensitive when it comes to talking about our mom."

I bite my lip, the urge to pry flooding over me. But I

remember Bea's advice and force it back down. "I'm sorry. I didn't know."

He shakes his head. "Don't worry about it. He'll be okay."

We float there next to each other, the sound of Brady swimming echoing off the walls. I wonder if I should go talk to him or if that would make it worse. Seth fidgets, like he wants to speak. "Brady was born strong, you know," he finally says. "Just like you were born invisible."

"Makes sense." I'm not sure where he's going with this, but I hope he'll just tell me already.

He grins. "You're being so quiet."

"I'm trying to listen." I wince, worried my attitude will change his mind.

He sighs. "Okay, good, because I'd rather not have to talk about this again." He looks to the other pool. "Brady . . . killed our mom."

It feels like the wind got knocked out of me. I'd never even thought about it, but it makes perfect sense.

The bump in Seth's throat bobs. "Not on purpose, of course. He was just a fetus. The doctors said she had to abort him, and she wouldn't do it . . . at least that's what her journals say. I wasn't even one at the time.

"Anyway, when he got too big, the bruises became bleeding and broken bones and eventually . . . yeah." He sniffs, then coughs like he's covering it up. "Brady blames himself, no matter how many times I've told him it's not his fault. It was her choice, and it was a pretty noble one."

I can't get out words. I feel like such a jerk for talking badly about my mom in front of him, even though I didn't

153

have a clue. What if I didn't have her? The thought hurts more than I expected.

Without her, Dad would still have complete hold of me. She's the one who's tried to escape. She's been trying to protect me. Maybe she kind of sucks at it, but she has tried. She's not leaving Dad for herself; she's doing it for me. I'd never have tasted freedom without her.

I'm the most ungrateful daughter in the world.

I want to tell Seth I'm sorry, but if I open my mouth I'll choke on my tears and give myself away. Despite my best efforts, a sniffle escapes.

He startles. "Are you crying?"

"No." I squeak.

His arms come around me, stronger than I expected. "Don't cry over us. Sure, it sucks, but we deal with it. Way better than our dad, too. He's still a drugged-up mess."

"I'm not crying over you." His skin is warm, surprisingly comforting. I'm tempted to put my arms around his waist, just to know how it feels to hug someone besides Miles. Before I can think better of it, my hands are on his back. He flinches, but then relaxes again.

My whole body tingles, and I feel slightly guilty about how much I enjoy the feel of him against me. I like Brady. Seth's *brother*. At least I think I do. But I can't seem to stop myself. I need comfort, and he's here for me. I put my head on his shoulder, confused as hell. "I'm such an idiot."

"No, you aren't. You didn't know. Brady only left because he can't talk about it without crying, and he hates crying."

I don't answer, figuring that sounds better than the real reason I feel stupid.

I can't stop thinking about Mom. I left her, just assumed she wanted to go back. Without thinking twice. I wish I could apologize, save her, stop all this from happening. But I can't do it by myself. I take a deep breath. I have to say it now or I won't have the courage later. I have to trust him. "Seth?"

"Hmm?"

I pull back a little so I can look at him, but he doesn't let go. "I need to tell you something, and you can't tell Brady or Bea or anyone."

"What is it?"

"Do you promise?"

He rolls his eyes. "Do you even have to ask?"

"Ugh. What did I say about the eye roll?"

He does it again. "Sorry."

I scrunch my lips so I don't laugh. This is not the time for him to act like a dork. "You were right about me. I did work for my dad. I stole things, spied . . . hurt people. All the time." It hurts to say it out loud. I wait for him to lecture me. To gloat about being right. Something.

"But that wasn't you."

I stare at him, surprised. "It doesn't bother you?"

"Fiona." Seth's fingers tighten around my waist. "You would never do that, not when you're free from your dad's influence."

"I should have tried harder to resist, though." I never realized how guilty I felt until I put it in words. How ashamed. I swallow hard and force myself to keep it together. I'm exposed enough as it is.

He shakes his head. "You're being too hard on yourself."

155

"Right. I forgot that's *your* job." I splash some water at him.

He smiles. "See, this is you—joking around, at ease. Whatever you did, like I said, that wasn't you."

For some reason, him being this nice makes it harder to say the next part. "I think my dad might be coming for me. Maybe even tonight."

The smile drops. "What?"

I recap what Graham said. "I need a place to stay. Miles told me not to go home. Do you know somewhere safe I could hide?"

He nods slowly. "We'll take you to Bea's."

"I don't want to put them in danger."

"You won't. It'd be more suspicious if anyone saw us running into the desert to give you supplies. It'll be easy to sneak you out of Bea's house if he comes looking. Do you think he even knows about us?"

"No. Just Miles; he's the only person I trust completely." I gulp. "Will that be okay? Tomorrow's Sunday and she said they don't—"

"Are you kidding? It's not a problem. Alejandro and Rosa are the nicest people in the world, and they won't turn you out just because it's Sunday. I don't know what Brady and I would have done without them after . . ."

"You told her?" Brady's voice comes from behind. I push away from Seth, suddenly worried about how that hug may have looked. It didn't mean anything. Or did it? I don't know anymore.

"Yeah," Seth says. "You may continue pretending to be happy."

Brady smiles. "Great."

As he jumps into the water, I realize he's not the guy I thought he was. But somehow, it makes me admire him all the more. It takes a strong person to smile through that. "Sorry about what I said."

Brady shakes his head. "No worries. Now, where were we?"

"Forgetting our problems, I think."

His eyes meet mine, undeniable mischief crossing his face. "Right."

A splash war follows, and I end up using Seth as a shield half the time. Brady pummels us with water, thanks to his massive arms. As another wave comes, I jump behind Seth, grabbing on to his waist. I keep doing that, wondering if maybe this time I won't like it. But I still do.

Chapter 23

It takes a second to realize the sound filling my ears is a blow-dryer. I open one eye and see Bea standing at her long closet mirror. She didn't even ask why Seth brought me over at almost midnight. All she did was complain about the guys trying to steal her friend; then she rolled out an air mattress, and we talked about my trip to the pools until we passed out.

I stay still, watching her. I'll admit I like spying on people, even if it's wrong. It's fun seeing how they act when they think no one is looking.

It's weird seeing her in a dress, but at the same time the lavender makes her more beautiful. She sticks her tongue out a little as she runs the brush through her hair. Then she puts on a necklace, the pendant a glittering cross.

"Why do I even try? Like he'll notice," she mumbles to herself.

My breath catches. I had no idea Bea liked someone. She's not the kind of girl to gab about boys, at least not with her brothers always around. I wonder if she means Miles, since she said he was cute. They seem to get along well, though I'd rather he didn't hit on my one female friend ever. Or could it be Brady? She doesn't flirt with him, but they are best friends. I'm suddenly relieved she can't see how much I stare at him.

She turns when I cough. "Sorry, did I wake you?"

"It's okay." I sit up, the feel of her silky pajamas strange on my skin. "Probably should be getting up anyway."

She smiles. "Yeah. Mass is in an hour, and it takes, like, thirty minutes to get there since it's two towns over."

"And you go every Sunday?" Religion has never been part of my life, and I find it amazing that she's so dedicated.

She nods. "Mom goes twice a week—she makes us go, too, if she thinks we need it. Like Carlos. He goes to Wednesday Mass *a lot.*"

The door swings open. Revealing Carlos, shirtless. "I heard my name."

"Get out!" Bea throws a brush at him. "And stop listening at my door!"

He dodges. "Hey, Fiona. I hope you had good dreams last night. Was I in any of them?"

Bea's makeup bag doesn't miss. "I said get out! I'll tell Mom you—"

"Fine!" He winks in my general direction. "I'll save you a seat at breakfast." Then he shuts the door.

"What is his problem?" I ask.

She rolls her eyes. "No clue. He's always liked girls, even when he was little. I mean, we're talking he kissed some poor girl when he was in preschool." She points over her shoulder. "You can shower in my bathroom. Pick whatever you want to wear. I'm gonna eat."

"Okay." The second she leaves, I jump for my phone to text Miles.

Is everything okay?

I wait a few minutes, but no reply. I figure it'll be fine if I shower quickly, as long as I leave the phone on the bathroom counter. The water is freezing, since all seven Navarros have probably showered already. I stare at my phone as I dry off, willing it to beep or ring or *something*.

It doesn't.

I rummage through Bea's clothes for something that fits, which isn't an easy feat, since she's several inches shorter and a size or two smaller than me. Finally, I manage to find a longish green tunic and some black leggings.

My phone still hasn't made a sound. I check the battery and signal, just in case. My fingers sweat as I make sure I sent the text to Miles. It all seems to be working.

Something is wrong—it has to be. I almost send another message, but force myself not to. I take in a deep breath; I'm probably overreacting. It's only fifteen past eight, and he's not exactly an early riser. Maybe he just slept through it. I'll start worrying if he hasn't answered in a few hours.

Carlos really does save me a seat at breakfast, and I have no choice because all the other ones are full.

"I swear I tried, but he wouldn't let me sit there," Bea says.

"Because it's Fiona's seat!" Carlos passes me a box of sugary cereal. "Here, it's my favorite."

"No thanks." I grab a banana, since cereal kind of grosses me out.

He frowns. "But I saved the last bowl for you."

I stare at him, his yellow cat eyes almost earning my

160

sympathy. At least until he attempts to play footsie with me. I kick him. "Will you quit it?"

"Quit what?" He grabs his foot, his face contorted in pain.

Hector rolls his eyes. "Please tell me you weren't doing what I think you were doing."

Tony takes the cereal box from Carlos and pours the last bowl for himself. As Carlos sulks, Joey shakes his head. "You better take the hint, bro, before Fiona sneaks up on you and beats your ass."

My eyes go wide. "I wouldn't do that!"

Joey flinches with surprise, and then it clicks. "Oh, Fi, I didn't mean it. Just because of your past . . . uh . . ."

I squirm in my chair, wanting to leave. Maybe they're just like Seth—they know I'm a criminal even if I haven't said it. Maybe they're only being nice because they're afraid.

Hector clears his throat. "I think what Joey is trying to say is that you'd beat Carlos not because you're syndicate-born, but just because he's that annoying."

"Yes!" Joey says. "And pushy."

"And pigheaded," Bea adds.

Carlos smiles, as if the insults don't even register. "Don't forget devastatingly handsome."

Everyone groans. "See, Fiona?" Joey says. "We all want to beat his ass, so really we'd just consider you part of the family if you did."

I laugh as warmth spreads through me. "So that's how you become a Navarro?"

They all nod, even Carlos.

I can't help but smack the back of his head. Hard. He

gives me this shocked look, but then they're all laughing and so am I.

Just like that, I *feel* like I'm part of the family.

"So," Bea says. "You can either come to Mass with us or hang out at Brady and Seth's house."

Carlos clasps his hands. "Mass!"

"Hmm." I tap the table, like this is actually a hard decision. "I think I'll hang out with Seth and Brady."

"Surprise, surprise. C'mon, I'll walk you over."

No one answers the first time we ring the doorbell. I'm starting to wonder if the Navarros are the only ones up this early on a Sunday.

"Stupid boys." Bea rings it three times in a row, and finally I hear heavy footsteps coming. She runs a hand through her hair. I shuffle from side to side, surprised by how anxious I am to see Seth. I need to tell him about Miles, so we can figure out what I should do.

The door swings open, revealing a shirtless and groggy Brady. I can't deny that he looks even cuter this way, but I'm still looking over his shoulder for Seth. I don't see him.

Brady smiles. "Hey, my two favorite people. Even if you woke me up." He runs his eyes over Bea. "Look at you, Trixy. I forgot you wore dresses."

Bea scoffs, though a smirk still touches her lips. "Only because Mom makes me." She pushes me forward. "Fiona doesn't want to go to Mass, just like you heathens."

"Ah." He opens the door wider. "You can hang out with me, then. Hell just got a little better."

"Better or not, it still sucks." Bea takes a step back just

162

as a car honks. "See you later. Unless, of course, the apocalypse comes first."

Brady nods. "Either way, wear the dress."

She laughs as she disappears around the corner.

Brady lets me inside, and I'm glad he can't see my reaction. The place is a disaster. No flooring, some walls torn out, wires hanging out where lights should be. I knew they were remodeling, but I pictured something more like redecorating. "Sorry about the mess. Though you should have seen it last week. Seth had me pull out all the old drywall; the place was basically one huge room."

"Wow." I almost say something about how amazing it is that they got so much work done so fast, but then remember it's Brady. His hands are wrecking balls.

"Let me grab a shirt. You can wait in the kitchen."

"Sure." The kitchen is the only thing intact, and it looks like something out of a showroom. Smooth granite counters reflect the morning light, and the brushed metal appliances all look new.

The first thing Brady does when he gets back is open the fridge. "You had breakfast? I'm starving."

"I ate at Bea's."

Brady proceeds to devour a whole box of cereal and three bananas. I watch, fascinated by how much he can eat and how fast. He must need more food than normal people to maintain that body.

I search for conversation topics, but nothing comes to mind except questions about his mom or worries over Miles. Neither of which I should bring up.

"Where's Seth?" I finally choke out.

"Grocery shopping, probably some other errands, too."
Brady tosses the empty cereal box in the trash. He sighs.
"Dad's passed out. I found an empty liquor bottle in the
trash this morning, so I guess we weren't the only ones
busy last night."

"Oh."

He rolls his eyes. "Stop being so quiet. I know you're
worried about what to say, but don't be. It is what it
is."

"Okay." I only speak because I don't have glasses or a
headband or anything to show my nodding.

He shakes his head, like he's not satisfied with my answer.
"You wanna watch TV or something? We moved the old
furniture to the study while we clean up out here."

"That sounds great."

I follow him down a narrow hall to a room packed with
tacky stuff that looks decades out of fashion. I almost poke
fun, but then I wonder if their mother picked it out, and
they're just starting to replace it. That must be it—that's
why Bea said Seth was renovating the house. His dad probably wouldn't. Couldn't.

Brady sits on the long brown couch, his weight making
it creak. I sit next to him. We're finally alone, which is what
I've wanted for weeks, and yet . . . it's not what I thought
it would be.

He grabs the remote. "Any preferences?"

"Not really."

He flips through channels and settles on a baseball game.
"This okay?"

"Sure." Despite Miles's efforts, I'm still not a baseball

fan, not the gifted league or the normal league. It just seems so blah.

As Brady watches, I find myself more interested in my phone than him. It still hasn't rung. I want more than anything to believe Miles just slept in or forgot to charge it or something, but in the back of my head the worry creeps in.

Miles is hurt.

Graham lied.

This is my last day of freedom.

The last day ever with my friends.

My last day with . . . Seth.

The thought hits me right in the gut. I did not see this coming, but now that it's here I can't ignore it. I should be worried about Mom and Miles—I am—but I'm dying here with just Brady and no Seth. He's the one I want to be around. The one I can talk to and be real with.

After who knows how long, Brady sighs. "You're doing it again."

"What?"

He lets out a short chuckle. "You're brooding, just like Seth."

That only makes me blush harder. "Why would you say that?"

He tilts his head. "Why not?"

"It's just . . . you can't compare me to your brother." I try to compose myself. Brady can't see what I'm feeling, so he doesn't know that I ever liked him or that I just realized I don't so much anymore. Sometimes it rocks to be invisible.

165

"It's not a bad thing. He's my best friend."

I pause, my heart warming. "He is?"

"Of course he is." Brady leans his head back. "We've been through everything together. I know he can be intense, but he's so used to being the grown-up, it's hard for him to chill out. That's not him, though. That's the person he has to be to get us through stuff."

So that's what Brady meant when he said they have different ways of coping. "Seth likes to fix everything, doesn't he?"

He nods. "Dad's been useless since . . . you know. Without Seth and the Navarros, we'd have probably ended up in foster care, which is a fast track to a syndicate when you have abilities like ours."

"Ours?" My eyebrows rise. "What would they want with Seth?"

He fidgets with his collar, then nudges me. "Last I heard, money was important to syndicates. Seth would make an amazing accountant."

"True . . . I guess. But what are you not telling me?"

His eyes go wide. "Nothing!"

A crash sounds from the front of the house, followed by crackling plastic bags. "Brady! Get your lazy ass out here!" Seth calls.

My heart stops at the sound of his voice, and whatever we were talking about is forgotten.

Chapter 24

Brady rushes out to help Seth, but my legs don't seem to be working properly. I walk slowly down the hallway, my heart pounding at my rib cage. As much as I want to see him, I'm scared at the same time. If I tell him how I feel, there'll be no going back.

"I told you to get him up!" Seth yells, and I pause in the hall, unsure if I should interrupt. "He can't do this again. I don't care if he doesn't like the changes; it's time to freaking move on."

"Yeah, but—" Brady starts.

"No buts! I'm so sick of this." A cabinet slams. "We just have to make it until I graduate and then—"

"Seth! Will you shut up for just one second? I have to tell you something!"

"What?" he says as he follows Brady's gaze to me. His eyes go wide, and he turns red. "Oh, Fiona. I didn't realize you were here."

I open my mouth to say something, but nothing comes as his blue eyes look for mine. Then guilt immediately strikes. Seth is so stressed out dealing with his own stuff, and here I am ready to drop all of my problems on him, too.

"I'm, uh, gonna go mow the lawn." Brady bolts for what I assume is the garage door. It slams behind him.

"Did something happen?" Seth asks.

"No. Nothing." I squeeze my eyes shut, refusing to let the tears come at the thought of how little time I could have left.

"Nothing? You haven't heard anything about your dad yet?"

"No."

"Okay . . ." Seth stares at the floor, hands in his pockets. I'm pretty sure he didn't want me hearing about even more of his problems.

I search for something neutral to talk about. "Do you need help with those?"

"Sure." He grabs the bags, seeming relieved. "These go in the fridge."

We unpack the groceries in virtual silence, save for his directions on where to put things. After he stuffs the plastic bags in a drawer, he leans on the counter and starts sifting through bills. I sit on a stool, unsure what to do. I hate to be in the way, but I don't have anywhere to go. And if I'm being honest, I don't *want* to be anywhere else. If Miles would just text me back, I'd know if it was safe to relax with Seth.

He sighs, shoving the envelopes away. "I'm sorry, okay?"

"Huh?"

"I know I was being a jerk to Brady. I'm not gonna bite your head off, so you don't have to be so quiet. I just . . ." He practically crumbles onto the counter. "Damn, I'm just so sick of this."

"I . . ." I'm not sure what to say. Seth never shows weakness, but it looks like he's about to break in two.

"I can't do this anymore, Fiona. The only reason my dad still has a job is because I make sure he's dressed every morning. He'd rather spend all day in his room than talk to us. I've done everything I can think of to make things better, and nothing works." He looks up at me, and I can almost see him sucking in his feelings, putting the pride back in place. "So, sorry. I'm not mad at you."

I look down. "That's not why I was being quiet."

"Oh." Seth and I seem to have become masters of the awkward silence. "Then what?"

"I texted Miles this morning, and he hasn't answered yet. I'm worried something happened to him. I wanted to tell you, but I didn't want to stress you out more."

He lets out a little laugh. "Well, aren't we a pair."

I manage a smile. "Our families are jacked up."

"And there's nothing we can do about it."

"Ugh." I run a hand over my face. I'm sick of this, too. I'm sick of living in fear, sick of worrying myself to death, sick of being so helpless. Just thinking about stewing all day makes me tired. This itch runs through my bones, like I might snap if I don't move. "Seth."

"Hmm?"

"Let's get out of here. We could drive to that movie theater in Saguro and get lunch after or something."

His cheeks go pink. "What?"

"We both have stuff we need to forget for a while. So let's just have fun."

He purses his lips. "But we were supposed to put in the floors today."

"Lame excuse. Brady can do that himself. Just leave a note." The more I think about this, the better I feel. Get out. Run away. Forget. I just want to hang out with Seth and not think about what could be waiting for me at the house. This could be the last day I ever see him, and I have to know if what I'm feeling is real.

"I don't know. He might not do it right, and then I'll have to—"

"Oh, c'mon!" I stand up, grab his arm, and head for the door. "We both deserve one day of slacking off."

He pulls back. "That was last night."

"Seth Mitchell." I put my hands on my hips. "Stop being so anal. When was the last time you did anything for yourself?"

"Fiona . . ."

I can tell he doesn't even know the answer. He's doing everything he possibly can to take care of the people he loves. He never thinks about himself. It's always give, give, give until he's got nothing left but fatigue and agitation.

All I want to do is make him smile.

My hands drop off my hips. "Just come, okay?" I look at Bea's flip-flops on my feet. "Can't you hang out with me today?"

He lets out a long sigh. "Fine."

"Really?"

He goes back to the counter, scribbles something on a piece of paper. "C'mon."

On the way down, Seth cranks the radio, and I let my

fingers hang out the window. The air catches them, and I move my hand up and down like I'm making waves. Today it doesn't feel like the sun is trying to melt me to death. The desert is perfect as winter approaches, cool mornings and warm afternoons. Just staring out at the distant mesas puts me at ease.

We don't say much, but there's this freedom in the air I can't get over. My problems are falling further behind every second. Madison isn't even in sight anymore, just endless desert. I almost want to ask Seth to keep driving until the tank runs dry.

The Saguro movie theater is a tacky dollar place that looks about eighty years old, but I don't care. I haven't gone to a movie in forever—not since Miles was living at home. And the place is empty this early in the day, so I can put my feet up on the seat in front of me.

"Man, this movie's lame," Seth says about fifteen minutes in.

"Shut up." We picked the only comedy, figuring we should keep with the fun theme of this outing. It's about some ultragifted guys trying to go undercover as normal—hilarity supposedly ensues. "That joke was . . . totally not obvious."

He smiles. "Ten bucks that guy falls in a vat of something at some point."

"Twenty if it's chocolate."

"You're on." He laughs, which I hope means he's actually having a good time. I am, too, even more now that he's smiling. Then he bumps my elbow on the armrest. "Oh, sorry, I didn't realize . . ."

"No worries." That tingling thing is back. I can't believe

how much I like being with him now, and I have to know if the feeling's mutual. I take a deep breath. "You know, we don't have to fight for the armrest. I think we've learned how to share."

He looks at me, clearly surprised. Maybe this wasn't such a good idea—maybe I'm totally misreading him—but then he smiles. His arm slides up against mine, and he leans in a little. "Look at us, getting along."

I smile. Being this close to him is electrifying, and I find myself wishing he'd hold my hand. "We better find coats, because hell has probably frozen over."

"And umbrellas, because flying pigs drop some serious shit."

I laugh louder at that than anything that's happened in the movie.

The rest of the show is lame, but it doesn't matter because criticizing it is half the fun. It's almost like a game, with Seth and I competing for best snarky comment.

"He got hot fudge poured on him! That should count!" I protest as we leave the theater.

Seth shakes his head. "But the vat was marshmallow. You owe me lunch."

My shoulders slump. "Fine."

We decide to walk to the diner, since getting in the hot truck and driving there would be more uncomfortable. The perfect weather makes me want to go for a long run.

"So, train one is going fifty miles an hour—" Seth starts.

"No!" I shove him. "Math is *not* fun. We're not doing math today."

He smirks. "But I think math *is* fun, and we still have to figure out how to get you to pass that test."

The test is the last thing on my mind at this point. "Why do you like math so much? I mean, you're good at it, yay, but I'm good at robbing jewelry stores, and I certainly don't love that."

He laughs, though I didn't realize I was being funny. "Math is . . . I don't know."

"C'mon, you do, too."

He sighs. "Fine. It's the answers, okay?"

"Answers?" I look up at him, realizing just how tall he is. For most guys I don't have to crane my neck.

"Yeah." He chews the inside of his cheek. "Once you know the rules, there's always an answer to an equation. All you have to do is follow the steps and then, just like that, you have an answer."

"I see. . ." I don't see.

He rolls his eyes. "Liar."

I wish I could stick my tongue out or something. "Just keep talking, jerk."

He doesn't for a second, and I wonder if I've pushed him one step too far. It's not like he talks about himself all the time. But then he takes a breath. "I can't fix anything in my real life, not Dad or Brady or . . . myself. Math has answers. I can fix any problem in math. So sue me if I like it."

I smile. "I guess I can understand that, but I still hate it."

A diner is in sight, one that had to be built in the fifties by the look of its old sign and retro style. There's even a classic motorcycle parked out front, one that reminds me of . . .

173

"You don't have to like it, you just have to—"

I put my hand on Seth's arm. "Wait."

"What?"

I gulp as I scan the diner's windows. I'm being paranoid. There are probably hundreds of electric-blue motorcycles in the Southwest. Just because there happens to be one here doesn't mean *he's* here.

"Fiona, you're freaking me out. What?"

I freeze when I look in the farthest window to the left. Graham's there, sipping his usual beer, but that's not the worst part. He's there with a man I'd recognize anywhere. Curly hair, fair skin, and an aura reeking of power and money. I turn around immediately, dragging Seth with me.

"Will you tell me what the hell is going on?"

"My . . . my . . ." I feel sick, but my legs propel me forward. *Run. Just run.* "My dad's in there."

Chapter 25

Seth doesn't say another word as we sprint for his truck, and I'm glad. I don't think I can explain or even speak in an intelligible manner. My dad's right there. If he'd looked out the window, he would have seen me. Everything I have here would have been over the second I breathed in his scent.

"Where to?" Seth asks when we jump in the truck.

I'm surprised that I know the exact place I need to go. "My house."

His eyes go wide. "Are you kidding? Don't you want to get out of here? I can drive you to Tucson or something; you can hop a train or a bus to anywhere from there."

It makes sense, and I'd be lying if I said I didn't want to on some level. But I can't.

"I have to get Miles and my mom out if I can. Maybe we can beat Graham home if they just started lunch. I can't leave Miles. I . . . can't leave her."

The truth of it hits me. We might not have the best relationship in the world, but she's still my mom. What little freedom I've had I owe to her, and I've never even said thanks. So I have to at least try.

"All right." Seth revs the engine. "I'll drive as fast as this piece of junk can go."

That would be approximately seventy-one miles an hour. The truck shudders down the long stretch of road, and I tell myself it's fast enough. If I don't, then I'll be too scared to go back. I don't have time to second-guess myself.

I pull out my phone to text Miles.

Call me, please.

I can't text the details, in case Dad is already spying on our words remotely. But it doesn't matter, because he still doesn't text me back. Hugging my knees to my chest, I can't help but think the worst.

But even if it is a trap, I still have to go.

Maybe I can sneak in and free them. It's not like I'm completely helpless. I have lots of training, and kidnapping shouldn't be much harder than stealing, especially if the people want to be stolen.

We pull up to my house. Everything looks normal. Miles's car is parked in the driveway; the blinds are all shut tight. No extra vehicles, no evidence of what might be happening inside.

"Are you sure about this?" Seth asks.

I take a deep breath. "Stay here."

"What? No way." His brows are set low over his eyes.

I swallow the lump in my throat. "Look, I appreciate the chivalry and all, but you can't get mixed up in this any more than you are. It's better if you just go home and forget about everything."

Then if I get taken, everybody else will be safe. It'll be like I was never here. If I have to leave, that's how I want to go.

"It'll be fine." He turns off the truck and gets out.

"Wait!" I follow him to my door, blocking it. "You are *not* coming."

"Yes, I am. You asked me to help you figure this out."

I put my hands on my hips. "I asked you to help me find a place to stay! I didn't ask you to throw yourself in harm's way."

"Isn't it the same thing? Aren't I already in danger?"

I pause, angry that he has me. "Just . . . don't talk. It's bad enough if anyone sees your face."

He straightens, his full height almost intimidating if he weren't so thin. "Fine."

I reluctantly open the door. The cold air seems fitting for the empty living room. I step in slowly, scanning the dark. There's not a single sign of life. Not even coffee in the coffeemaker. My heart beats harder. They're not here. They really did get taken. Graham and Dad were probably celebrating, or plotting how to find me. I force myself to keep looking, since I don't have solid proof yet.

"What's that?" Seth whispers.

"I thought I told you not to talk."

"I know, but . . . is that music?"

I stop in the hall, trying to listen over the blowing air conditioner. There is something, and a flicker of hope rushes through me. I head for the garage door, ripping it open.

Mom's hippie-dippie music blares out. She bobs her head as she waves her graceful hands. A clay pot twirls in mid-air, growing at her will.

I sigh in relief. At least she's not tied up. Maybe we still have a chance. "Mom!"

She jumps, spinning around. But her eyes don't find me; they zero in on Seth. "Fiona! Who's this?"

"Is Miles here?"

She sets down her pot. "I think he's still sleeping. Is something wrong? You sound worried."

"I saw Dad."

"What?" she shrieks.

I run to the guest room, part relieved and part angry that Miles slept through both my messages. Mom follows, begging me to explain, but I'd rather not have to repeat myself. I push my brother's door open and throw on the light.

Miles shoots up. "Damn, Fiona, where's the fire?"

I toss him a shirt. "We have to go. I saw Dad in Saguro."

His eyes go wide. "Shit."

Mom shakes her head. "There has to be some kind of mistake. What were you doing in Saguro anyway?" She eyes Seth, and my face heats up.

"I saw his bike, and then I saw *him* through the diner window eating lunch with Graham."

"I knew it." Miles pulls the shirt over his head. "I'm gonna kill him."

"No . . ." Mom puts her hand over her heart, like the information is physically painful. "There must be an explanation. He said—"

"He was lying, Mom!" I stamp my foot, frustrated that even with so much proof she believes Graham over me. "I told you he was bad! But we can get out of here. We still have time."

Miles stands. "I have a full tank. If we leave right now, we can at least get a head start."

178

Mom wipes a tear from her face. "Graham said to stay here at all costs. He said he'd protect this house."

My chest tightens, but this time it isn't anger. It's sadness. She's so messed up. After all those years of being manipulated, how could she not be?

"Mom, he *lied*."

"He didn't! Why would he keep us safe this long just to turn us in? Why would he get me a job? Make sure my employers keep quiet? It doesn't make sense."

"No, it doesn't, but there has to be some kind of reason." Miles folds his arms. "Whatever it is, it's not good."

"You're wrong!" Mom holds back tears. "It's always been you two against Graham, but he's not a monster. He's my son—your brother. He wouldn't give us all of this just to take it away. He was probably distracting your father from looking in this area. They weren't *here*."

I can't believe she's doing this. I thought maybe she had changed, that I'd misjudged her. "You really do want to go back, don't you?"

She stares at me, searching for my eyes. "No."

"You're hoping Dad comes here! You want him to find you, because that means he still loves you." I force my hands to stay at my sides, so they don't find anything to hit. "News flash, Mom. He doesn't love you. He never has! I don't care if you love him—you're just a tool!"

Her mouth drops open, but she doesn't say anything.

"He doesn't want you back because he misses you. He wants you back because he needs your ability to pad his pockets. He . . . doesn't want me, either." The thought hurts, even if I don't want it to. "He wants his invisible henchman."

179

Mom looks at her hands, the hands that have stolen millions. "You think I don't know that?"

"Then let's go while we can." I hold out my hand. "Please, Mom."

She stares at my sleeve, and then runs a hand through her wild hair. "Fiona, I can't. That's not—"

"Fine. I get it." I want to scream—she's being such an idiot—but at the same time I fight back tears. Suddenly I understand what Seth was saying about answers. No matter what I do, I can't fix my mom even if I try. But she's not dragging me down with her. Not this time. "I'm out of here. Have fun with Dad."

I head to my room and grab the biggest bag I have. I can feel Seth behind me, but he doesn't say anything. Miles, on the other hand, does. "Where are you going?"

"Either with you or back to Bea's, I guess." I hate taking advantage of the Navarros's hospitality, but it's the only other place I feel safe.

"If you don't mind, I'd like you to stay with The Pack. I have . . . a contact I need to see, and she doesn't like strangers."

I raise an eyebrow at him. "Who?"

"Fi." Miles's face is so serious it scares me. He hardly seems like the brother I know. "You know who."

"Spud?" It comes out in a whisper, as if even my voice can't believe he personally knows the most infamous hacker alive.

He nods. "I have an idea, but I don't know if it'll work until I talk to her."

"What about Mom?" I hate the idea of leaving her, but what else can I do?

180

"I'll stay with her today, see if I can convince her it's not safe. Hopefully Dad won't show up."

"Please just go now." I shove in every dress I brought. Forget pants. "I couldn't stand it if you got hurt for not telling them where I am."

"I don't know where you're going, do I? So there's really no reason for a beating."

I know he's trying to be funny, but it isn't working. "That won't stop them. And could you please answer your freaking phone? It would have been nice to know you were alive this morning."

"Will do." He pulls it from his pocket and winces. "It died. Oops."

"Good one, Miles." Why is it that I'm the only one panicking? Maybe it's because I stand to lose the most if Dad comes strolling through the door. Stupid me, getting attached to this place.

"Don't be like that," Miles says. "You'll be safe. That's what matters most to me. Seth, you better take care of her, at least until I can get more information."

"I will." His voice is soft.

"I told you what's really going on. Graham is ratting us out to Dad right now." I sling my bag over my shoulder. I'm determined not to say good-bye, but Miles grabs me into a hug.

"That's why it's time to pull out the big guns. Lay low; I'll email you when I know more."

"Whatever." I nearly choke on the word. Why won't he just get himself out? He might be worthless to Dad, but that won't keep him safe. He has to know that.

"Love you, Fi."

I can't say it back. I won't cry. The only thing I can do is squeeze him tighter, and then I let go and head for the door. Seth starts the truck. We're almost to his house before he says, "What are you going to do?"

I'm not really sure. I don't want to leave Madison, much as I should. The idea of never seeing Bea or Seth or Brady again makes my heart ache. "I should probably run."

"Maybe . . . maybe you could stay." He parks the car, but his hands still grip the steering wheel. "What your mom said could be true. Graham could have been throwing him off the trail."

My jaw drops. "You're siding with my mom?"

"No!"

I glare at him. "Then what?"

"I guess I'm just saying give it a few days before you disappear. Maybe it *is* a misunderstanding, and . . ." Seth bites his lip.

I'm not in the mood for these pauses. "And?"

"There are lots of people here who'd miss you if you just upped and left. I'm assuming I'm sworn to silence here, but Bea would probably rip my balls off if she found out I knew you were running and didn't try to stop you."

I wince at the image. "Jeez, can you be more graphic?"

"I'm serious. You think the Navarros let people in like that often? Well, they don't. They care about you. We all do."

I stare at him. He might not be looking at me, but I can see the worry in his brow, the desperation in his locked jaw. He . . . doesn't want me to leave. My heart warms, even if I know staying for a boy is about as reckless as it gets. But I already wanted to, and this seals it. I have to at least try. "Two days."

He nods. "Fair enough. But if there's any word that things are safe, you have to promise to stay."

I sigh, wishing I had the willpower to say no. "Okay."

"Bea should be back home now. We'll tell Rosa you're having family problems. It'll be okay."

I follow him to the Navarros, hoping he's right.

Chapter 26

It's Tuesday. Day two. I check my email after school, since I don't dare use Seth's or Bea's internet connection. Nothing more to tie them to me. Seth sits at the nearest table, eyeing me. Even if he can't protect me, I feel safer with him nearby anyway.

As I log into my account, my fingers feel slick against the keys. There are three messages, two of which are spam for ability-enhancing drugs. Radiasure may be illegal, but that doesn't stop people from making new, "safer" things that supposedly boost powers. Either they don't do anything, or they're really bad for you.

The third message is from HotMulletMan1. I click it, my heart pounding. Please be good news.

BritBunny, The Big Man never showed. The Lap Dog left yesterday, according to Mom. He was waiting for you—he's not happy that you don't come home at night. He started asking a lot about where you're going, who you're with. He thinks he should keep better tabs on you to make sure you're "safe."

I'm back in Tucson, and I'm meeting up with my contact in the next couple days. Tell me if there are signs of trouble. For now, it seems like you're safe. Just be careful.

I hate to say maybe he's not lying (I know that'll piss you off), but I can't rule it out. I just don't know why he'd want to protect you so much. I'm gonna dig deep this week, promise. (And no, I'm not gonna get killed so chill out.)

Love, HotMulletMan1
(P.S. Bag the phone. Lap Dog grabbed mine and saw your messages on it.)

I let out a long sigh. It doesn't feel like enough, but Miles did say I'd be safe. I guess that means I'm staying for now, but I'm not sure how long this can last. There's no way Dad's given up—not even Graham could convince him to do that.

The second I log out, Seth's in my face. "So?"

I pull out my phone and drop it to the ground. My flip-flops definitely won't break it. "Could you crush that for me?"

"Um, sure." It cracks under his tennis shoe.

"Hey! There you are," Bea calls from the library entrance. She looks between Seth and me with a sly smile. "Did you two forget about tutoring? Everyone's about to leave."

"Oh yeah." My shoulders slump. "Math. Forgot."

Bea's smile fades. "Is something wrong?"

"She's . . ." Seth gently puts his hand on my shoulder, and I savor the sensation. He keeps touching me like that, and I wish he'd just say he liked me so I wouldn't have to wonder if we're more than friends or not. "Not feeling well. Maybe we should take you back to Bea's."

Bea raises an eyebrow. "Seth, are you actually saying you're going to ditch tutoring?"

"No." His face goes red. "I . . . maybe."

"I can deal. Don't worry." I head for the math room, not particularly interested in explaining myself. Seth has the sense not to ask, but he does spend most of the class working with me, since my test is tomorrow. I wish I could say I cared more—at this point I'm mostly doing it because Seth thinks I can, and he actually smiles when I manage to get a problem right. I owe him at least that after all I've put him through.

Besides, he's really cute when he smiles.

"Ugh." I put my head on the desk after he excuses the others. The thought of doing this for another hour is physically painful.

"How are you feeling?" Seth puts his hand over my apple-green bangle, and even that gets me all fluttery.

"Do I have to stay longer? My brain is fried."

"You've been drilling her like crazy, Seth," Bea says. "She deserves to go swimming or something. We should all relax."

Floating in the water, letting the stress wash away for a second. "Sounds nice."

Seth purses his lips. "Well, you did manage a C on this worksheet, so theoretically you should pass tomorrow. But . . ."

"But?"

"You're going to take this test, right? You won't play sick to avoid it or anything?" He gulps, and I realize he might think I'm leaving. I did have him destroy my phone.

"Oh, yeah, I'll be here. Whether I want to be or not."

He smiles, seeming relieved. "We could go swimming, then."

"Really?" Bea looks between us suspiciously.

Seth shrugs. "Sure. I'll go get Brady and meet you guys there."

"Okay, see you!" Bea drags me out the door, as if she's worried Seth will change his mind. "I don't know what you've done to him, but thank you. I've never seen him so happy."

My heart does a couple of flips. I'm not sure what Seth and I are, except that we are closer than I ever thought we'd be . . . and I like it. "Do you have any one-piece swimsuits? I didn't grab a suit in my rage-packing."

She laughs. "No, what about a T-shirt over it?"

"It always comes up, and then it looks like someone just left a shirt in the water. I've been groped as a result."

She winces. "Better not give Carlos that excuse. Would it be so bad to make a quick trip to your house? Maybe your mom's cooled off by now. She probably misses you."

My stomach turns at the thought, but I can't tell Bea. As far as she knows, my mom and I got in a big fight and that's why I've been at her house. I can't tell her the whole truth. She'd be too worried. She'd want to help. It's scary enough having Seth so involved. I can't put anyone else in danger.

"If it's quick, I guess. Maybe she won't even be home," I say, since I'm kind of pinned into going. Unless I want to explain it's not my mom who's the threat.

She hops in Sexy Blue. "I won't even put her in park."

We don't speak, and I can tell she's thinking about something. She's not stupid; she has to at least know I'm stressed out. Even if she can't see my expressions, she has an uncanny knack for picking up my vibes. "Did, um, something happen with your syndicate?"

I force myself not to react. "Why do you ask?"

"I don't know, you've been so quiet and secretive lately. You seem . . . scared." She takes a sharp turn onto my road. "I wondered if your dad was on to you or something."

"It's nothing you should be worried about." I can't tell her the truth, even if she's zoning in on it. "I just . . . the math thing is stressing me out."

She doesn't look convinced. "Is it Seth?"

I freeze. Talk about a subject change. "What?"

"I'm just saying, you two have been spending more time together, and you seem to be getting along pretty well . . ."

"And?" I want her to say it. Maybe if she says what I'm hoping, then it won't sound as crazy as it does in my head.

She shrugs. "Those two Mitchell boys have a way of going straight to your heart, don't they? Like lost puppies you want to take home and keep forever."

I watch her as she parks in front of my house, and then it clicks—Brady. She has to like Brady, and she's testing the waters to see if we can talk about it. "They are pretty annoying that way. And cute."

Her eyes light up when she smiles. "I know, right?"

"I'll be right back." I hop out of the car. "And then we'll talk more."

"We better!" Her voice carries in my ears, even as I open

the front door. I rush past the living room, ignoring Mom's cries for information. As much as I want to smooth things out with her, I can't risk it. I won't stay here, not until I get concrete information from Miles.

My suit still hangs on the bathroom doorknob. I grab it, resisting the urge to find my favorite pair of jeans. I am so tired of wearing dresses. When I round the hall corner, I'm met with an angry face, auburn hair wild like fire. But it's not Mom.

It's Graham.

Chapter 27

Graham folds his thick arms over his chest, blocking the entire hallway. Even if he didn't, it wouldn't matter—it's not like I could run fast enough to get past him. And Bea's outside. If he saw her . . .

"Fifi, there you are." His smile is so fake, it hurts. "Going swimming?"

I clutch my suit. "No. I just need to wash it."

When his smile drops, I know he doesn't buy it. "Not your best lie, sis."

"It's none of your business." I head back to my room, but he flies over and shoves me into the wall.

"What did I say?" His breath is stale and hot on my face. "Everything here is my business. If you ever get that close to screwing this up again, I swear I'll ship you right back to Dad."

I can't seem to find air. "What?"

"Who was that boy? What were you doing in Saguro?"

"You . . . you saw me?" If he saw me, there's little chance Dad didn't. My knees get weak, and the only thing keeping me up is Graham's arm on me. "D-did he—?"

"No, you idiot. Do you honestly think you'd still be here if he did?" He pushes on my stomach, making it hard to breathe.

"Then . . . you're using him as punishment if I don't do what you say?"

His lip curls. "See it however you want. The boy lives around here, doesn't he? I'm sure it wouldn't be hard to find him, what with that light red hair and those gangly limbs."

My insides go cold at the thought of him hurting Seth or any of my friends. "Graham, please, don't. He doesn't know anything."

"Your lying is pathetic today. Either you can take me to these supposed friends of yours, or I'll have to deal with them on my own." He doesn't have any names. It would take him time to find out who they are. Maybe I could figure out how to keep them safe.

"There's no way I'll—"

The doorbell rings. Bea said she wouldn't even put Sexy Blue in park, but obviously I've taken way too long inside.

Graham raises an eyebrow. "And who might that be?"

He lets go, flying down the hall before I can grab a full breath. I rush for the stairs, but Mom's already at the door. "How can I help you?"

"Um . . ." Bea spots me, and her eyes widen when she recognizes Graham from the SuperMart incident.

Graham points to her, all fury. *"You."*

I don't have time to think. She's the best friend I've ever had, and that's enough to muster my courage. I throw myself at Graham and wrap my arms around his waist. My surprise extra weight throws off his balance, and he hits the floor.

"Run!"

Bea takes off without a second thought.

"Fiona! What on earth?" Mom says.

Graham rips me off him, but maintains a strong grip on my arms. "Don't worry about it, Mom. I'll take care of her."

She purses her lips. "Graham, don't hurt her. Give her a chance to explain."

I stare at Mom, shocked that she's defending me over Graham.

He scoffs. "I gave her a chance. She decided to be difficult."

"Graham!" Mom yells, but the door slams behind us. Before I can fight him I'm fifty feet up, with Graham's arms the only thing between me and falling. My stomach turns, and I close my eyes to block out the shrinking earth. Higher and higher we go, until the air feels thin and cold.

"If you sold out to another syndicate, consider this your last few minutes," Graham says.

"I didn't! Why the hell would I do that? They're just friends!" I venture a peek at his face. He's dead serious about this; he really would kill me. Not like that's something new for him, but it's terrifying all the same. I'm in his way, and he can get me out of it.

"I need more proof than your words. So you better tell me where to find your 'friends.'"

I stay silent too long, my fear of heights making it hard to think. He finds my wrist and lets go of everything else. I scream as he dangles me above the desert by one arm. "Graham! No!"

"Tell me!"

"They don't work for anyone, I swear!" My wrist feels like it's about to snap. I can't help but picture my skin ripping free of my hand, how it'll feel to plummet to the hard ground below. He's always caught me before, but this time I don't think he will. The tears refuse to stop. "Please . . . don't drop me."

"I want to meet them. Now." His grip loosens.

I don't want to die. I wish I could be that noble, but I can't sacrifice my life to keep them safe. I don't know what that means—if they're not really friends or if I'm just a horrible person. I suck in my sobs. "They're probably at the community pool."

"That's a good girl." Graham slings me over his back, and he soars toward the pool. Seth and Brady will be there at least, which means there's a good chance The Pack will as well.

The smallest twinge of hope flickers in me. Brady . . . if anyone could stop Graham, it'd be him.

We begin to descend, which is far worse than going up. My stomach rolls so badly I almost lose it. When Graham sets me on the ground, my legs buckle, and I end up on top of the grassy hill. Splashing and laughter surround me, and I open my eyes. A few people stare, but other than that it seems all's well.

"Fiona!" Seth's voice comes from behind.

I turn, finding him, Brady, and the entire Pack running toward us, Bea included. A flood of emotion crashes over me as I stand and run. If I can just get to him, I'll be safe. Seth grabs me—hugs me—and I gasp and sob into his chest.

"Thank God." He runs his hand over my hair, which is

surprisingly calming. "Bea told us what happened, and we thought . . ."

"And you would be?" Graham says.

Brady gives him the coldest stare I've ever seen come off his face. It's honestly frightening. "Stay behind me." He pushes Seth and me back.

"Are you okay?" Seth whispers. "Did he hurt you?"

"He . . . he . . ." I still feel like I'm about to lose it, so I wrap my arms around him for support. "I'm sorry I brought him here. He was going to drop me, and . . ."

"Don't be sorry. You did the right thing. We don't want you dead."

"Please, don't let him take me." My voice is a shaky whisper.

"I won't."

Graham hovers in front of Brady, a sick smile on his face. "This is all very cute, but I'm gonna need information now."

"What makes you think we're willing to give it?" Bea's hands go to her hips, like she's ready to tell him off.

Graham narrows his eyes. "Who are you with?"

"Who says we're with anyone?" Brady asks.

A small crowd has tuned in, even if they're pretending not to listen. This conversation needs to end fast.

Graham smirks. "C'mon, let's not play games." He nods at Bea. "She imitates voices, which is way up there on anyone's list of good attributes. You look pretty strong, so I'm assuming the rest of these people are gifted as well. Not a bad little gang, don't you think?"

Brady flexes. "I suggest you leave Fiona alone. And if you don't, you better believe you'll pay for it."

"Oh? You think you can make *me* pay?" He laughs in a way that says no one can beat him. It makes me sick.

Brady reaches out, grabbing Graham by the neck. Graham's eyes bulge as he tries to pull away, but just like I hoped, he can't overcome Brady's muscle. The sight almost makes me smile. Serves him right.

"Don't mess with her." Brady lets go. "I don't want to, but I *can* make you pay."

Graham flies out of his reach. He rubs his neck, glaring in my direction. "Nice friends you have there, sis. You better hope they're enough to keep you safe."

He shoots off.

Chapter 28

The last thing I want to do right now is take my math test, but it plops onto my desk anyway. I stare at the cover sheet, wishing I could keep what's underneath a mystery. Bea squeezes my shoulder, as if she can see the panic on my face. "It'll be okay, chica."

I let out a breath. "I hope so."

Opening the test, I try to block out what happened yesterday with Graham. I have to do my best—not for myself, but for Seth. He put in so much work, and I can't give up now. Every problem feels like a mountain to climb, but I keep going, not really knowing if I found the right answers. At least I have an answer to every question before the bell rings. That's more than I can say for past math tests.

"How'd it go?" Seth asks at lunch.

I shrug, honestly unsure of what to say. "I need to get in touch with Miles. You coming?"

He nods and follows me down the hall. I expect him to ask more about the test. He's silent. Something is off, but I'm too drained to bother asking. It feels like I've used all my brainpower. I wish I could skip the rest of school and take a nap, but I have to tell Miles about what Graham did to me yesterday. He's not on instant message, so I type out a quick email, telling him to call Bea's house if there's an emergency.

When I plop down in the seat next to Seth, he gently puts his hand on my back. It doesn't feel like enough. I want to crawl into his lap, wrap my arms around his neck, close my eyes, and feel safe with him.

"Should I just grade your test now?" he asks.

I sit up. "Can you do that?"

"Yes."

I smile. "Please. One less thing to worry about."

We rush to the math room. Ms. Sorenson is at lunch, but the morning tests are already piled neatly at the TA desk with a note for Seth. He riffles through them for mine and grabs the key out of a locked filing cabinet. I can't watch as he takes out a red pen and starts comparing, but I hear the scratch he makes for each wrong answer.

There are a lot of scratches.

Finally it's quiet, the ticking clock the only sound. I wait for the verdict, but Seth doesn't talk for what seems like forever. Finally he says, "Are you ever gonna turn around? I'm getting tired of holding this up for you to see."

I cringe. "Did I fail?"

"Why don't you look?"

"I can't."

He sighs, and the chair squeaks when he gets up. I close my eyes, too scared to know, but I can feel him in front of me. The paper touches my nose. "Open your eyes, Fiona."

I whimper.

"Don't make me open them for you."

I force my right eye open to peek, and then I grab the paper because I can't believe what I'm seeing. That can't be a C- on my test. I look at him. "You didn't miscalculate?"

"Yes, I suddenly forgot how to figure percentages." He rolls his eyes, but smiles. "You passed!"

"I passed!" I'm dancing over a math test, but I feel victorious. If I can beat my messed-up brain, I can beat anything. And then my arms are around Seth's neck. "You really are a genius!"

He laughs, his hands wrapping around my waist. "You're the genius."

"Whatever." Suddenly we're very still, to the point that I'm not even sure he's breathing.

"It's true," he says quietly. "I remember numbers—you have to relearn math every time you sit down to do it. That takes a lot of intelligence."

I bite my lip, the intensity in his eyes making me blush. "You mean that?"

He nods, but then his face fills with worry. "Fiona, I have to say something, and it can't wait anymore."

"Is it bad?" His hands tremble, and now I'm anxious, too. "You're scaring me."

"Sorry." He pulls away from me, biting his nails. Finally he takes a deep breath. "I haven't been entirely honest with you, and I wanted to come clean today."

I gulp. "Not entirely honest how?"

"I . . ." He looks away. "I like you. I have since day one."

"Is that all?" I put my hand over my heart as if that'll slow it down. Smacking his shoulder, I laugh. "I thought you were going to say something horrible!"

He offers a wary smile. "You don't think that's horrible?"

"Not at all." I feel like my face might break from smiling so wide. Seth likes me. He's always liked me.

He holds out his hands, and I take them. "I hoped you'd feel that way, but you hated me so much at first I thought maybe I was reading too much into it."

"It wasn't just me—you hated me, too."

"Never."

That only makes me smile wider. "Then why were you so mean?"

He sighs, some of his nervousness coming back. "I didn't know how to handle it all. I kept saying the wrong things, and then you seemed more interested in Brady than me—"

"What?" My face heats up. How did he pick up on that? I never told anyone but Miles. "I didn't . . ."

"Don't worry about it, okay? Brady makes a much better first impression than me. I just consider myself lucky you stuck around long enough to give me a chance."

I slide my hands away from his. Something isn't adding up here. And then it clicks—why Brady always brought Seth, always talked about him, always invited me places where Seth would be. "Wait. Are you saying you and Brady planned everything?"

His eyes widen. "No! Well, maybe. You wouldn't have come if I asked, and Brady knew I liked you, so he helped me. Is that so bad?"

Anger and sadness well up inside of me, to the point that I end up pacing the room instead. Seth watches me, clearly worried about the direction this has gone. I can't believe he deliberately made me think Brady liked me. "You manipulated me."

"No." He tries to come closer but I step back. "Fiona, I would never. I just wanted to be around you. I wanted you to like me back before . . ."

"Before what? Before you revealed all your plots to mess with my emotions? I thought you actually cared about me!"

"I do!" His voice sounds desperate. "I didn't *make* you like Brady! I only noticed that you did."

"And used it to your advantage."

That cuts him short. He leans on a desk, his fight suddenly gone. "You're right; that was a mistake, a really stupid mistake. I wanted to make it an easier transition, not make your life harder than it already is."

I let out a wry laugh. "Of course, because in the end, I'm just another problem for you to fix."

"No, Fi—"

"I don't want to hear it! You know what your problem is, Seth? You really do think people are like math problems; you still think there's an answer to why they're messed up." My nails dig into my palms, but I don't mind the pain. "Well, guess what? There isn't. Some people are just messed up. I'm not an equation. You can't fix me with your plots and nice words and . . . and . . ."

"And?" A smile creeps onto his face, as if he knows I'm thinking about all the times I've let him be closer to me than anyone. Part of me is screaming to stop fighting with him and let it slide, but I can't. He tricked me, and he knew more than anyone how I've been tricked my whole life.

"I gotta go." There's too much flooding my brain as I

head for the door. I can't think, can't breathe, with him looking at me like that. For the first time in a while, home seems like a haven.

"No, I haven't told you everything yet." Seth follows me, but I don't turn.

"I think you've said enough."

"Just wait!" Seth grabs my hand, and it takes a second to process what that means. First I realize I'm wearing my favorite purple halter. Then I remember I didn't put bracelets on today. And then I comprehend that there is no possible way Seth could have grabbed my *hand*—not my shoulder, or arm, or elbow—unless . . .

I whirl around, pulling away as I do. Seth's eyes meet mine directly, and I know. He's not guessing, not getting lucky. He can *see* my eyes.

He looks away. "I messed up. Big time. I should have told you sooner, but I was scared. I didn't want you to leave or hate me even more. I didn't want you to feel exposed."

Except I do feel exposed. That's *all* I feel. Everything else is gone. It takes me a moment to find a word to describe the new sensation coursing through me. I'm . . . naked. This is what it feels like. Even wearing clothes I want to cover myself, to hide from him. Normally I'd strip and run, but that would only make it worse.

I always imagined that being seen for the first time would make me happier than anything else could. I was wrong. I don't feel at all happy. I'm terrified to know the answer to what I've wondered my whole life. What does he see? I can't bear to ask. I can't handle him looking at me and seeing what I can't.

He lied. All this time he's known, and he lied. He could see my emotions—that's how he knew I liked Brady—and he used them. How could he hide something so huge from me for so long?

"I . . . I gotta go, okay?" I finally choke out.

"I never wanted to fix you," he says softly. "Whether you knew it or not, you've been fixing me."

"Oh." I don't know what else to say.

"Can I at least take you to wherever you're going? I want to make sure you're safe." His voice cracks. I refuse to think about what I might be doing to him. I've hit my max, and I can't hide from it like I usually do.

I shake my head. *Holy shit, that's all I need to do.* He doesn't need me to say no; he saw me shake my head. I wrench the door open and break into a run, not looking back.

Chapter 29

My sandals slap the pavement as I run from school, from Seth. I can't get his eyes out of my head no matter how hard I try. They're like windows into who I really am. I thought he already knew too much, but he knows *everything*. He knows more about me than I do. It's not fair.

I run harder, like that might help me forget.

Everything looks the same when I see the stucco house, with its shady tree and slightly dry lawn. Home never looked so good. Then it hits me. This is home now. I've never thought of one of these getaway houses that way. I'm not sure if I like it or not, because losing a home would hurt more than losing a house.

When I open the front door, Mom spits out her coffee. "Fiona!"

"What are you doing here?" I throw my schoolbag down, frustrated. She was supposed to be at work. I shouldn't have to deal with her, too.

"I have the late shift today." Her eyes well up with tears. "Where have you been?"

"It's none—"

"Of my business. Right." She sets her mug on the table. "I'm just . . . happy you're safe. I've missed you."

Part of me wants to run to her and beg her to make it all better, but I don't. "I need to lie down."

"Fine." She stands awkwardly, like she wants to hug me or something. "Will you be staying long?"

"Yeah."

I rush to my room and recommence freaking out. After putting on layers of clothes, I hole up in my bedcovers and try to pretend everything is the same. It's not. I still feel naked. I can't stop thinking about how Seth looked at me. *At* me. Not through me or near me. The idea is everything at once—I feel like I'm ripping apart in a thousand directions.

On some deep level, I think had suspicions. I just couldn't believe it. That first day in tutoring, he acted surprised when I gave him my name. He knew I was the invisible girl, except not to him. He probably thought he had to hide his real ability from me. Maybe that's why he was so mean at first.

And how does he see? Is it like X-ray vision? I've heard of infrared and night vision like Carlos, but never someone being able to see through things like good old Superman.

Every moment we spent together has changed. I want to die when I realize he saw me standing there naked that night I hid in the desert. That's why he wasn't looking for me.

He could see my scowl when Brady called me "Fifi"; that's why he called him on it. He could see all the expressions I never thought to hide—every time I glared or smiled or rolled my eyes at him. He could see everything, and he must be able to see through more than just me. That's how he found me so fast the night we played sardines.

Speaking of sardines, that's probably what Brady and Bea were whispering about at Taco Bell. They were trying to get us alone. Does everyone know he likes me? They do; they have to. That's why Brady told Carlos to back off. Not so he could make a move, but so Seth could. I am such an idiot.

I've never felt so blind in my life. And blind to the one person who can see me, no less.

The worst thing is part of me wants to go back there and see him. I left him hanging, and I don't have a clue how to make contact again. I don't dare talk to Brady, who willingly tricked me for his brother. And I can't face Bea when she knew this the whole time, too. She even hinted at it! I was just completely distracted by Brady. I'm so stupid. Stupid, stupid, stupid.

Sleep finally tugs at my fried brain. I don't know what time it is, but I let it take me away. I can't think any longer without losing my mind.

When morning comes, things don't seem as bad. My dreams were surprisingly calm. I feel a little better, and I decide maybe I can go to school, almost convince myself it's fine that Seth can see me. What's the big deal? He obviously likes what he sees. And even if he did lie, I know him well enough to understand that he thought he was doing the best thing. Maybe it was—if I knew he could see me from the start, then I'd never know if I liked him because of that or because of *him*.

I wish I could deny it, but I still like him. As annoying and stupid and messed up as he can be, I do.

I manage to get in the shower, even with the tingles of

fear and doubt. But that's when it all comes crashing down. I scrub my armpits like usual. Except everything is different because I realize Seth can *see* the hair under my arms. The hair on my legs! I panic.

Should I shave? No. Not only would I cut myself like every other time I tried, but he'd *see* that I shaved. And he'd know the only reason was because he could see me, which is so lame and vain. I consider wearing pants and a long-sleeved shirt, but then I'd sweat up a storm and he'd see that! I practically collapse when I realize he's seen every sweaty, hairy, unclothed moment since I met him.

By the time I dry off, I've changed my mind. There's no way I'm going to school. What if I have a pimple or my hair is a disaster or my teeth are the color of egg yolk? I can't see him. I can't see everyone else because they'll definitely know what happened. So I throw on a tracksuit, socks, gloves, and a hat just to feel covered. Then I crawl back in bed, ignoring the gnawing in my stomach, which is made stronger by the fact that I'm starving. But the thought of eating makes me sick.

I don't know how long it's been when Mom knocks on my door. "Fiona? You okay?"

"No. I'm sick." My voice sounds terrible, dry from not drinking anything since yesterday.

The door clicks open, and her weight makes my bed creak. "Do you need me to get you anything?"

I pause, wondering what she's up to. I glance up to find her blotchy, tired face, but it's strangely clear of her typical glazed-over expression. She's not faking this—I can tell she

206

is genuinely worried. Something has changed. She isn't the mother she was in Las Vegas.

"Sweetie?" She puts her hand on my shoulder, and I stop breathing. She rarely touches me, and for a second I consider telling her everything. But I can't. She'll be excited; she'll force me to talk to Seth so *she* can know what I look like. I don't want her to know after all the times she said it was okay that I would never be seen. "Should I call a doctor?"

"No. But maybe some juice?"

"Okay." She rubs my shoulder gently. "Just rest."

She's back with juice and a box of Pop-Tarts in minutes. She doesn't say anything else, like she knows I'm too "sick" to talk. When she leaves, I sit up and chug the juice. It doesn't sit well in my empty stomach. I lie back down and hope it'll stay put. Throwing up would just add insult to injury.

I only get out of bed to pee. The rest of the day my brain replays everything that's happened with Seth in the past couple months. The more it plays, the stupider I feel until all I comprehend is my complete idiocy.

I could leave right now and never have to face Seth again. He'd get over me for sure, and in time I'd forget, too. Then I'd never have to know if I have a lazy eye or ears that stick out too much. I could just keep being whatever I wish I were, instead of what I am. I could forget everything that happened here. Forget this stupid person that I am.

Starting over would be easier. I'm invisible. I can be whoever I want. Why in the world would I want to be myself?

The garage door slams, and I can hear Mom's car keys clank on the counter. Then her footsteps pound the stairs. She leans on the doorjamb. "Feeling any better?"

I sit up, taking a deep breath. I know once I say it, it'll all be over. But I'm ready. "Yeah. I want to leave."

She tilts her head. "What?"

"Let's move again."

Chapter 30

Mom lets out a small gasp. She sits on the end of the bed, staring at the beanie I'm wearing. "Did something happen?"

Yes. I can't face the boy who can see me. "I don't want to talk about it. I just want to leave. You don't even have to come. You can go back to Dad if you want."

She looks at her hands, picking at the clay under her nails. You'd think she'd stay clean with her ability, but it's always like that when she gets in her creative moods. She says she likes to "dig in" and feel the medium. "Fiona, I don't think you understand. I'm never going back."

Now I'm the shocked one. "Look, I get that you were doing this for me all these years, this whole trying to escape thing. Thanks, but I don't like this place. It sucks. So you don't have to pretend you want to be here anymore, okay?"

She sighs. "But what about your friends? I know seeing Graham has been rough on you, but other than that you've seemed so happy here."

She's right . . . at least she was until yesterday. "I'm not."

"Can you explain?"

"Ugh." I lay back in my pillows. She was supposed to say yes and skip off to her room to pack. I search for a subject change, something to make her angry so she'll leave me alone. "Miles told me you chose to be with Dad—that you loved him."

She doesn't answer for a minute, just stares at the floor. That expression washes over her, the desperate one that makes her look pathetic. "I do love him. I hate that I love him." She glances at me, her eyes wet. "Sometimes you love things that are bad for you."

I hate that I get what she means about Dad.

"They say love can heal anything, and for a long time I believed that. Your dad . . . he's not as tough as he looks. You should have seen how hurt he was the first time I told him I wouldn't date him. That's when I realized, with a power like his, he probably had no understanding of what real love was. Even his own mother was taken in by his ability. He could get anything he wanted without trying."

She lies on the bed, almost touching me. "That was my biggest mistake. I pitied him. I wanted to show him that love could be real, even with an ability like his. I thought he would love me back if I could prove it.

"Sometimes love isn't enough, Fi. It took me a long time to figure that out, but I finally get it. If your father wanted, I think he could have changed. He could have loved me the right way. He could have grown into a good man."

"But he doesn't want to," I say.

She nods. "Love can only heal someone who *wants* to be healed. And that's why I won't go back, sweetie. I finally know that deep in my soul, and I can't give any more of myself to your dad."

"You're really serious." How did I miss the fact that Mom was changing right along with me this whole time? It makes sense now. We've both been away from Dad long enough that his drug is out of our systems; we can think for ourselves again.

She sits up. "I am serious. The other times we ran, you're right: I ran for your sake, because I love you despite all the hell I've put you through. I'm sorry for bringing you into that horrible world; you never had a chance for better. I've always wanted to give you as normal a life as I could, but by then I couldn't get over his hold.

"This time . . . this time I left for myself, too." She smiles a little. "I think that's why it worked, why I can actually sit here and say I like living in Madison. And I hope you can say that as well."

I fold my arms, glaring at her. It's easy for her to say because she hasn't found *new* problems here. But she is right about one thing: Love is hard. "Well, I can't say that. I'll leave without you if I have to."

She sighs. "I really don't think that's a good idea. It seems like something happened, and you can't run away from your problems forever."

"Why not? We ran from Dad."

"That's different." She pinches the bridge of her nose. "Look, I know you probably think I'm not qualified to give you any advice, but do me one favor?"

"What?"

"Really, *really* think about it. I don't think it's a good idea, because if you run, you might never have this chance for a normal life again. You might never be this safe. That's a big decision, and it shouldn't be a rash one."

I stare at her, trying to believe that the person in front

211

of me is my mother. She's so calm. So reasonable. It's annoying. "That's it?"

"Yeah. I trust you, Fiona. You know what's best for you. I just want you to be happy." She heads for the door. "Do you want dinner? Spaghetti?"

"Um, sure."

"Okay. I'll call you down." She shuts my door as she leaves.

I hate admitting her little speech got to me. Am I over-reacting? Could I forgive Seth for going about things in every possible wrong way? I don't even know if it'd work between us. We'd probably fight all the time. So what if there's chemistry? I shouldn't let that cloud my judgment. I need to be practical.

It would never work.

I pause, clutching my blankets. Even after all the ugly moments, he said he cares about me. He said I was fixing him. Mom said love only works when someone wants to be healed, and Seth's spent his whole life looking for answers. For healing.

So maybe it would work. Plus, he can see me. What are the chances of finding someone else who can do that?

I shake my head. "No. Stop it."

Mom's spaghetti isn't half-bad. I can't remember her ever making it before—ever making anything but coffee, really.

"I'm going to visit Miles," I tell her, just to get it over with. "Maybe it'll help clear my head."

Mom sucks in a breath and nods. "Is that a nice way to say you're leaving?"

"No. I'm still thinking." Every other minute I change my mind, but Miles will help me figure it out.

"He'll take care of you."

"Yeah. Can I use your phone to call him?"

"Sure." She grabs her phone from her purse and slides it to me. "He's number three."

I hold down the number and listen to it ring until it goes to voicemail. I call again, and still Miles doesn't answer. After waiting ten minutes with no reply, I try again, and this time it doesn't even go to his cheesy message.

His phone is disconnected.

Chapter 31

By the next morning, Mom and I have called Miles forty-seven times, hoping his voice will magically answer. She hands me a slip of paper. "This is the bowling alley's number. Call if you hear from him, okay?"

"Of course." I call again right then, but by now it's clear there's something terribly wrong. He said he was going to "pull out the big guns," and I worry they blew up in his face. I try to pass the time watching TV, but it doesn't help. Every time a commercial comes on, I'm calling him and hoping for an answer besides, "We're sorry, the number you dialed is no longer in service."

At about six, there's a knock on our door. I look through the peephole, afraid I'll see Graham or Dad, but it's Miles, his curly hair bursting out of a baseball cap. I open the door, planning to cuss him out for letting his phone get cut off without warning, but then he pulls the cap off, revealing the blackest eye I've ever seen. "Hey, sis. You guys have ice, right?"

I pull him closer to get a better look at his eye. He shouldn't have driven here—it's almost completely swollen shut, and what I can see past the fattened, black lid is bloodshot. "What happened? I thought you were dead!"

He shrugs, like it's no big deal, as he limps to the kitchen. "I got hold of Spud to see if she could hack Graham."

I still can't believe he knows how to contact Spud. She is an enigma in the crime rings—probably within the government, too. All anyone really knows about her is that she's a girl, she can hack just about anything, and she'll make you pay for it.

"How did you come up with the money?"

"It was more of an exchange." He shovels ice into a bag and puts it on his eye. "Ahh, that's better."

"So, what? Her thugs beat you in exchange?"

He smiles slyly as he limps to a chair. "Nah, she owed me."

My jaw drops. Spud . . . owed him? Spud doesn't owe anyone. Maybe I don't know Miles as well as I thought. "Owed you for what?"

He shakes his head, laughing. "That one's going with me to the grave, Fi. Sorry."

There is only one reason I can think of for Spud giving away a hack. Miles has to know who she really is. "So who did the beating?"

"Dad's people jumped me after work. Let's just say Spud found what I was looking for—but Dad's men found out I was looking. Or suspected me, at least. It wasn't really clear. You know how it is: They beat anyone suspicious *before* asking questions."

I sigh. "What did you find?"

He glances at the garage door. "Mom here?"

"No, but she should be home soon. She told me to call if I heard from you."

"Don't." He stands. "Let's go to your room and turn up some music, just in case."

As I help him up the stairs, my mind races through the possibilities. It has to be huge if the beat squad was dispatched. Beatings are warnings—back off or expect to find yourself at the bottom of a desert pit without water. They love slow deaths like that.

He turns on some loud punk music and crashes on my bed, looking exhausted. "So I found out you're safest here. Trust me. I discovered Dad basically wants to kill you and Mom."

I freeze. "What?"

Miles rolls his eye. "You heard me. That's why Graham's been helping you guys out—he knew what Dad was planning, and as bad as he is he couldn't let his mom and sister die."

I shake my head. It doesn't make sense. "Why would Dad want to kill us? What would he gain by doing that?"

He sighs. "Well, not intentionally kill you, but there's a rumor going around that some syndicate lord in China has figured out how to manufacture Radiasure again. Not that cheap imitation stuff, but the real thing. There's this rare, secret element that has supposedly been left out of the existing formulas. It was top secret stuff. Dad wants that formula, and he planned on sending you and Mom all the way to China to kill the man who has it, and steal it."

Could that be true? America may be Shitsville these days, but it's paradise in comparison to organized crime in China. Even the "good guys" there want Radiasure to boost their powers. Mom and I would have made a great team for a job like that, but it still would have been suicide. Getting in would have been practically impossible. If we got the formula, maybe we could have managed to send it via the web. But getting out? We'd have to kill a lot of people to even stand a chance.

Would Dad really have sacrificed us like that? He's cruel and greedy and all-round horrible, but surely he'd see it wasn't worth the risk. His last command comes flooding back—kill Juan's daughters. Maybe he was prepping me for the plans to come. Maybe it really was a test. He wanted to see if I would kill for him. He needed to see how loyal I was.

I can't swallow. Why just have an invisible thief? Why not an invisible assassin?

Of course that's what he wants. The stealing and spying were only the first steps in my training, not my ultimate end. Once I could break into anything and steal anything, I could kill anyone easily. I just had to be dead enough inside to do it, completely under his control.

Miles sits up. "Graham's using a decoy here to explain all his trips. There used to be another town close by named Radison—and its sole purpose was to manufacture Radiasure. They evacuated it and blew up the factory once the drug riots started. Madison grew up out of the ashes, so to speak. Anyway, Graham claims there's still a Radiasure storage at the old factory, and the reason he's here all the time is to find it. But really he's been smuggling some of Dad's own supply there. He's supposed to "retrieve" it this week, and then Madison will be totally off the map."

It sounds good. I've seen the factory with my own eyes,

and it's a logical cover. The place looks just as Miles described, and the battered buildings now make perfect sense.

But something tugs at me. "How do you know this is real?"

He tilts his head. "What?"

"Maybe what you found was fake. Maybe Graham and Dad knew we'd go looking, and they're trying to put us at ease. I don't see why Graham would have any more motivation to save us than Dad, and I don't see Dad throwing away two of his most valuable people, for that matter. He may not love us, but he's not that stupid."

My brother's jaw drops. "Are you saying you don't believe me? You don't think Spud would break through stuff like that? This is the most solid info we could hope to get!"

I shrug. "I'm just saying it could be a lie. There's no guarantee that I'll be safe if I stay here."

Miles doesn't move, but I swear I can feel him thinking, fuming. "What happened to you?"

"Huh?"

"You're being completely irrational!"

"I am not!"

Miles shoots to his feet. "This place is good for you, Fiona. Can't you see that? And this information shows that you're safer here than anywhere else."

"I don't want to be here anymore." I shrink back, because even if Graham does have one last shred of decency in him, that doesn't remove Seth from the picture.

Miles puts his hands on my shoulders, startling me. But it's not forceful or angry. His fear seeps into me. "Fiona, did someone . . . do something to you? Did Brady . . . ?"

"No!" I pull away. "Don't be ridiculous! Brady would never, *ever*. Ugh."

He's getting closer to the truth, zoning in like a sniper. I head for the door, but he blocks it. "Something happened, though. Something that has you running, right?"

I keep my mouth shut. If I open it, I'll burst into tears.

I can't stop thinking about how much Seth smiled that day in Saguro. The way he'd glance over at me during the movie when I laughed at his jokes. The feel of his arm against mine, steady and warm. How close he walked next to me down the street. He . . . enjoyed being with me. He wasn't there to fix me or manipulate me. Not that day. He was there because he wanted to be.

But he's so obnoxious, and he thinks he's better than everyone. . . .

Except that's not true. He doesn't work so hard because he wants to be better than other people, but so he doesn't let people down.

No. Stop going in circles. No more thinking about him.

"Fiona," Miles whispers. "You're scaring me. Please tell me before I start picturing Carlos going too far or something."

"Nothing happened," I manage to say, though I squeak.

"You're lying. You tell me everything—why not this?"

I shouldn't tell him. I don't have Seth's permission, and it's obvious he's kept this a secret from practically everyone. I'm not even sure Bea or her brothers know. Brady does, though. He almost slipped that Sunday, when he said they both had abilities criminals would want. I knew there was something fishy about that.

But I can't hold this in any longer. I can't do this by myself. As I look into Miles's working eye, I know he has my back no matter what. He'll fight for me even if he shouldn't. And there's only one reason why: My brother cares about me.

Seth protects me, fights for me even when I'd rather give up, treats me like a real person, not an invisible girl. He's not manipulating me—he's reacting to my emotions because he can see me, inside and out.

Seth cares about me, and I care about him.

I burst into sobs, and Miles wraps his arms around me. "Seth likes me."

Miles pulls back. "What?"

"Seth. Brady was just his wingman, and I totally read it wrong and everything blew up. But I like him, too, and I can't face him."

He laughs. "Is that all?"

"I've never done this before!" I feel horrible for half lying to him, but Seth has kept all my secrets, so I should do the same.

"It'll be fine." He kicks my shoe. "You already know he likes you. I totally approve."

"Really?"

"Yeah. You can't run because of that. Seth is a good guy, and I don't think Graham's lying. You'll never be safer than you are here."

I sigh. "Why do you have to be right?"

"C'mon, I'll drive you there."

Even though I feel sick, I can't help but smile.

Chapter 32

Miles opens the car door for me, but I can't seem to move. Seth's house is right there. Somewhere inside, he's probably installing cabinets or painting walls or whatever else you do in renovations. What if he sees us out here and freaks? What if he's changed his mind?

Now that I realize how much I care about him, I'd rather not see him if he doesn't like me anymore. I already feel stupid enough after running away, especially since he put it all on the line.

You were fixing me.

The thought makes my face warm. If I weren't so mad and freaked out, hearing that probably would have been incredibly romantic. It should have been. I should have let go of all my fears. But I ran. I hurt him. How am I supposed to face him again?

Miles holds out his hand. "Are you coming?"

"Do I have to?"

He sighs, leans over to unbuckle my seat belt. "Yes. You do. I kind of hate saying it, but he's perfect for you. You *need* him."

I shove him away. "Punk."

He laughs. "C'mon! You can't tell me you don't like him.

I've seen how you guys are. Haven't you always wanted this?"

It's true, but wanting and having are different things. Now that it's a reality, I can't idealize it anymore. "Yeah, but—"

The front door slams, and I whirl around, heart pounding. It's not Seth. It's Brady. He walks down the path, his hands in his pockets and his eyes on the ground, as if he's trying to act chill. It doesn't work. He's biting his lip. "Long time no see."

"Uh-huh," I manage to get out.

Brady turns to Miles. "That's quite the black eye."

"Probably the best I've ever had." My brother pushes me forward, like he knows I might bolt any second.

I haven't *prepared* for this. If I had it my way, I would have spent lots of time getting ready. I would have removed leg and underarm hair, dressed up in something nice, tried to tame my wild mane. But here I am in freaking Christmas-patterned pajama bottoms, a hoodie, and a grungy white tank.

Seth will think I look like crap. I *have* to look like crap.

"So, did she tell you?" Brady asks Miles warily.

"I told him Seth liked me," I say, hoping he'll get that I didn't tell Seth's secret.

"Ah." He nods, clearly relieved, and heads for the house. When I don't follow, Miles drags me with him.

The place is starting to look like a home. A nice one with personality and class, but not over-the-top like Dad's penthouse. So Seth has been busy the last couple days. "He's waiting for you out back."

222

"Okay." My heart pounds so hard it hurts. I force my feet to go forward, and I'm out the door before I can change my mind and run.

My breath stops when I see their backyard. It's prettier than I expected. White paper lanterns light the patio awning. Flowering vines climb up the posts. Tall trees shade most of the lawn, which is as manicured as the front. There are rosebushes everywhere and in every color.

Seth leans on the porch railing, and I freeze when our eyes lock. I'm not sure what makes me blush more—the fact that he's really looking at me or that I completely forgot how cute he is. He's wearing a nicer shirt than usual, making me feel even grungier. The blue color matches his eyes exactly. His hair's almost red in the fading light.

I missed that shy side smile more than I thought. It makes me want to run over and hug him, cry on his shoulder, and feel his arms around me. But I don't. Not after the way I acted. So I attempt humor. "Your water bill must be insane with all those roses."

His smile grows. "My mom loved them. She planted every single bush. Have to keep one thing to remind me of her."

I nod, unsure of what else to do. It's still weird that he sees my reactions. I wonder if I should try to hide them, but I'm not sure I can.

He pulls out a chair for me. "Do you want to sit?"

"Okay." I can't seem to get my words out after that. There's so much to say and no good place to start. He watches me, and I can't help but worry I have something on my face.

He frowns, looking away. "This is really hard for you, isn't it?"

"Yes."

"I'm sorry."

"It's not you, really. There's just a lot to get used to. I have to think about things that never mattered before."

"Like?"

I sigh. "If I'm sweating like a pig or eating like one. Then there's every facial expression I'm not used to people seeing, and this feeling of . . . I don't know, being exposed, naked, *visible*. It's scary." I hug myself, a wave of it coming over me. I miss hiding. "And you've seen me actually naked, haven't you, in the desert?"

His face goes bright red. "Yeah, but that time was unavoidable. It's not like I spend all my time undressing people. When I was younger, clothes were hard to hold on to. Trust me, it's not pleasant to see your old, fat second-grade teacher naked."

I can understand that, though it's not completely comforting. "But how do you see through? How can you, um, keep my clothes on but see through my invisibility?"

He shrugs. "It's hard to explain, but I guess it's like layers. I can peel off different layers or put them back on. Some layers—thick ones—are harder to get through. I get killer headaches if I spend too much time using it to see through thick walls and stuff like that. But your invisibility is nothing. It's hardly there, thinner than a spider's web. I have to work hard to see you invisible, actually."

"Huh." I always felt being invisible was more like being

surrounded by a cement barrier. "That's why you didn't realize who I was that first day."

He nods. "To me, you were just some beautiful girl walking into class."

"Whatever." I wish he couldn't see me blushing.

His fingers wrap around mine tightly, sending goose-bumps up my arm. I peek up at him—his eyebrows are pinched with concern. "Fiona, I know this has to be hard, and I'm sorry I messed up so much and made it worse. I probably can't understand at all, but you have nothing to be embarrassed about." His eyes run over me, and his face softens. I can tell he honestly likes what he sees. "If you only knew."

His touch feels even better than before. Somehow, it clears my head. I know I want this. I want him. It's still scary, liking someone so real and messed up, someone who knows your weaknesses. But at the same time it's intoxicating. He likes me—I like him—despite all the bad stuff. We both want it to work, and maybe that will make it happen.

I take a deep breath and squeeze his hand. "Okay. Tell me."

He glances at the French doors, which is when I notice Miles and Brady are right there talking. "Let's sit on the grass."

He lets go of my hand, and we leave the deck. We sit on the cool grass under a tree, facing each other. In the dark, it feels like we're miles from everything. All I can hear is crickets and my own breathing.

"What do you want to know first?" he asks.

"Oh, um . . ." I hadn't really thought about that. For some reason I pictured knowing it all at once, like looking in a mirror and finally seeing my reflection. "I guess my hair. Is it as crazy as I think it is?"

He smiles. The moment before he speaks, my insides flip upside down. "No, it's not crazy." He runs a hand through my curls, and it sends tingles down my neck. "It's wavy, some times more curly than others, but always pretty."

"What color?"

"Dark blond." My face involuntarily scrunches and he laughs. "Is that bad?"

"No, I just . . . dark blond? That's the nice way to say dirty blond." I feel stupid for being disappointed. I *know* my hair color for the first time in my life. I should be happy. But boring, mousy blond?

"Don't call it that; I like it." He takes a few strands in his fingers. By the way they tug at my scalp, it feels like they're near my forehead. "Besides, the pieces closest to your face are golden. Sometimes they catch the light, and I swear they glitter."

He looks at me like I'm the most beautiful thing in the world, which makes me feel like I am. "Well, when you put it that way."

"What next?" He lets go, probably since he can see how nervous I am. But I want to hold his hand again. Am I allowed to just take it?

"Hmm. Skin?"

He purses his lips. "Let's see . . . how do I explain that? You're a little tanner than me, but not as dark as Bea. Maybe like caramel?"

226

I smile wide. "Caramel. I like that."

"Me too. And you have these really cute freckles."

"I do?" I might pass out. The hair color was a little let-down, but knowing I have even one freckle makes up for it. "Where?"

He looks down. "You'd have to take off your hoodie so I can point to them for you."

"Okay." The thought of my caramel skin having freckles shouldn't be motivation for me to strip, but for some reason it is. I have the hoodie off in seconds.

He lets out a breath. "You never look bad, do you?"

"Shut up, I look like crap."

"You really, really don't." Seth leans in closer. I can't breathe right as he takes me in. It's getting easier, but my heart hasn't slowed. He touches a spot on my forearm, and the sensation radiates through me. "There's one right here." He moves his finger along my skin and stops on my upper arm. "One here." Then he moves to my shoulder and points out four. There's three on my other shoulder and four on that arm. He also points out two on my back.

I sigh, some of the nerves subsiding. At least I have freckles. The rest of me can be butt-ugly, and I wouldn't care. Okay, maybe I'd care a little. "That's so great."

He smirks. "You sure have a thing for freckles."

"I do. I really like yours." I get daring and put my finger to his cheek. He doesn't flinch with surprise. It's still hard to process that.

Seth puts his hand over mine, pressing it into his cheek. I can't help but smile as he wraps his fingers around mine and lowers our hands from his face. I like holding hands.

It feels right. "I always got teased for them as a kid."

"Well, those kids were stupid."

"Next?" He pulls at my arm like he wants me to come closer, so I move from facing him to sitting next to him. Our arms touch, just like in the movie theater. He smells incredible, something like cinnamon but not as sweet.

"Eyes?"

"Brownish hazel, but not as dark as your brother's." There's an edge to his voice when he says "brother," so he must mean Graham.

I nod. I kind of expected brown, since all my family has brownish eyes. "What about my face?"

"You're gorgeous." He picks at the grass, his smile growing as he thinks. "Let's just say everyone would be after you if they knew."

I laugh. He has to be exaggerating, but it doesn't matter. He's the only judge. "You're pretty smooth, you know that?"

"Nah. I'm just telling the truth." He puts an arm around me, and I know we're together without either of us having to say it. All my nerves are the good kind, the ones that tell you incredible things will happen. We stay like that for a few moments before he talks again. "It's really your expressions that make you, though. It's a shame people can't see. I feel sorry for them."

I look up at him. "What do you mean?"

He stares at the night sky contentedly. "Well, take your lips. Very nice, by the way, full and pink. But they're just lips until you smile; that's when they're *your* lips. Your smile is intoxicating, and your pout is painful. I hate seeing you sad."

I stare at him, taking in the words. They're so simple,

but they change something inside me. I'm real now. Whole. I never have to wonder again if there's something underneath my invisibility. Someone sees me—all of me. I don't know what to do with the happy current pulsing through me, so I lean my head on his shoulder. "I'm sorry I ran away. It was so stupid, because I already liked you so much. I just didn't know what to do. I was so freaked out."

"Don't worry about it." He leans his head on mine. "I totally understand. That's why I was so scared to tell you. I knew there was a good chance I might never see you again. Why would you want to be around someone who lied to you? I wanted to say it so many times, Fiona, but then I thought about you leaving and . . . I couldn't."

A laugh escapes. "I think that was the first selfish thing I've ever heard come out of your mouth."

"Yes, you've turned me into a horrible person. I like being around you too much."

"Heaven forbid you think about your own happiness." Just one of his arms around me isn't enough, so I climb into his lap and wrap my arms around him. He squeezes me tight, burying his head into my neck.

"I don't think I've ever been this happy in my life," he whispers.

"Me either."

Before we say anything else—or *do* anything else—a soft whistle comes from the house. Seth tenses as he looks in that direction, then his eyes go wide. "We gotta hide."

"What?" He's already pulled me to my feet and toward the side of the house.

"Graham's here."

Chapter 33

We duck into a thick bush as I fight to restrain my panic. *Don't scream.* Seth wraps his arms around me, and I bury my face in his chest. I can't seem to stop gasping for breath. How did he know where to look? Why is he looking? Supposed noble intentions or not, there's no good reason for Graham to be here.

Seth stares into the wall, his face set into a hard glare. I'm not sure if it's from trying to see through the wall or from what he sees on the other side. I hope Miles is hiding, even if his car is outside. He doesn't need another black eye.

"He looks pissed," Seth whispers. "He's trying to search the house, but Brady's blocking him."

"Is Miles okay?"

"He's under my bed."

I gulp. If Graham really did save us, maybe he can be reasoned with. "I should talk to him."

"No." Seth's grip on me tightens. "It's too dangerous."

"But—"

His eyes stop me, practically burn my retinas with their intensity. "You didn't see the bruises, the ones on your neck when we were at Taco Bell. Like someone had choked you. That was Graham, wasn't it?"

I nod.

"Your skin was purple where his fingers had been. And the ones on your arms and wrist after his pool visit? It killed me not to ask if your wrist was broken. It was that bad." He puts his head on my shoulder. "I . . . I can't see you beat up like that again. Please."

My lungs won't take in air. I remember my neck being sore after Graham threatened me that day, but I'd never thought of how it looked. And that was nothing compared to what I'd been through working for Dad, but no one cared because they couldn't see it. Even I didn't care as much as I should have. "Okay. I won't."

"Thank you," he whispers.

It's not like I know Graham's good anyway. He *might* be, but considering his track record I'd prefer to have solid proof before I approach him. And there's only one way to know for sure he's on our side. "We need to—"

"Shh," Seth hisses. "They're coming out here."

Brady's voice cuts through the silence. "It looks like they went for a walk in the park or something. Guess you're out of luck."

Graham floats over the lawn, searching the dark. He spots something that almost makes me swear. My hoodie. He picks it up. "A walk, huh? Why didn't she take this? I won't find more of her clothing strewn around, will I?"

I gulp, positive he thinks I stripped down to hide. It wouldn't be the first time. He'd assume that, since he doesn't know Seth can see me.

Brady folds his arms. "They are together; it's not my business."

"Maybe I'll look around a second." Graham flies to the bushes along the fence farthest away from us.

"Or you could be considerate. You don't have to talk to her right now."

Graham jets back to Brady and hovers in his face. "Actually, I do. And I'd love to leave her alone, but she's in deep trouble."

I wish I knew what for. Either he's pissed about the hack, or Mom told him I wanted to leave Madison and he's mad about that. I can't quite tell, but either way I'd probably get hit.

"You might wanna back up," Brady growls. He seems bigger, stronger, than usual. With all that rage building, he could probably take out the house with one punch.

"Or what?" Graham comes closer.

In one swift motion, Brady reaches out to grab my brother. Graham tries to dodge, but he isn't fast enough. Brady has him by the ankle, gripping him tight enough that Graham winces. A smile creeps onto my lips—seeing him bullied will never get old. My brother tries to wiggle out of Brady's iron hold, but it doesn't work.

"Where do you think you're going?" Brady gives one tug, and Graham slams into the ground with a loud thud. He coughs, trying to get air back in his lungs. They stare at each other for a few seconds. "You're not the only one who can do threats."

That cunning grin plasters Graham's face. "You can beat me—so what? You have no clue what you're up against. The O'Connell Syndicate has plenty of other tools."

He shoots up in another attempt to get away. Brady

lunges, grabbing him by the arm. Graham's legs fling forward like he got swept up in a gust of wind, but he doesn't go anywhere.

"Whoa, hold on there." Brady plucks him out of the air and forces him to stand on the ground. "Again with the threats. What ever happened to brotherly love?"

"I tried to protect her!" Graham looks at the ground, visibly shaken. "If you won't help me find her, let me go."

Brady releases him. "I hear anything about you hurting her again, and I'll rip you right out of the sky. Now, I'm going back inside. You have one minute to get off my property—and for you Flyers that means at least one hundred feet in the sky, right?"

"Right." Graham picks himself up off the ground. He watches Brady go into the house as he hovers.

"Brady's still watching." Seth's lips almost touch my ear as he whispers, and it makes my skin prickle.

Graham sweeps the yard once, flying right over us. I'm glad his vision isn't the greatest. He might have the speed, but he's never been good at finding me once I'm hiding. He stops in the middle of the lawn.

"I'm not stupid. I know you're here. We have a lot to talk about before you make more mistakes." He rubs his hands over his face. "Fiona, if you don't stop this crap, I'll make sure you don't jeopardize Mom's safety anymore. This is your last warning."

He rockets off, but I still can't breathe. Whether he has good intentions or not doesn't matter. He's still Graham, and he'll sell me out the second I don't do exactly what he says. Maybe I'm not living under Dad's roof, but it's only a slightly nicer prison with my brother in charge.

Seth's hands are on my face. He moves my head so he can look into my eyes. "He has to be lying. He's trying to get to you."

"He's not lying." My voice sounds stronger than I expect. I feel stronger. I know what I want, and for once I'm not afraid.

He looks up. "I don't see him anymore. Let's go inside, okay? You're getting cold."

I nod, and he pulls me out of the bushes. After grabbing my hoodie, Seth keeps an arm around my waist as we rush to the porch. I half expect Graham to dive-bomb us, but he doesn't. Seth sits on the leather couch they must have just bought, but I can't stop pacing. An idea clicks into place with each step, along with the determination to do it.

I won't live here under Graham's terms. I won't leave, and I'm certainly not going back to Dad's. This is my life, and I should be free to live it however I want. With whoever I want. No more threats or fear or indecision.

Miles appears from the hall and leans on the kitchen table. "What's the plan?"

Seth starts to speak, but I talk over him. "We're going to the factory. Get The Pack."

If Graham thinks I'll lie down and trust him, he's dead wrong.

Chapter 34

When Brady comes back with The Pack, part of me feels like hiding. Their voices fill the house, bouncing off the walls and warming the place up. Seth squeezes my hand. "Don't worry. They miss you. I told them you needed a little space."

"Fiona!" Bea's voice booms through the house. When she rounds the corner, glaring daggers, I'm fairly sure I *should* be worrying. I cower into Seth's shoulder when she points at me. "You are so dea—wait, are you guys . . . *together?*"

Seth glances at me, like he wants to make sure we are. I smile and give him the nod. He laughs. "I guess you could say that."

Bea lets out a sigh. "Well, finally! I was getting so sick of not telling you!"

"Seriously," Hector chimes in. "I was this close to ratting him out."

"Gee, thanks, guys," Seth says.

I groan. "You all knew?"

They laugh, and I try not to feel stupid.

"Yeah, yeah, whatever." Carlos plops on the love seat, frowning. "So what's with Brady calling us all over here? Please don't tell me it was just to announce *that*." He glares at our clasped hands, though it looks more like Seth is pretending to hold something. I wish I could see what it looks like to him.

"Fiona's brother paid us a visit tonight," Seth says.

"Duh, he's right here." Joey taps knuckles with Miles. "Nice shiner, by the way."

Bea slaps Joey's arm. "Obviously he means the jackass, dumbass."

"What'd he want?" Hector asks.

I take a deep breath and give them the whole story, everything from what I really did for my dad, to what Graham's done to me, to Miles's hack and what he found. "Sorry I didn't tell you what I really was. I didn't want you to hate me."

"Psh. Not your fault," Joey says. "Not like we're saints."

"We're banned from the mall in Tucson," Hector says.

"And the bowling alley in town," Carlos says.

"Don't forget the Saguro theater," Bea says.

They all laugh.

I smile, deciding not to tell them that doesn't really count, all things considered. Can't burst their bubble. "So what do you think: trust Graham or not?"

"Hell no," Carlos says.

"Who's to say he'll stop threatening you?" Hector folds his arms, thinking. "Sure, he could be separating you from your dad, but what if he plans on starting his own syndicate?"

Miles raises an eyebrow. "Interesting theory, but I doubt it."

Bea frowns. "Don't kill me for saying this, but I don't

know . . . he's your brother. There's something about that blood connection. You can't throw out the possibility that he's trying to do a good thing."

I sigh. "I know, but I need proof. I hate asking you guys—you shouldn't be this involved—but I need backup."

"Anything," Bea says, and they all agree.

The eagerness in their eyes hits me. I still don't get why they'd jump to put their lives on the line. Maybe they don't fully understand. Maybe they really are crazy. "Why do you always say that?"

And then, for the first time, Tony speaks. "Because we like you. Isn't that enough?"

I smile, wishing they could see it. "Yeah, it is."

After some preparation, we pile into Seth's truck and Sexy Blue. The plan is simple: Drive out to the factory and find the Radiasure. If it's there, then we know Graham's telling the truth. If not, well, we'll have to get him to leave by force. He can't even handle Brady, let alone the rest of The Pack.

"If Graham happens to show up," I say as we bounce and bump over the desert, "jump him. He flies by emitting hydrogen, and he can only handle so much weight."

Seth puts his hand on my leg. "It'll be okay. There's no way he can take all of us."

"I'll pound him if I have to," Brady says.

"Right." I take in a deep breath, focus on the desert around us. It's been a while since I've been on this side, and it brings up strange memories. When the broken strip mall comes into view, I realize how much I've changed since hiding there.

I'm finally learning how to fight for myself. I've learned that I'm worth fighting for.

The headlights make it hard to see anything not directly in front of us, but the sky still shimmers with stars. I can't help but smile at them. I'm small, but not alone. I'm surrounded by people who care about me. And strangely, they make me feel more important than anything ever has.

We park in front of the factory and hop out. "Spread out. Go in twos."

"Right." Brady grabs Bea, and I'm glad, since she's the smallest and most vulnerable. "You're coming with me."

Bea smiles wide, happily holding on to Brady's arm. I can't believe I didn't notice sooner how much they care about each other. "No complaints here."

Seth takes my hand, and Miles follows closely behind. The Pack pairs up evenly. I have no idea what to look for, but we start with the biggest tumbleweeds and pieces of scrap metal. Not surprisingly, there's nothing there.

"How much is supposed to be here?" Seth asks.

"At least a whole crate." Miles pulls up a piece of metal.

Seth whistles. "That's a lot, isn't it?"

"A good three million bucks' worth, at least—maybe up to five," Miles says.

"Sick, huh," I say. Radiasure . . . Dad still takes a pill every day. He'd never say it out loud, but sometimes I wonder if he doesn't think he's strong enough, even with a power like his. One time, I overheard him saying to Graham, "I'm not all-powerful. I'm only half-powerful. My ability doesn't even work on males."

Some people never have enough control, I suppose.

"There's nowhere to hide anything here!" Seth says after searching for fifteen minutes. I must admit I expected him to find it easily. But it is night, and I don't think he can see through darkness very well. "It's bare—"

"Hey! Over here!" Brady calls from the opposite side.

We rush over, my heart racing more from hope than from the jog. I can barely make it out in the dim light, but it looks like Brady is in some kind of hole.

"Underground, of course," Seth says, as if he actually feels stupid for not thinking of it sooner.

I nudge him. "You can't get 'em all right."

"Don't remind me."

"I only noticed because I'm so heavy," Brady says as he steps down deeper. "It sounded hollow when I walked over it. Looks like there's a smaller hole. There's no way I can fit."

"My turn!" Bea climbs into the hole and disappears under the dirt wall closest to me. After a lot of cursing, she emerges with a box.

Relief fills me as I take it from her. I lift the lid, and the blue glow shines from the glass bottles. So Graham had a plan, and it was actually a good one, too. "He wasn't lying. He really did mean to help us."

"Doesn't matter now, does it, Fifi?" Graham's voice sends a shiver down my back, and I whirl around. I drop the box when I see he's not alone.

He sets another man on the ground, a man I can recognize even in the dark. He saunters into the beam of our flashlights, completely at ease. I wish I could move, but my legs won't cooperate.

"Well, well, isn't this a nice surprise." My dad's smile is just as I remember, all silk and honey, but never reaching his eyes. "It's been a long time, sweetheart."

Chapter 35

We stand there, staring at each other. It can't be real—my dad is not here, not seeing all my friends' faces, not putting the puzzle together.

But, man, he looks good in that leather jacket.

I shake my head. He's definitely real if I'm thinking creepy thoughts like that, and it's only a matter of time before I'm high on his scent and not thinking straight. I take Seth's hand, hoping that'll keep me focused. He squeezes too hard, but even that doesn't get a sound out of me.

My father takes a step forward. "You didn't say good-bye. How do you think that makes me feel?"

I almost apologize, but I choke it back down. I'm not supposed to feel bad for leaving him. Or am I? "W-what are you doing here?"

"What do you think, idiot?" Graham seethes. "After everything I—"

Dad pulls out his favorite silver gun and points it at Graham. "Traitors don't get to talk."

"Dad, let me—"

Dad pulls the trigger, and Graham lets out a primal scream. Clutching his leg, he crashes into the ground. A small pang of guilt hits me, and it grows as I watch my brother suffer. Brady hurting him was one thing, but Dad shooting him means something totally different.

It means Graham had almost pulled off his plan, and I just ruined it.

Suddenly the reasons why he wanted to help us don't matter like they did before. He put his neck on the line for me, for Mom. Dad might actually kill him for this. As much as I hate Graham, I never wished him dead.

"It was a brilliant plan, though, son." Dad stands over him, and Graham sounds like he's crying. "Bringing me this close to them, using the perfect decoy—that takes guts, smarts."

When he points the gun at him again, my voice finally wells up inside. "Stop!"

Dad's attention snaps to me, and he smiles. "But Graham missed one thing, didn't he, sweetie?"

I shrink back, unsure of what I should do. "I don't know what you're talking about."

"He didn't realize what a pain in the ass you really are." He takes a step forward, the gun now at his side. "How headstrong . . ." Another step. "Rebellious . . ." And another. "Independent . . ." He reaches his hand out, finding my shoulder and then my face. "How hard to control, just like your damn mother."

I can't find air as I search his dark eyes, and The Pack's words are muddled against his perfect voice. His fingers are soft, forgiving. I must have caused him so much trouble. What did he do all this time without me? What if he missed me? What a horrible daughter I've been, leaving him. Maybe if I apologize he will forgive me. I want him to.

Seth pushes his hand away. "Don't touch her!"

I gasp at the sound of his voice. What am I thinking? It's Seth who cares about me. Seth would miss *me* if I left, not just my ability. I hold on to the thought. "Dad, just take the Radiasure and go. I don't want to have to hurt you."

He laughs. "You? Hurt me? How?"

"I have no problem hurting you." Brady steps in front of me, and The Pack surrounds me from the sides. Thank goodness I brought them; otherwise this would have been over already. I watch Bea, worried that my dad already has her under his spell. She stares at him, but her glare is hard and unwavering. Hopefully that means she's trying to resist.

Dad frowns. "You'd let these punks beat up your own father?"

It does sound pretty heartless, but I focus on Seth's hand in mine. "Yes."

"Tsk, tsk." He takes a step back. "Perhaps I should have sent you to finishing school."

"What do you want us to do, Fi?" Carlos whispers to me.

I gulp. I wish it was an easy answer; it should be. My dad is alone, and he was stupid enough to shoot his ride. I can't think of a time he's been this vulnerable—and he knows it. I can tell by the way he stands, right hand tightly gripped on his gun. But he's still my dad. And more than that, wouldn't beating or killing him make me a fledgling syndicate boss? That's the last thing I want, to become like him.

"Just . . . restrain him," I finally decide. "Watch for the gun."

"Carlos, there's rope in our truck," Seth whispers.

"Got it."

The boys tense around me. I can feel them preparing for the worst. Dad won't hesitate to kill—never has, never will. But if we can tie him up, maybe we can work out a deal or turn him in or something. At least I could get away and clear my head, so I can make a real decision.

"Go!" Brady yells.

Carlos goes for the truck, and everyone else charges, save Seth. He pulls me toward the nearest brush, while my senses fill with the commotion. The Pack yelling. The feel of dirt flying up at the footsteps. The sight of my friends throwing themselves at one of the most powerful men in the West.

Dad doesn't move, doesn't even go for his gun, and I swear I can see the gleam of his crooked smile.

My blood chills. Something is wrong.

That's when I notice Bea has stopped. She stares at my father. Then she opens her mouth.

The noise is unlike anything I've ever heard, a sound so loud and horrible it feels like my brain might explode. It warbles at a high pitch, completely inhuman. I cover my ears, but it doesn't keep them from burning. The Pack stops cold, crumbling from the pain.

I close my eyes, sure my eyeballs might pop out if I don't. I had no idea Bea could do that, and there's only one reason she would. The noise stops, but my ears still ring. I check them for blood.

"He just misses his daughter! Is that any reason to tie him up?" Even Bea's normal voice hurts now.

"That is a lovely gift, dear." My dad unplugs his ears. "Where did you learn it?"

She tips her chin up. "I used to cry like that as a baby. My parents had to wear earplugs until they could teach me not to."

"A natural talent, of course." He holds his hand out to her. "I'm so glad someone here understands me."

She smiles when she runs into his arms, and he caresses her hair. "My brothers can be total dumbasses. I'm so sorry."

"Not to worry. It seems you taught them a lesson, beautiful."

We slowly pick ourselves off the ground, backing away from my Dad. He has Bea. Every bad thing he's done to me . . . that could easily be her fate. Or worse. What do we do now? I'd hoped she could resist the lure long enough to get out of here, but I'd forgotten how easily most women fall.

Don't panic. Don't panic. I'm so panicking.

Brady stays out front, his eyes filled with horror. "Trixy, you need to come with me right now."

She glares at him. "You were going to kill him, weren't you?"

"You know I would never." He holds his hand out. "Beatrix, please. I beg you."

Her eyes go wide, a split second of recognition filling them, but then she hardens. "Why should I?"

"Because . . ." He falls to his knees.

My dad laughs. "I think, my dear, that he's trying to say he loves you." He runs a finger along her cheek. "But he doesn't, does he? Not like I do."

245

"He pushes me away," she says. "Always just friends, even though I've been there for him through everything. I'm not afraid of his strength, but he doesn't believe me."

"I do love you!" Brady punches the ground, and the shock wave vibrates under my feet. "I just don't want to hurt you! You know better than anyone what I can do. Just the smallest mistake and . . . I can't hurt you."

Tears fall from Bea's face, even though she looks angry. "Well, you do. Every minute hurts. All I ever want is you, and you never cared, not really."

"Bea . . ." Brady slumps forward. "Stop this. You're not thinking right."

"Cruel boy." Dad hugs her. "Don't worry. I would never do something like that to you. You're too special."

"Bea," Joey says. "C'mon, we're your brothers—you know you can trust us."

"Yeah," Hector says. "We love you, too."

"You can't leave us," Tony says. "We're family."

Bea frowns, as if she's searching for more justifications. "But I'm always on the outside. The only girl. Always treated differently."

"That's not true and you know it!" Carlos says.

She does know it; at least she would if Dad weren't here.

Dad catches her gaze. "There are lots of girls where I live. And they would love you like a sister."

"Dad!" I can't take it anymore. Watching him do this to Bea makes my whole life too clear. He never stops spewing lies. That's all I have to remember and I'll be fine. "Stop. Right now."

He raises an eyebrow. "And why should I? This is finally

getting fun. Your friend is quite beautiful, and useful, too."

Standing tall, I convince myself I can do this. "Me and the Radiasure—all you have to do is give her back and promise no one here gets hurt."

I know he'll take the deal; as powerful as Bea is, there's only one of me. The Radiasure is icing on the cake at this point, though it's technically already his. Dad's eyes gleam, as if that's what he planned all along. "Sounds fair."

Seth tugs at my arm. "Are you insane?"

My heart aches at the thought of leaving him, but it's the only way they'll be safe. "Trust me, okay?"

His eyes glisten as he pulls me closer. "He's tricking you, too. You can't leave."

"He's not, I swear. You heard him—I have some resistance. I'll figure this out." I kiss his cheek, savoring the slightly rough feel of it. "I know what I want now. I want you to be safe and happy—same goes for everyone. I'll come back, promise."

"Fiona . . ."

"I know. I don't want to, either, but you can't say I'm not doing the right thing." I give him one last hug. If I don't go now, I won't.

"I hate you," he whispers.

I smile. "I hate you, too. Also, we're stealing your car."

Seth shakes his head as he hands me the keys. "You better bring it back."

"I will."

As I pull away from Seth, everything feels wrong. It hurts deep in my bones, but I savor it. This is real. I can't forget that.

"Done with your good-byes, sweetie?" Dad calls, his voice sickly happy.

"Miles, get the crate." I walk over to my father, determined not to lose myself to him again. This time, he's the one who'll get played. Once I figure out a plan, at least. "If you'd be kind enough to help put Graham in the truck bed."

Dad complies. Graham grunts as we get him in place, but he doesn't fight. There's so much blood, and he's shaking. Sweat beads his face. I hop in the truck bed and pull off my hoodie.

"What're you doing?" Graham croaks.

"What do you think?" I wrap it around his leg and pull tight.

He winces.

"Fiona," Dad calls. "Up front."

"But—" *Graham needs help. Bad. Because of me.*

"Don't waste more time on that traitor." He motions to the cabin. "Now."

I watch my friends grow smaller and smaller as I drive away. Tears stream silently down my face as I realize I may never see them again.

Chapter 36

Dad wastes no time being his usual self. Since Graham is still bleeding and possibly dying in the back, he's got the gun pointed at Miles. He knows if I have any plans that'll snuff them right out. "Take me to Lauren."

"Don't do it, Fi," Miles says.

Dad puts the gun to my brother's temple. "You know, you're the stupidest one here. I'd practically forgotten about your worthless ass."

He scoffs. "Is that supposed to make me feel bad?"

"Don't push it."

Miles lets off a horrible smell, something like crap mixed with gross perfume. "Maybe *you* shouldn't push it."

Dad tightens his fingers, and I know he'll pull the trigger eventually if I don't do something. It was bad enough watching Graham get that. "I'll take you to Mom, okay? Just don't hurt him."

He takes the gun away from Miles's face. "That's my girl."

He probably thinks I'm caving to his presence. I'm not; at least I don't think so. I'm just buying time to form a plan. If Mom really doesn't want him back—and I'm pretty sure she's serious—then that's one more on our team. I have a feeling Graham might be, too.

I check the rearview mirror. Graham's feet bounce and bump back and forth. I can't stop thinking about when he first showed up, how he grabbed me by the neck and threatened me. He told me not to get mouthy until I could fight back. The delivery was crap, but I think I finally get what he meant, what Miles meant when he said Graham was right.

I'm a runner. I've spent my whole life taking the path of least resistance. Before living in Madison, I never had to face anything. I did what Dad told me to, and when I wasn't doing that, I numbed myself to the horrible things I'd done. I ran from my problems, not realizing I was on a treadmill. They've always been right behind me, waiting for me to slow down so they can destroy me. Never once did I think I could stop altogether, turn around, and fight them. Maybe that's what happens when you don't know who you are or what you want.

But that's not who I am anymore.

Dad has no idea what he's up against, and he won't as long as I put on the best act of my life.

When I pull up to the house, I take a deep breath to calm myself—there's no turning back now.

"Get your brother," Dad says to us.

When we reach the back of the truck, Graham looks dead. I check for a pulse. It's there, so he must have passed out from the pain. Miles hops into the back of the truck, despite his slight limp. I take Graham's legs, and we heft him down the path to the front door. For a guy who flies, he's shockingly heavy.

Dad bangs on the door, the gun still pointed at us. It

seems like an eternity passes without Mom answering. Dad pushes the doorbell twice. Finally, the lock clicks. When Mom sees who's waiting, her face goes white. She almost shuts the door, but she catches sight of Graham. Then, maybe for the first time ever, she glares at Dad. "What did you do to him?"

"I was merciful, considering he's a traitor." Dad pushes his way in. "Be warned, Lauren, I don't have much mercy left."

Mom ignores him, heading for us instead. "Put Graham on the couch."

Dad laughs. "You think I'd let you stay in here with this many escape routes?" He waves the gun. "A windowless room. Now."

Mom doesn't move, as if she wants to fight back, but then she heads for the laundry room. Still, it gives me hope. If Graham weren't shot, if Miles didn't have a black eye, she would have fought back. Maybe her kids really do come first.

Dad shoves us in there with a grin. "I'm calling for an escort. Then we can have a little family reunion."

After he shuts the door, I hear something shoved in front of it. Probably a chair, since his muffled voice sounds nearby.

"How did he find us?" Mom whispers through tears. She strokes Graham's hair, all her strength replaced by fear.

"It's my fault." As hard as it is to say, it's true. I didn't trust Graham, and now we're paying for it. "We don't have time to talk about it—we need to get out."

Mom sighs. "You think?"

"I'm not kidding." I crouch down and check Graham's

251

breathing. When will he wake up? He has to at some point. I refuse to think he's lost too much blood. "Dad has us all thinking he's stronger than us, but we can do this. We're some of the most feared thugs in the world."

Miles smiles like he was waiting for me to say that. "I was starting to think it would never happen, but it's time to implement The Plan."

I tilt my head. "The Plan?"

He nods. "You have no idea how long I've been waiting for this chance."

"Miles, what are you talking about?" Mom asks.

He rolls his eyes. "Haven't you ever noticed that Dad's never touched me? I've never gotten close enough to smell his cologne. The ride here? First time he's ever sat next to me."

Mom frowns. "He's touched you. . . ."

Miles gives her a flat look. "When? Does he even know my name? Because I haven't heard him say it since I was maybe six, and even then I'm pretty sure it was a lucky guess. I'm just "That Worthless Boy." In fact, that's probably what he has written next to my phone number, for the few times he's called looking for you guys."

She opens her mouth, but it seems she can't remember a single time. "Miles, I . . ."

"Nah, don't apologize. As a kid it used to eat me away inside, but I figured out pretty quick that being neglected by him was a good thing." His smile turns wicked. "It's payback time now. Just you wait and see."

He talks like it's all a joke, but I wonder if he means it. I'd never thought much about what it was like to be Miles in our family. He's like the ultimate middle child. All of us were powerful and important to Dad, and he didn't get so much as a pat on the back or a hug from his father his whole life. And not because Dad wasn't around, but because he just didn't care. No matter what Miles says, that has to hurt.

I walk over and hug him. "I love you the most."

He lets out a small laugh. "I know, and that's why—"

Graham groans. We hover over him as we wait to see if he'll come to. His eyes flutter open, and he startles when he realizes where he is.

Mom puts a finger to her lips. "Dad's right outside the door."

"What happened?" His voice is strained.

"Dad shot you," Miles says.

"And now we're trapped in the laundry room?"

"Yup."

Graham tries to sit up, but opts to put his head back on the floor. "You should have listened to me, Fiona. You ruined everything. You could have been safe here—all you had to do was trust me."

"Shut up." I don't need to be reminded. The pit in my stomach is enough to do that. "You could have told us Dad was trying to kill us. You could have trusted us, too, and you didn't. You decided to act like a dictator instead, so stop preaching like you're some kind of saint."

Mom's eyes water. "What are you talking about? He's trying to kill us?"

Graham points at her. "Right there. That's why I couldn't tell. Unlike you, I prefer not to cause Mom pain. She's been through enough."

"We all have!" I stop, realizing my voice is too loud. The silence overcomes us as we listen. Dad's still talking. "Look, we don't have time for this. I just need to know one thing."

Graham pinches the bridge of his nose, either in pain or annoyed with me. Probably both. "And that would be?"

"Why did you do it? All this—why would you plan this elaborate escape for us?"

He looks away, his mouth forming a tight line. And then, ever so slightly, he bites his lip. "I know you think I'm the bad guy, but all I've ever done is make sure you and Mom survive. You know what Dad told me that first day he came for me?"

"What?" I ask.

"He said he could make Mom kill herself. He said he could convince you to jump off a building. He said he could make you violently murder people, or use your bodies in ways I can't even repeat. He said if I didn't do what he said, you guys would pay the price. It would be my fault."

It feels like there's a cue ball in my throat. All these years . . . "So you did what he said for us."

"Someone has to do the dirty work, and I'd rather it be me than you." He pauses, turns his head so I can't see his face. "Dad told me he thought it was time you became an assassin like he's always wanted. And then came this China mission. I couldn't let it happen. Killing people . . . it messes you up beyond repair. I know. There was only one way to stop it—I had to get you out."

It's not an act. Not because I wish for it, but because he would have looked at my face if it were a lie. That's the secret about criminals. They can lie right to your face.

They can look like they believe it completely. But it's the truth that makes them turn away, ashamed.

I don't know what this means for Graham and me, but for once I don't completely hate him. That's something. "So you're in?"

He looks back, quizzical. "In?"

"We're bust—" Miles stops when the doorknob turns.

Dad comes in with his chair and sets it in front of the door. He holds his gun casually, like he's not threatening his own children. "You've been very problematic. We won't all fit on the chopper, so I had to organize a full road escort through Juan's territory. You'll have to pay me back for all the trouble."

And then, out of nowhere, Miles throws himself on Dad.

Chapter 37

"It's my fault!" Miles wraps his arms around Dad, burrowing into his neck. My mouth hangs open, and Mom wavers between him and Graham as if she can't figure out who will die first. Dad has never looked so surprised, but that doesn't stop him from raising the gun to Miles's head. "I'm the one who kept telling Fiona she could escape. I just wanted her to have a normal life. Don't hurt them. Please."

"Get off me," Dad growls.

"Not until you promise." Miles sucks in air, like he's scared and trying to keep in tears. "Take it out on me. I don't care what you do, but it's not their fault."

"Such a sweet story." Dad tries to shove Miles away, but Miles clings to his jacket, looking absolutely pathetic. "Except that doesn't explain Graham."

Miles takes in a deep breath, sighing it out. "I tricked him. I told him about the Radiasure, but wouldn't give him a location until he agreed to bring Mom and Fiona for the job. I was going to take them away, but he figured it out. He's been trying to get them back ever since."

Dad's eyes narrow. It sounds semi-plausible, and for a second I think he might believe it. Then his finger goes to the trigger. "Get off."

"I . . . I just wanted you to notice me. I thought if I could be smart enough, maybe you'd see I'm useful." Miles drops to the floor, groveling at Dad's feet like a slave. It makes my blood boil. What the hell is he doing? He's never sought Dad's approval before.

Dad scoffs. "You're worthless and a fool."

Miles purses his lips. Without another word he slinks back next to me, burying his head in his lap. His ears rise slightly, which makes me think he might be smiling.

Smiling? It clicks, and I stifle my gasp. He was getting his scent! Why hadn't I thought of it before? If Miles could imitate Dad's smell—even strengthen it—then maybe it would sway Mom and me to him instead of Dad. Miles usually has to practice a scent to get it right, but hopefully it'll at least buy us time.

My brother is a genius.

"Lauren, baby, c'mere," Dad says in his smooth way.

Mom tenses. "No."

He smiles. "But I missed you. It's been so long since I held you."

"Forget it, Jonas." She busies herself with caring for Graham, grabbing a washcloth and wetting it in the sink. "It's never happening again."

"We'll see." Dad leans into his chair, satisfied with the answer. He knows "never" isn't an option. He can see as well as I can that her hands shake.

That's the thing about Dad. He doesn't like to use force. Not with women. He likes watching them break down. He revels in how determined they are to resist, how his presence slowly chips away their resolve. He doesn't have to push; all he has to do is wait. It doesn't help that he's so good-looking. He's pale, but in a good way, with smooth skin and dark, dark eyes. Eyes that capture your attention and never let go.

I shake my head, realizing my ridiculous thoughts. I hope Miles can nail that scent, because my resistance is already fading.

Think of Seth. He cares about me, knows me. Dad doesn't know me. He turns me into a tool, a monster. But I don't want to be that person anymore. I want to be a person who trusts her friends. A person who can love. A person who is comfortable in her own invisible skin. If I want that, then I have to make it happen.

Dad looks at his watch. "We have a little time until our ride gets here. Get cozy."

I force myself to say, "Sure thing."

He smiles, proving how easy it'll be to fool him. "You have anything soft in here?"

"Maybe some towels." I open the dryer, glad to find the last load there. I toss him one, and he makes it into a pillow.

"Thanks, sweetie."

"No problem." Handing out the other ones, I tell myself I'm playing a game. I'm not doing this because of his ability. I'm tricking him.

I wish I had more confidence in my own mental state.

Time passes in silence. It must be really late by now, because I can feel the tug of sleep in the back of my head. I fight it, knowing this could be the moment. If Dad lets his guard down, it could be our only chance.

I'm the only one awake, though. Miles snores next to

me, wedged awkwardly in the corner. Graham is long gone, wincing every now and then from the bullet in his leg. Even Mom has dozed off. My eyelids feel swollen, heavy, but I keep forcing them back open. Dad's not sleeping. He's watching us, gun at the ready. But he must be tired. How can he look so alert?

And then, sweet miracle, he yawns. I pounce on the situation. "There's some Coke in the fridge, Dad, if you're getting tired."

He perks up, seeming pleased by the honey I put in my voice. "Fiona?"

"Yeah, Dad? Is something wrong?" I stand up and come closer. I can feel his anticipation, as if he's finally got it how he likes.

"Make sure they don't go anywhere. I'll be right back." He stands. "Right back."

"Of course, no problem." My heart stops. I didn't think it'd be that easy. Or is it? Is this some kind of test? I try to read his face, but I can't tell.

He opens the door and pats the chair. "Sit here, hon."

"Okay." When he shuts the door, I take the seat. My legs bounce as I try to figure out what to do. I don't have more than a minute. Probably less. And I'm wasting time already.

"Fiona."

I about fall out of the chair at Miles's voice. He's awake, and so are Mom and Graham. "Wait, were you all faking?"

"Of course," Graham says.

"Huh." So my family really is a bunch of con artists.

Miles comes closer, scrutinizing me like he can see my face. "Fi . . . are you still with us?"

"Yeah. I was faking." I kick him. "Stop looking at me like that. It's creepy. Have you been trying to mimic his scent, or was that embarrassing display for real?"

He smiles. "Glad you caught on."

"I think it's working, whatever you did," Mom says. "I still can't stand looking at your father."

Miles bunches his lips. "It took some retooling, but I think I have most of it. Here, let me ramp it up to make sure."

The room fills with this intense, musky scent, kind of like a bad version of cologne. With sweat. It doesn't smell very good. Maybe he has it wrong. "That's it?"

"Yeah." He puts his hand on my shoulder, searches for my eyes. I'd forgotten how intense his stare could be, since he's usually laid-back. Strangely, it looks good on him, that smoldering look. Even if he's my brother, he's pretty hot. "Kiss me, Fiona." I lean in before I can think, but Miles pulls back. "Oh gross, it worked!"

I cover my mouth as the scent wanes. I should not be blushing this much over my own brother. "Miles!"

Dad's knock makes us all jump. "Fiona? Everything okay in there?"

I get the door, trying to steady myself. "It's nothing. Miles was just being stupid."

By the time he comes in, Graham and Mom are back to fake sleeping. Miles has a defiant look on his face, but he doesn't say more. I can't help but feel a glimmer of hope. Miles pulled it off. With Mom and me safe, we at least have some time. What would Dad do if he knew that someone could beat him at his own game? Might be *better* at it than he is?

"Here, sweetie, I got you one, too." Dad holds out a Coke, his smile all charm.

"Aw, you didn't have to do that." I take it from him and crack the cap.

"I know, but you deserve it."

I take a long drink. He's awful. The second he thinks he has me, he turns into this amazingly kind person. He's calm, a pleasant smile on his face like he has everything under control.

It's infuriating.

"Dad, is it okay if I lay down? I'm so tired," I say after I finish off the Coke.

"Of course." He points to a spot at Mom's and Graham's feet. "We still have a little time. Soon enough you'll be back in your old room with your big, soft bed. Right where you belong."

I don't actually sleep. I lay there on the hard floor, thinking of a way to get out. I'd hoped it'd be easier, but there's no time to plan with him watching over us. The next chance we get—if we even get one—we have to take.

Fabric shifts behind me, but I don't move. I figure it's Mom, since Graham is still weak and Miles is fake snoring. "I need to go to the bathroom."

I hold my breath, wondering if Dad will let her, hoping this is our chance.

"Use the sink." His voice is cold.

"Jonas," Mom says it softly, the smallest hint of flirtation. I try not to shudder. "Please. Fiona will watch the door for you, and I'll be fast."

There's a long pause. I venture a peek, just because the

silence seems to go on forever. He glares at her, but then his face cracks, making it look like he actually cares. "You better be quick." Dad shakes me hard. "Fiona."

"Huh?" I do my best groggy voice.

"Watch the door again."

"Of course."

The second he leaves, I get to work undressing. This is it—our last chance to get the upper hand.

"What're you doing?" Graham asks.

"Hide those under your pillow." I toss him my clothes. "Miles, find some kind of weapon, something to throw. I'm going to try and get him from the back."

"Fi, I don't know if that's such a good idea," Miles says as he grabs the jug of laundry detergent. Kind of a pathetic defense, but we don't have much else.

"We're not wasting this opportunity. Shh." I climb onto the dryer by the door, get a firm footing so I don't have to move. My heart won't stop pounding. If I fail, Dad will kill us all.

Out of nowhere, it sounds like a wrecking ball hit our house, complete with walls cracking. I gasp, realizing what— or who—it is. Without another thought, I jump off the dryer and out the door. Dad's in the hall, his fingers dug into Mom's arm. He points his gun, but I can't see around the corner.

"Fiona!" Seth cries.

Dad pulls the trigger.

Chapter 38

Seth. Everyone's saying his name. Tony's voice stands out, just because I've only heard it a couple times. Carlos sounds like he's crying, the way he repeats it over and over. Brady whispers it like a prayer. Joey's the only one yelling for them to take cover. I don't have to see to know what happened.

My dad shot my boyfriend.

Rage. Years of it boil to the surface as I charge down the hall. I tackle my dad from behind, managing to get his arms locked behind him. "Mom! Get his weapon!"

"Fiona!" he cries. "I'm gonna kill you!"

I know he means it, but I focus on keeping his arms down. Mom holds her hands out, and Dad grunts as he tries to resist her telekinesis. Another shot fires, this time into the floor.

He's strong, far stronger than me. The attack only worked because I took him off guard, and I can't hold him much longer. "Mom, hurry!"

"Trying!" She pushes her hands down, like she's panto-miming.

"You little bitch," Dad spits. "You conned me! Your own father!"

"You've conned me my whole life!" As hard as I fight, I'm losing ground. He pushes back, and I know I'm about to slam into the wall.

But instead, he flies out of my arms. I look up, surprised to find Brady. "That's enough."

The gun floats by Dad's head, pointed with precision. Mom smiles. "You shouldn't have come, Jonas. I hate seeing you like this."

"How?" he says through his teeth.

Miles coughs, and we all turn to find him standing in the hall, still holding the detergent. "I guess I'm not exactly worthless after all. Finally got your scent, which is just what you always feared, right?"

Dad stops fighting Brady's hold, his face slack with shock. I can't imagine what's going through his head, and I don't particularly care. I have other people to worry about, others who need protecting. "You . . ."

My brother stands face-to-face with him, and for a second I'm taken aback by how much they look alike. "I know that's why you made sure to tell me I was worthless, why you stayed as far away from me as you could."

Dad's eyes are hard. "I should have killed you."

"Yup." Miles smiles wickedly. "But I seemed too stupid and apathetic to notice, didn't I? Why get Mom and Fiona worked up over nothing? Couldn't risk doing something so horrible even your smell couldn't make them listen to you again."

Dad says nothing, which says it all.

I stare at them, stunned. For years, my unassuming brother patiently waited for the right moment to get his revenge: the moment he could ensure our freedom.

"Miles, is there rope anywhere?" Brady says. "If I hold him any longer I may end up doing something I really don't want to do."

The reality of Seth, bloody and lying on the kitchen floor, finally registers. I run for my clothes, trying not to think about how I was standing there naked in front of a bunch of guys . . . one of whom can see me. I shudder anyway.

Once I have my clothes on, I push my way through The Pack. "Seth!"

"Fi . . ." His eyes meet mine, and suddenly I'm crying.

It looks so bad. His entire shoulder is red. "Why did you barge in? I told you I could handle it."

He gives me a weak grin. "You're lecturing me? Really?"

Stupid boy, making me smile. I know why he did it. He could see my dad wasn't near me at that moment. He thought he could give me an opportunity to escape. I put my hand on his chest, trying to push back this crying fit. "This is exactly what I didn't want to happen."

"Fiona." Hector puts his hand on my shoulder, his face too close to mine. "It'll be okay."

"What?"

"It. Will. Be. Fine." His eyes are determined, so much so that I have to believe him. "Just get your dad out of here. As fast as you can."

"Okay." I head over to my dad. He doesn't look threatening at all. His hair is messy, and sweat beads at his forehead. The lines around his eyes seem more prominent. Without his charming ability, he's just a man. An old man.

He's pathetic, and yet I'm more disgusted with myself for not seeing it sooner. We might have been able to take him down years ago, if we were more of a family and hadn't played into his games. It's like he knew the second we united, he wouldn't be able to handle us.

"It doesn't matter if you run," he says. "My men will be here soon, and we'll hunt you down."

I scoff. "Oh, we're not leaving. You're going back to Las Vegas and pretending this never happened."

Now he's the one laughing. "Like hell I am. I will kill you all. With my own hands."

"I don't know, Dad." Miles folds his arms. "Sounds like a pretty good deal to me. You leave us alone; we leave you alone."

"Or I could murder you all, teach everyone what happens when you defy me."

I sigh, knowing we have the upper hand whether he'll admit it or not. "Miles, maybe you should call Spud right now, let her know Jonas O'Connell got whipped by his worthless son. Make sure all the syndicates know there's someone out there who can nullify his charms, maybe even lots of people if Miles wants to share the scent. What do you think? The whole world could know in, like, an hour?"

"Eh, thirty minutes."

Dad's lip curls. "You're bluffing. You don't even know her number."

Miles smiles. "Oh, I know her number, and what her bedspread looks like, if you catch my drift."

"Liar!" Dad yells. "You really think I'd believe Spud would look at you?"

Graham clears his throat, and we all turn to find him

266

leaning against the wall. "Remember that last hack? It had Spud written all over it, though the handle was SweetBabyM."

Miles curses. "So that's how you guys guessed? That's what I get for calling in a favor. It's like she *wants* me to come back and yell at her."

Dad's mouth hangs open. Maybe our deal isn't sounding so bad anymore.

"So what do you say, Dad? We'd rather not let this get out—it's not good for you or us. We don't want syndicates poking around. We just want out." I sit on the couch and try to act like this is a normal conversation. "You can go back and say we're working on expanding your territory. No one has to know you got duped by your own family. No one has to know we can take away all your power in a heartbeat."

He's silent, but I can tell he's considering. It's more than fair. I'm not looking to save the world here. I just want to protect my family and friends. I want to be free. Dad can go on doing what he does. For now. His syndicate is way too big to take down in one day anyway.

Finally, he lets out a long breath, almost like a growl. "You don't talk. I don't talk."

"Hold out your hand so we can shake on it," I say.

He glares at me, and in his eyes I see fury. He plans to make us pay, but he won't. Not if I have anything to say about it. I take his hand and smile. I really do like this winning thing. It feels great.

Dad's men pick him up fifteen minutes later, and he's gone. I don't have time to celebrate, not with two wounded people groaning in my house. Especially since they're dying

267

because of me. "What do we do? The hospital will ask so many questions . . ."

"Seriously, when Hector said don't worry, he meant it." The black bulletproof car is barely out of the driveway when Joey puts his phone to his ear. "Mama." He goes off in Spanish for a few seconds, and then says, "Adios."

"What's going on?" I ask.

"You'll see," Carlos says. "This is the Navarros' biggest secret, by the way."

"We really might kill you if you tell," Hector adds.

Seth and I lock eyes, and it's clear he doesn't know what they're talking about, either. So we just have to wait, I guess.

Bea arrives with Rosa not ten minutes later, her flour-smeared apron still on. She rushes over. "Move. Make room." We do as she says, and she inspects Graham and Seth's wounds. "Are the bullets still in there?"

"Yes," I say.

"We need to get them out first." She looks to my mom. "Do you have a large pair of tweezers?"

Mom shakes her head. "No, but I can get them out." She frowns. "It will probably hurt."

"Hurry," Rosa commands. "The pain will be temporary."

Mom raises her hands, concentrating on the pieces of metal inside Seth and Graham. I watch, though I keep wondering if I'll lose it. The queasiness comes in waves, but the thought of leaving them stops it. Not after all they tried to do for me. I owe them more than that.

They scream when the bullets emerge from their skin. The blood flows anew. I crumble slightly, only to find Bea's arms around me. "It's okay, chica. Watch."

268

Rosa pulls a small knife from her pocket. She runs it across her palm, making a deep cut. Then she lets the blood drop onto each wound. More screaming, but it quickly subsides.

I can hardly believe my eyes as the wounds close rapidly. There cannot be a person in this world with that kind of power. I have never heard of such a thing, and yet here it is. How many secret abilities are out there, I wonder, abilities so valuable no one dares speak of them? "Alejandro isn't injured. You're hiding out here. This is the real reason you pay Juan to leave you alone."

They all nod.

"There was a really close call when he played soccer. She healed his knee, and people started to suspect. So he got reinjured and left. Dad won't risk anyone finding out about Mom," Tony says. "Wars could be started over stuff like this."

Seth sits up, rubbing his shoulder in disbelief. "Thank you, Rosa."

She smiles, putting her already-healed hand to his cheek. "You are like a son to me, Seth." She glances at me. "What's important to you is important to me."

His grin lights up his whole face, and he holds his arms out for me. "She's pretty amazing, isn't she?"

I tackle him and kiss him, not caring what it looks like. "If you ever get shot again, I'll kill you."

Everyone laughs as Seth whispers in my ear, "Thanks for fixing what I couldn't."

I nuzzle into him. "Thanks for seeing what I can't."

Those old family pictures fill my head again, with the

kids huddled around a fireplace waiting to hear a story. I never thought I could be part of those pictures. Hell, I didn't think I could have the blurry, bad-quality version. But now I feel like I'm standing in the scene right where I belong, surrounded by people I love. People who love me.

It's the best feeling in the world.

Read on for more about
Natalie Whipple . . .

Q & A with Natalie Whipple

Where did you get the idea for TRANSPARENT?

I've always been a huge fan of superheroes, and growing up my favourite TV show was *The X-Men*. But I've always thought that invisibility was handled in an 'easy' way in a lot of comics and shows, and it led me to wonder how it would feel to be permanently invisible instead of invisible at convenience.

Fiona's voice originally came out of those thoughts, and she blossomed into a character I just had to write a book about.

Who is your ultimate superhero?

In my actual life, I have to give that spot to my mom. She has always taught me to go for my dreams and to be confident in who I am. She is such a hard worker, and always thinks about others first. She makes the world a better place.

As for traditional comic superheroes, I will always have a soft spot for Wolverine from *The X-Men*. Regeneration is an awesome ability to begin with, but the fact that he's not perfect and even a little bit bad appeals to me. I think that concept shows a lot in TRANSPARENT, where many characters toe the line between good and bad.

Also, on the playground as a child I was a bit of a bully, and the boys nicknamed me Wolverine because of my sharp nails. Which I was never shy about using. I was rather proud of that back then; now I feel bad.

If you could have a superpower, what would it be?

Teleportation. I know a lot of people pick flying, but I'd rather just be there instantly. I've always wanted to travel, but I've never quite had the funds to do so. It'd be so nice if I could just appear wherever I wanted. Then I could visit friends too far away, eat the best authentic food all the time, and see everything I've ever wanted to.

What inspires your writing?

Everything—songs, movies, books, news, people, nature, conversations. There are stories everywhere if you care to look. You just have to be bold enough to write them down.

How did you first become an author?

I became an official author (as in actually paid for a novel I've written) in 2011, when I sold TRANSPARENT to my US publisher, HarperTeen. It took me five years of trying to get published, ten completed novels, four attempts at securing an agent, and a book that failed in submission before it happened.

It was a hard journey. There were times I didn't think I'd make it, times I seriously considered giving up, times I wondered if I was any good at writing to begin with. But

I kept going. And while I may have nine novels that will never see the light of day, all that work was worth it to finally reach my goal.

All in all, it will have taken seven years from when I started writing seriously to when TRANSPARENT is released upon the world.

What was your earliest career aspiration?

When I was little I wanted to be a writer. As I grew I also added teacher, comic book illustrator, animator, theatre designer, and linguistics professor to the mix. Somehow I ended up back at the childhood dream, as if it was waiting for me all along.

What advice would you give to budding writers?

Work hard. It's one thing to dream about writing, and it's another thing entirely to actually pursue it. The dream is filled with ease and wonderful things. The actual pursuit of writing is a lot of hard, tedious work. If you want the dream, put in the work to get it.

Also, have fun. Which seems contradictory, but you have to enjoy what you're writing, otherwise you won't have the passion necessary to get through all the hard work. It's not worth it if you don't love what you're doing.

What were your favourite books when you were a child?

I was a big Narnia fan. It's really the only series I can remember reading as a child, though I know I read other things. I always came back to Narnia, and even now it's the only series that I've ever reread.

Where is your favourite place to write?

I end up writing in bed mostly, since I have three small children and it's the only place I can hide for a little peace and quiet. My husband is wonderful enough to watch them while I steal a couple hours to work.

Natalie Whipple

Natalie Whipple, sadly, does not have any cool mutations like her characters. Unless you count the ability to watch anime and Korean dramas for hours on end. Or her uncanny knack for sushi consumption. She currently lives in Utah with her husband and three children.

Follow Natalie at

betweenfactandfiction.blogspot.co.uk

Twitter @nataliewhipple